HADLEY BECKETT'S NEXT DISH

Center Point
Large Print

Also by Bethany Turner and available from
Center Point Large Print:

The Secret Life of Sarah Hollenbeck
Wooing Cadie McCaffrey

HADLEY BECKETT'S NEXT DISH

BETHANY TURNER

CENTER POINT LARGE PRINT
THORNDIKE, MAINE

This Center Point Large Print edition
is published in the year 2020 by arrangement with
Revell, a division of Baker Publishing Group.

The text of this Large Print edition is unabridged.
In other aspects, this book may vary
from the original edition.
Printed in the United States of America
on permanent paper.
Set in 16-point Times New Roman type.

ISBN: 978-1-64358-635-9.

The Library of Congress has cataloged this record
under Library of Congress Control Number: 2020932648

To Kelly
Thank you for a lifetime of better

HADLEY BECKETT'S NEXT DISH

Prologue

HADLEY

"Okay, everyone! We're back in twenty. Places, please."

"You okay, Had?" Stuart, my longtime friend, collaborator, and, on this set, the assistant director, asked me with concern as he crossed from Max's kitchen space to mine.

I smiled. At least, I *attempted* a smile. My competitor was rapidly taking away my reasons to smile, one by one. But that wasn't Stuart's fault. "I'm fine, thanks. I'm less sure about our friend Chef Cavanagh over there."

Stuart rolled his eyes and nodded. "I'm so glad this is our last segment." He backed away from me with a grimace and then shouted, "Ten seconds!"

I cleared my throat and straightened my apron, looking down at my coconut-curry chicken and naan waffles one last time to make sure I wasn't missing something important, like the chicken. Or the waffles. I figured I could make just about anything else work for the judges—and with how stressful the day had been, thanks to my fellow chef's antics, I figured if the main ingredients made the plate, I could call the day a success.

Stuart's verbal countdown ended after four, and

I kept my eyes on his fingers—three, two, one. I was ready to hear the outcome of a long day in the kitchen, and I was more than ready to put an end to a miserable two days of filming alongside Max Cavanagh.

First there were eight. Now there are two. Which of these landmark, on-the-brink-of-legend chefs will be crowned America's Fiercest Chef? We're about to find out.

I tried to listen to the host, Xavier Stone, as he gave a quick recap of all we had been through over the course of our two days of filming, which would play out as six separate episodes, spread out across six weeks of Culinary Channel can't-miss viewing. But, as I had been for the entirety of two days, I was too distracted by my competitor to focus on a single thing happening in the moment.

"I'm sorry," Max muttered, actually turning and facing my direction, not seeming to care one little bit that the cameras were on us. "Did he just say 'on the brink'? Did he say we're on-the-*brink*-of-legend?"

"Oh my gosh, please stop!" I seethed through my teeth.

"Cut!" The director called out the command, and everyone in the studio groaned. It was a familiar call-and-answer of which we'd all had enough. We'd all be professionals and prepare to do our jobs, Max Cavanagh would decide *not* to be a professional and *not* do his job, then we'd all have to stop and repeat the cycle from the top—over and over for two days, like a chicken on a rotisserie grill.

"Chef, what's the problem this time?" Glenn, the director, asked from his chair.

Max shoved his knives aside and hopped up on the counter. As he did, the knives tumbled to the ground, taking a beautiful cut of unused Wagyu ribeye with them.

"The problem *is,* Glenn, that it's insulting for you to refer to us as on-the-brink. I mean, considering the ratings we get for this network, and considering my nine Michelin stars, I'd say we deserve better. You're with me on that, right, Hayley?"

Oh, where to begin.

I shook my head and opened my mouth to speak. I was prepared to tell him that I most assuredly was not *with him.* I couldn't have been less *with him.*

Until two days ago, I had looked up to him as a brilliant chef and a masterful businessman, not to mention an engaging television personality. At thirty-six he was only three years older than me, but he'd reached pinnacles in his career that I didn't anticipate reaching until I was no longer young enough to enjoy them, if I ever

11

reached them at all. It was amazing how quickly the awareness that he was a complete and total jerk had gotten in the way of my esteem. He wasn't legendary. Jacques Pépin was legendary. Wolfgang Puck was legendary. Julia Child was a legend among legends.

Maxwell Cavanagh was a spoiled little boy with a haircut he stole from Hugh Grant, circa 1994, and a propensity toward underseasoning his stocks and bases.

"It's Hadley," I mumbled as I crossed to his kitchen space to pick the gorgeous, expensive meat off the ground. *And I have two Michelin stars of my own, thank you very much.* I didn't say that, of course. How pretentious that would have sounded.

"Hadley, Stuart's got that," Glenn called out.

Stuart was, indeed, fully capable. In addition to working on *America's Fiercest Chef*, he was the director on my weekly show. He also happened to be my oldest friend and probably the only reason I was on television, so I knew him to be *extremely* capable.

I handed the meat to Stuart after he had carefully scooped up Max's MAC knife set and gingerly passed it to a production assistant to take and clean. "Here you go," I whispered with an apologetic smile.

"Thanks," Stuart replied, once again rolling his eyes.

As I stood back to my feet and realized Chef Cavanagh was towering over me from his perch just a couple feet away, I questioned what I was doing there. I don't just mean picking up the steak. Why had I stuck around for two days of demeaning treatment from a chef I had once admired but whose cooking skills were actually very much on the same level as mine, apart from the underseasoning? Yes, *To the Max* was the number-one show on the network, but *At Home with Hadley* was number two—and gaining ground all the time.

Why hadn't I corrected him more vehemently when he called me Hayley for the eighth time? Why hadn't I told him that his béchamel needed more nutmeg? And why had I picked up the blasted meat that had landed on the floor as a result of *his* temper tantrum?

"Thanks, doll." He hopped down from the counter and leered at me as he returned to his mark, as if nothing had happened.

Doll?

"Did you seriously just call me doll?" I asked.

Glenn, who was typically heard and not seen, was suddenly standing beside us. He leaned in closer to Max and softly asked, "What would you prefer, Chef? Would you rather we just go with 'legendary'?"

I scoffed, and they both turned to face me.

"Is there a problem, Hadley?" Glenn asked.

I lifted my hands in the air and, as my jaw dropped, looked around the room. *Seriously? Is anyone else hearing this?* My level of confusion and frustration grew as I realized both Glenn and Max were looking at me with accusation in their eyes—as if *I* was slowing down production—and yet no one else seemed to be clued in.

Why am I just now hearing it?

"Chef," I corrected him hesitantly.

"Yes?" Max answered.

I shook my head and cleared my throat, focusing entirely on Glenn and doing all I could to pretend Max wasn't there. "No, I mean . . . you should call me Chef. You refer to Chef Cavanagh that way, and I'd appreciate it if—"

They turned away from me. Turned away!

I took a deep breath and attempted to tune out their discussion regarding the proper usage of the term legendary.

Anise. Broiler. Colander. Dough. Egg timer.

My tried-and-true trick of calming down by alphabetically listing items found in the kitchen had failed me spectacularly before I got to *fondue set,* and I felt heat rising in my cheeks. Just about the time the rushing blood reached my temples, resulting in a *whoosh* pulsing through my ears—similar to the sound of the ocean but ever-so-slightly tinged with the ambiance of chainsaws and screeching owls—Stuart entered my periphery with a kind smile.

"Had?" He put his hand gently on my elbow and escorted me back to my cooking space. "I'm sorry that this has been such a nightmare," he whispered, his eyes flashing over toward Glenn and Max pretty much continually.

I wondered if he was worried Max would hear him call it all a nightmare, or if he was worried Glenn would hear him apologize. Maybe, if he was a true friend, he was just trying to size up the best moment to go over and thump Max on the head.

"Why is Glenn coddling him? He should have been kicked off the set a long time ago." I matched the quiet tone out of respect for Stuart—no one else.

He shrugged. "You know how it goes. We're so far into production now that all anyone wants is just to finish it up and move on."

"I get that, but—"

"Okay, people!" Glenn shouted. "We're ready. Back to your marks, please. We'll pick it up there again."

Stuart repeated his eye roll from earlier and then returned to his spot. He repositioned his headset and called out, "Ten seconds!"

First there were eight. Now there are two. Who will be crowned America's Fiercest Chef? Will it be Maxwell Cavanagh, the legendary restaurateur who, at thirty-six, is the youngest-

ever recipient of nine Michelin stars, or will it be Hadley Beckett, the sweet and sassy Southern belle of the kitchen? We're about to find out.

My eyes flew open, and for a moment, I thought I heard a familiar bubbling. I briefly wondered if Max or I had left a burner on, but I quickly realized it was only my blood that was boiling.

Cool your jets, Hadley, I warned myself. Sure, I had been downgraded from landmark and on-the-brink-of-legendary to "sweet and sassy," but all I really wanted was to wrap up the shoot, move on with my life, and leave Max and his nine stars to marinate in their pomposity.

A camera-ready smile still plastered on my face, I tilted my head to look at him and his dish. *Well, that should be enough to feed a three-year-old. Are Michelin stars awarded by toddlers, Chef?* I caught a groan as it threatened to escape. I'd never understood the gourmet food industry's propensity for starving its customers while charging them the price of a month's worth of groceries.

As my gaze wandered upward, however, and I observed the smug expression on his face, I resigned myself to his soon-to-be-announced victory. There was a part of me—a pretty big part, if I were being honest—that really wanted to win. I mean, *of course* I wanted to win. From the beginning. I wouldn't have left Nashville

16

and flown to New York in the first place if I didn't intend to win. I got paid handsomely and publicized excessively win or lose, of course. But to be named Fiercest Chef? I'd already outlasted some of the greatest chefs in the country, and if I could defeat Max Cavanagh—the "Playboy Gourmet" as he was "affectionately" called by the media—well . . . that was the kind of validation and reputation-builder money couldn't buy.

Plus, I really wanted to see that smug, infuriating smile melt off his face.

Chef Beckett. Chef Cavanagh. Please bring your dishes forward.

I was pretty sure I would never get used to being a chef on television, no matter how long I did it. My competitor, on the other hand, seemed to feed off of the attention like one of those hungry toddlers eating their tablespoon of duck ballotine. Or, you know . . . something a toddler would actually like. As soon as it was his turn to *present*—his creation or himself—he shifted into a higher gear.

Eh . . . maybe not higher. Higher implies better. And as awful as I had discovered him to be when the cameras *weren't* rolling, he was so much worse when they were.

"Okay, hold it there, please," Glenn instructed

as soon as we had approached the judges' table, like two attorneys on *Law & Order* approaching the bench.

My mind wandered as Stuart and a production assistant adjusted the angles of our hands and dishes, and the cameras zoomed in to capture various shots of the way we had each chosen to plate. I held perfectly still, as instructed, and wondered if *Law & Order* was still on the air. When was the last time I had watched TV? Had they launched any additional *Law & Order* spin-offs? Was *Law & Order: DMV* a thing yet?

"Hadley, we need you to look at camera two, please," Glenn stated.

I nodded and did as I was told, until I heard Max sigh. Not a restless sigh. An exasperated sigh.

I turned away from camera two and glanced at him, and wasn't surprised to see him looking right at me.

Don't engage, Hadley. You're so close to the finish line. Go back to looking at camera two, stop your hands from shaking so you don't have to reset your garnish, and just let it all finally be over!

"What! What is it, Max?" I asked, blatantly disregarding my inner sage's wise advice.

He looked me straight in the eye and had the audacity to say, "It's been a long day. Could you please stay focused on your cues so we can get out of here?"

Apron. Blender. Carafe. Dutch ov—

"Hey, Glenn, can you get me another bourbon? And grab one for Hayley too. She seems uptight." He winked at me, and I squirmed in disgust.

"You've been drinking?" I asked.

I was shocked, but I don't really know why. If anything, it made everything about the day make more sense. Yeah . . . nothing about the lack of decorum shown by Max could surprise me at that point. I guess I was just disappointed to be part of a project that had allowed such unprofessionalism to rule the day.

"We're almost done, Chef," Glenn replied. "Think you can hang in there just a few more minutes?"

Max nodded. "You bet I can. Just as soon as you grab me another bourbon."

Glenn chuckled. "Stuart, go ahead and get Chef Cavanagh a—"

"Are you kidding me?" I shook my head vigorously. I just couldn't take any more. "I—I—I mean, I've *never*—"

"Hadley, can I see you for a minute?" Glenn called out, as if summoning me to the principal's office.

Sure. I'm right here. Jump down from your special little stool and join me in my kitchen like you did Max!

I was so irritated with myself for, instead of saying any of that, setting my dish down on the counter and crossing the set to where Glenn sat. Stuart smiled apologetically at me as he passed by, a lowball of whiskey in his hand.

As I approached, Glenn jumped down and then gently pulled me aside. "What an experience this has been, huh?" he whispered. "You've been a total trooper, and I just can't tell you how much I—how much we all—appreciate it."

"Why are you indulging him?" I asked, not bothering to keep my voice down to match Glenn's. "This is ridiculous. I know he's the top dog and all that, but I don't think anyone is doing anybody any favors by letting him walk all over y'all. By letting him walk all over *me*," I added. "I get it. His ratings are higher. But *At Home with Hadley* is solid, and I really think . . ."

I kept talking. I know I kept talking. But I really don't know what exactly I said next. I got a little too caught up in the realization that my righteous confrontation was quickly morphing into a situation where I was on the verge of apology. I wasn't even sure how that had happened.

"That's not it," Glenn said as my attention snapped back into focus. "We love you around here. You know that. The network is *thrilled* with your ratings, and with the magazine launching next week, your audience is only going to grow. It's just that . . ."

"It's just what?"

He pulled me a little further away and lowered

his voice even more. "As you know, Max has had a bad week."

How in the world would I know? Why in the world would I care?

"Oh, I'm sorry. I didn't realize that Max has had a bad week. How can I help?"

"That's very sweet of you." Glenn squeezed my arm and smiled. "I think he'll be okay. I knew you'd understand."

Seriously? Was I even capable of sarcasm? I could have sworn that my offer of help had been dripping in it. That had certainly been my intent . . .

He continued, my masterful sarcasm having been artfully deflected. "I know you're the praying type. I'm pretty sure Max could use some of it."

What was I even supposed to do with that? I couldn't be offended that I was known for being the praying type. I *was* the praying type. But I did not want to pray for Maxwell Cavanagh. All I wanted was for my brilliant Indian/Southern infusion to walk all over his toddler-ready finger food/truffle/mashed pea/foie gras infusion, and then to get the heck out of there.

But when you *are* the praying type, it's not easy (or, probably, advisable) to refuse to pray for someone just because they're a nincompoop.

I groaned softly. "Can we please just finish this?"

"Stuart!" Glenn abruptly shouted, shattering

the veil of discretion. "Count it down! And get Hadley a drink if she wants one."

Max whooped, as if *now* the party could get started. But Stuart, thankfully, knew me, and just threw his eyes open comically wide as he passed and said, "On your marks, please. We've got the transition shots. Let's pick it up from there. Ten seconds!"

Chef Beckett. Chef Cavanagh. Please bring your dishes forward.

We completed the walk to the judges' table and set our creations before them. Finally. I looked over at Max's dish and felt simultaneous admiration and irritation. How? In the midst of all of the drama—all of *his* drama—how had he managed to create a beautiful jambalaya bourguignonne, an infusion dish he made up on the spot, just as I had made up mine, that looked as if it were ready to be served at any Michelin-starred restaurant in the world?

"Chef Beckett, please tell us about your final dish."

Why couldn't it be enough to just be really good at cooking? Or, in my case, really good at cooking and exceptionally good at baking? When had that stopped being enough? When had it been determined that in order to be truly successful in the food industry, you had to be on television?

I took a deep breath and prepared to explain the dish to the judges, and to all the world, I guess. I was so grateful that when I heard the sound of my voice, it seemed to be full of confidence. Confidence I really wished I was feeling.

"Today, Chefs, I have prepared for you a coconut-curry chicken, served on a naan waffle. And while the flavor profile is a little more on the exotic side, I think even exotic food should be comfort food. To that end, you'll see that you also have a side of warmed sweet and slightly spicy plum chutney. I'll ask you to pour that over the dish, as you would maple syrup over the traditional Southern version of chicken and waffles."

I held my breath as I looked down at my dish one more time, and then gently pushed the plate in closer to them. They poured the chutney and then cut into the chicken, and I released a bit of the air I was holding when I saw how easily it cut. My shoulders relaxed as the waffle sprung down and back again beneath the pressure of forks. And finally, my teeth freed my bottom lip from their clenches as three poker faces morphed into expressions of satisfaction and contentment.

"Thank you, Chef Beckett," the lead judge stated with a smile. "And Chef Cavanagh, what have you prepared?"

For the next two minutes I marveled. It was as if a switch had been flipped, and suddenly

Max Cavanagh, grade A jerk, was replaced by a culinary and presentational genius, seemingly worthy of at least some of the honors and commendations which had been bestowed upon him.

He was so smooth and nuanced, and he flirted effortlessly. With the judges. With the cameras. With all of America and the world, it seemed. The pompous, verbose egotist disappeared and a quiet, perfectly subtle Casanova appeared. It was almost indecipherable—and I imagined that to be on the receiving end of his charm would be completely disarming. You know . . . if you hadn't spent two days growing increasingly convinced that he was somehow the spawn of a serpent and a rabid raccoon.

"Thank you, Chef Cavanagh."

The judges looked just as satisfied and content after eating his dish as they did after eating mine, and I felt whatever confidence had developed slipping away. Ah well. The anticipation of a second-place finish wasn't so bad.

But man, oh man, I hated that *he* would be the one to beat me.

Ten minutes later Max and I were sitting at the Chefs' Table—a long, rustic wooden slat with equally rustic benches, none of which matched the decor of the "stage" area, but at least felt less cold and staged than the rest of the set. It was at the Chefs' Table where my opponents and I had sat during the filming of each episode, while our fates were determined. One camera crew was out filming the judges breaking down our dishes while another sat with us as we bantered. At least banter was the goal and expectation.

Max and I did not banter. Certainly not with each other.

"Hadley?" Stuart whispered my name from behind the camera. I looked up and saw him gesture for me to join him.

I hopped down from my bench and walked over to him. "What's up? I thought we were rolling."

"We were. But, I mean . . . you guys have to give us *something*."

I crossed my arms. "I think we've given you plenty. Right now I'm just grateful for the silence."

"Come on, Hayley," Max called out. "I think we can handle thirty seconds of small talk."

I glowered at him and sighed. "Fine." I returned to the bench as I added, "But please, for all that is good and holy, can you remember my name for those thirty seconds? Please?"

He downed the last of his drink—not even the same one he'd been finishing off a few minutes ago, I was pretty sure—and handed the glass to Stuart. "Of course I can, Harley." He laughed uproariously at his joke, which I was actually strangely comforted by. At least he knew Harley wasn't my name either.

"We're rolling," Stuart said. Nervously, I think. And still we sat in silence.

Okay, suck it up, Hadley, I lectured myself. *Be the bigger person. Again. If he doesn't want to put in any effort, it will all come across plain as day on TV.*

"Your dish looked really great," I told him, for the benefit of our future audience.

"Thank you," he said with a nod. "Yours looked better than I expected."

Out of the corner of my eye I saw Stuart shake his head and then bury it in his hands.

"And what did you expect, Chef?"

Max shrugged. "You don't have to be offended—"

"I'm not," I lied. "I would just be really interested in knowing what you expected."

"It's nothing personal, it's just that very few chefs can pull off all Southern, all the time. I mean, it worked for Harlan Sanders, but—"

I nearly choked on my indignation. "You're comparing my cooking to fast-food fried chicken?"

He shrugged yet again. "Well, I mean, it's not quite as flavorful as the Colonel's, of course, but you're just getting started. You'll get there."

"That's it!" I exclaimed, jumping up from the bench and stomping to the door. "I'm done."

Stuart placed his finger to his headset to put it closer to his ear. "They're ready for you. Come on, Hadley. It's almost done. This is it." He put an arm out to usher me back into the main studio.

Aioli. Breadbasket. Chopsticks. Dish rack. Espresso machine. Flour sifter. Gravy boat.

I was going to need at least the entire alphabet in order to actually cool off, but that was going to have to do for now.

"This was the closest competition in the history of *America's Fiercest Chef*," Xavier began as soon as film began rolling once again. "Ultimately, our judges chose one chef to carry the mantle and the title. One chef will be named victorious. One chef will . . ."

Oh my goodness, get on with it!

The rest of it was a blur, and not just because it was all so repetitive and melodramatic. Although, that certainly didn't help. I zoned out because I just couldn't take one more hyperbolic guarantee that the winner's life would completely change, and that they would never be bored or financially strapped or unknown or alone or, I don't know . . . stuck in traffic ever again.

So when I heard Xavier say my name, it took me a moment to remember the rules. Did they say the name of the winner or the loser first? The loser, right? I plastered on a disappointed-but-resigned-and-grateful-for-the-opportunity smile and took a step toward the judges, to shake their hands and say thanks.

"You're kidding me," Max said. At least that's pretty much what he said. His version was somewhat less family friendly.

I rolled my eyes. Really? He was even going to make a big deal about the fact that I hadn't shaken his hand and congratulated him first? Granted, that was the way it was usually done on these competitions. Granted, that would have been the polite thing for me to do.

But come on! He was lucky I didn't haul off and slug him.

I sighed and turned back to face Max, my arm extended. His arm extended as well, and for one fleeting moment I considered the possibility that we might actually end this thing with civility. But then I realized it was his left arm reaching out, and it wasn't meeting up with the right arm *I* had extended. He wasn't going to try to *hug* me, was he? He wasn't that much of an imbecile, surely.

I was wrong. He was so much more of an imbecile than I had ever imagined. He wasn't coming in for a hug at all. As bad as that would have been, the reality was even worse. He reached past me to the judges' table and with one fluid motion, struck the edge of my plated masterpiece and caused it to flip into Chef Aguste Bisset's lap.

I gasped and, regrettably, muttered, "Well, I never!" I was always so disappointed in myself when Southern colloquialisms dripped from me freely in the most stressful of moments.

I don't know a lick of French, apart from necessary cooking terms and the essentials to assure any French visitors to my restaurant that I'm merely ignorant, not rude. But I was fairly confident that Chef Bisset's exclamation was even less flattering than my Minnie Pearl–inspired outburst.

I heard Glenn call out "Keep rolling!" and I whipped around to glare at him, but he couldn't be bothered by my disapproval, I suppose. He was, after all, in the process of filming the Culinary Channel's first foray into *Jersey Shore*–level entertainment.

"Chef Maxwell," Xavier said, his voice sounding more confident than his cautious steps back from the table appeared. "We'll kindly thank you to control—"

"Her?" Max asked with a sneer and, if I'm not mistaken, disgust as he gestured toward me. "With her 'y'all come back' and her 'kiss my grits' . . . *her?*" He took another step toward the judges' table, causing them all to scoot back in fear of what he might do.

"I have never said 'kiss my grits' in my entire life!" I protested, quite possibly zeroing in on the wrong thing first. Although, seriously. Kiss my grits? I may have been a little too folksy at times, but I would not stand there and be accused of being a folksy grandmother.

Besides, I was prepared to add, *you won. You*

29

are the better chef, even if you are the lesser human. So kiss my ever-lovin' grits, Maxwell Cavanagh.

But before I could say any of that, a funny thing happened. My brain kicked into gear. Finally. They'd said my name first. I'd watched four seasons of this show, in preparation for my appearance. Back when I'd thought that my episodes would bear even a slight resemblance to any episodes that had gone before, I'd studied the patterns. What the judges liked, what they hated, what they were tired of, what they would view as fresh and innovative. Once my brain was working, I saw it all clearly. I knew this show inside and out.

And they always announced the winner's name first.

"I won?" I muttered.

Thankfully no one heard my muttering. They were all too busy being verbally assaulted by Max's deluge of insults. Not that I'm thankful about that part, of course.

In context, his temper tantrum made a lot more sense. I mean, it still made absolutely no sense whatsoever, but a temper tantrum over *winning* would somehow make less than no sense whatsoever.

A few moments later, about the time security was called in and Max was forcibly removed from the set, hurling accusations and threats all the way to the door and beyond, it began to really sink in.

I won. I defeated Max Cavanagh, who was generally regarded as the greatest chef of our generation. I had done it my way—with manners and a whole lot of butter and salt—when faced with unbelievable circumstances that would have caused even the cook at a firehouse to crumble. I'd proven that I was more than just a great pastry chef from Nashville. I'd made it clear that I could hold my own alongside the big guns.

It was just too bad the world would never know, since there was absolutely no chance whatsoever that *America's Fiercest Chef*'s tribute to *All My Children* would ever see the light of day.

1. *Freeze fresh ingredients for up to three months.*

HADLEY

"That's it for today, friends. I'm already looking forward to next time, when I'll show you some tricks for making biscuits that even your gluten-free friends will fight over. And before you ask, no. They aren't gluten-free. I never said it would be wise for your gluten-free friends to eat them. That's another story altogether!"

Movement caught my eye, just to the right of the camera. Though he stood in the shadows, I was instantly certain that I didn't recognize the silhouette. It was undoubtedly a man. Beyond that, I didn't have a clue. My little makeshift studio didn't attract guests very often, so my curiosity nearly got the best of me, but the silent snap of Stuart's fingers pulled back my focus.

"I'm also going to give you a peek into my tried-and-true methods for making sure big family events don't become overwhelming. It really is possible to enjoy hosting a houseful of people. Well . . . that depends on what your family's like, I suppose. Regardless, no one has to die!"

The unfamiliar guest's shoulders bounced up and down. Suddenly, his eyes shot upward, and he

33

began taking in his surroundings with seemingly newfound interest. My eyes followed his. I just couldn't help it. The intensity with which he began looking around left me no choice. He acted as if there could be a sniper in the rafters, and as desperately as I kept hoping the network would build me a new kitchen, that really wasn't the way I wanted to go about getting it.

"Until next time . . . I'm Hadley Beckett. Thanks for spending some of your precious time at home with me."

Ugh. I loved my show. I was grateful that I got to do what I loved. And without a doubt, the kitchen they had designed for me in the Brooklyn studio I inhabited was more spacious than any apartment in which I had ever lived. But that didn't change the fact that every time I had to act like I was actually at home when filming *At Home with Hadley*, I felt like I was selling my soul, just the tiniest bit. Each time I had to say it, I was always filled with this vision of a very Dorian Gray–esque portrait of me on the wall, which had begun as a cute and thin-despite-all-the-comfort-food Hadley of her twenties. But each time I sold my soul, the portrait began showing the years.

And certainly the pounds.

Why was it that unlike with Dorian Gray's arrangement, the reality staring back at me in the mirror didn't stay young and impervious to carbs?

"Hey, Hadley, there's someone here who would like to meet you," Stuart called out as he walked the stranger toward me.

Ah yes. The trained assassin sent to, hopefully, fire at will, not hit a single person, and completely destroy my outdated appliances.

"Hi there," I greeted him with a smile. As much as my sniper theory intrigued me, I knew it was much more likely that he had just won a contest in some fan group on the Culinary Channel's website or something. "I'm Hadley Beckett."

"Oh, I am *fully* aware of who you are, Chef Beckett. I'm a big fan, and I've been following your career probably longer than you have."

I chuckled, frighteningly aware for the first time that the line between groupie and trained assassin could be less discernible than I had ever suspected.

"Really? Well, that's flattering! I'm so glad you're able to be out here today. But I really must insist you call me Hadley. And what's your name?"

He put his hand out to shake mine. "Leo. Leo Landry."

"It's great to meet you, Leo. I don't think you caught the entire taping, but I hope it was worth the trip for you. I know it's quite the trek to get all the way out here, but hopefully you've got some visits to other studios lined up? They call this neighborhood Foodie Row, there are so many Culinary Channel studios around here."

"I know. I've spent a fair amount of time in the area. But I'm actually just here to see you."

I try not to think the worst of people. Really, I do. I try to be welcoming and trusting, and apart from occasionally wondering if a guest in the studio is an assassin, I think I do a pretty good job at that. But that didn't keep me from darting my eyes around to make sure I wasn't alone with Leo Landry, the stranger who had come to Foodie Row just to see me.

Of course I should have known that Stuart would always have my back. I spotted him about twelve feet away, apparently polishing a camera—something I'd never seen him, or anyone, do before. I smiled as I realized his eyes were fixed intently on Leo.

"Well then, what can I help you with, Leo?" I asked.

"Actually, I'm hoping we can help each other."

His hand moved slowly toward the inside pocket of his blazer, and my life flashed before my eyes. Well, not *my* life, actually. I'm not sure whose life it was, exactly, but it was definitely the life of someone from some movie in which Matt Damon was about to appear out of nowhere and tackle Leo, just in the nick of time.

The threat level in my mind receded as Stuart just kept on wiping down the camera, and Leo handed me a business card.

"Hadley, I've been watching you for a long

time," he said. Admittedly the business card I was now able to look down at made that sentence a whole lot less creepy. "I think it's time to take your career to the next level, and I believe I'm the guy to get it there."

Leo Landry. Landry & Associates Talent Management.

"That's very flattering, Leo. Really. But I already have a manager."

He nodded and chuckled. "I know. Your grandmother, right?"

I had the best business manager in Nashville. She'd managed Chet Atkins and Waylon Jennings, Patsy Cline and Kris Kristofferson. Dolly Parton had once dedicated an entire album to her. Sure, those were all musical acts, and she hadn't worked with any of them—or anyone at all—for at least twenty years or so, but there was no denying that she was justifiably a legend. The fact that she was working with *me,* a moderately successful chef with an undeniably niche audience? I was blessed. Blessed enough that sometimes I knew I just needed to hold my tongue and let it slide when my manager didn't treat me with the professional respect I might hope to receive from others in the business.

Besides, she only took 5 percent commission and still did my laundry for me when my schedule got too hectic.

But whenever anyone in the business seemed to

look down on the fact that my grandmother was my manager, I always felt a strange combination of embarrassment and indignation. Most of the time, no one had any idea. Sure, I'd occasionally have to explain how my manager's experience in the country music business in any way qualified her to be a player in the world of food, but that was always easy to defend. Apparently Dolly Parton and the career Meemaw had helped carve out for her was a universal language when it came to earning people's respect.

I hated that I could never seem to escape any conversation in which the grandmother factor was known without being made to feel like a little girl attempting to play in the big leagues.

"Yes, my grandmother," I said with a sneer. Well, I don't know if I actually sneered. I'm not sure my Southern manners would allow for a sneer. But I sure wasn't smiling, that's for doggone sure. "Does that amuse you?"

The smile dropped from his lips. It must have been the sneer.

"Oh no. No, not at all. Sorry. I think it's completely charming."

Charming? Ugh. Was I going to have to sing "Hard Candy Christmas" to get this guy to stop being so patronizing?

I was pretty sure that wouldn't actually work. Ever. In any situation.

"If you think it's so *charming,* what makes

you think I would want to make a change and be represented by you instead?"

"Because there's something very strategic, very precise, that needs to be happening in your career right now. And I do mean *right now*. Are you aware that *At Home with Hadley* is the number-one noncompetitive show on the Culinary Channel?"

I nodded. I was aware, no matter how difficult it was to believe, and no matter how giddy I felt inside to hear the words spoken aloud. And no matter how much I knew the current level of success was only a result of Chef Cavanagh's on-air tirade and subsequent suspension.

"It's because *To the Max* is on hiatus—"

"I'm going to stop you right there and give you a little free advice, before I'm even representing you. There is no justification needed. You shouldn't be minimizing the importance of that to anyone—or to yourself. *At Home with Hadley* is the number-one show. Period. So, let me ask you, Hadley . . . why are you in Brooklyn?"

"This is where the studio—"

"Oh, I know. But you shouldn't be in a studio. The show is called *At Home with Hadley*. Wouldn't it make sense for the audience to get to be at home with you?"

I snorted at the idea. No matter how many times I'd thought about that myself, I knew it just wasn't feasible. "Well, sure, that would be great, but my apartment isn't big enough."

He leaned in and whispered, "Then they need to be buying you a place that's big enough."

My breath caught in my throat. *No.* There was no way he was being serious. I was grateful for so many of the perks I received—top-of-the-line cookware, free flights to New York and a nice hotel room while I was filming, and even grade A prime steaks that had been showing up in a giant crate at my door every month for three months, ever since *America's Fiercest Chef* had aired despite my protests. I made good money, I was treated like a star, and having the show had done more for business at my restaurants than I could have done on my own in a hundred years. The thought of anything more was ludicrous.

"You think they'd buy me a bigger apartment?" I asked breathlessly.

Leo took a deep breath and smiled. "Look, Hadley, your grandmother has done a great job with your career. With getting you here. Truly. I'm not looking down on that at all. Besides, I did my research. She's had quite the career of her own. But the fact of the matter is that I could only get a country music superstar so far, and then I would need a music industry manager like your grandmother to step in if we really wanted to go all the way. I *only* represent the food industry, Hadley. Chefs, restaurateurs, critics. This is what I do. This is what I know. And what I know is that if the network's number-one personality-focused show is called *At Home with Hadley*, we darn well better be spending some time at home with Hadley. You know what I mean?"

Of course I knew what he meant. He was poking at the biggest sleeping bear in my heart. It wasn't just that the show was called one thing, and yet the reality was something very different. That was definitely something that nagged at me, but it went further than that.

Once, in the early days of the show, a producer had thought it would be a great idea to introduce viewers to my horse, Marigold. Despite the fact that Marigold lived with and was trained by a kind old man named Kent in upstate New York. Also, Marigold wasn't my horse. Also, I don't ride horses. I'd put my foot down on that—at least in part because Marigold looked like she would just as soon trample me as trot with me. Mostly I just didn't see what being an equestrian had to do with my skills with meringue. It was bad enough that I had to act like I was preparing to welcome friends and family into my Brooklyn studio dining room—which was, admittedly, gorgeous—for the Thanksgiving episode. It wasn't my home and, truth be told, I didn't have enough friends and family to justify preparing that eighteen-pound turkey, even if I had actually been preparing to play hostess.

But every time I mentioned those sorts of things to Meemaw, she said things like "beggars can't be choosers" or "don't look a gift horse in the mouth." Well, I *had* looked my gift horse in the mouth. Her name was Marigold, and she was terrifying.

I sighed. "What you're saying rings true. Trust me. I've had the same thought."

Some of the stage lights shut off and I looked toward the booth and waved at the technicians whom I'd kept there long enough by lingering. I began walking toward the door and indicated that Leo should come along. I patted Stuart on the shoulder to indicate all was well as I passed him and the shiniest camera this side of the Mississippi.

I stopped a few feet from the exit and turned back to face Leo. "But I can't complain. Really. I mean, like you said, the show is number one, so it's obviously working. Viewers are liking it; the network seems happy—"

"Of course the network is happy. They're tickled pink, Hadley. They're getting you for a steal."

I shook my head and smiled. "It's not really about the money for me."

He was silent for a moment as he observed me, making me truly uncomfortable in his presence for the first time—even more uncomfortable than when I briefly believed he was there to carry out a hit on my life. People staring at you in silence is just the worst. Not only are they probably judging you—or at the very least taking in every detail so they can pass judgment later—but they're doing it *silently*. They don't even help *distract* from the fact that they're judging you.

"I believe that," he finally stated assertively. As if his believing it meant that was the final word on the matter. "I can't tell you how many people have said that to me through the years, that they aren't in it for the money, but with you I actually believe it. And that's why you've *got* to let me manage you."

"I'm sorry, but I don't see how *that* is the natural conclusion there."

"People take advantage of you, I would imagine. Don't they?" He didn't wait for my answer. "They've got you pigeonholed into the perfect version of what *they* think you should be. And because you're so humble and real, you just feel grateful to be here. To be invited to the party. And *because* you're so humble, and *because* you aren't doing it for the money, they can keep you right where they want you. But what they don't realize—and what you certainly don't realize—is that if they'd just let you be *you*, if they let you be as real on camera as you are in life, you wouldn't just be the top noncompetitive show on the Culinary Channel. You'd be the top show. Period. You'd launch other shows. You'd become a brand, and the other networks—not to mention retailers—

would be fighting for you. All because we let Hadley be Hadley."

Let Hadley be Hadley.

There was instantly some Aaron Sorkin–related déjà vu happening in my head. I mean, Josh and CJ or whoever else on *The West Wing* hadn't used my name, of course, but I was pretty sure "Let Bartlet be Bartlet" was a thing they'd said about Martin Sheen as the president. And it wasn't just those few specific words. It was the whole speech. Leo's entire demeanor. By pulling him from the stage a couple minutes prior, I'd even provided him with a well-timed walk-and-talk.

"I appreciate it, Leo. And I'm flattered. Really, I am. And everything you just said, about having the opportunity to be a little more real . . . well, I can't deny that sounds lovely. But you've got to know there's no way I'm going to kick my own grandmother to the curb as part of a shrewd business deal."

If I ever became *that* person, I wouldn't be able to live with myself.

He nodded and smiled. "Now *that's* letting Hadley be Hadley." He thrust his hand in front of me to shake mine once again. "You do understand I'm going to keep trying . . ."

"And I will be flattered every time," I replied with a self-conscious laugh before ushering him out the door.

2. Thaw for one week.

HADLEY

"Meemaw? Are you home?"

"I'm up here, darlin'," she called out from a far and distant place I couldn't immediately comprehend.

She spent most of her time in her study, reading the celebrity tabloids she loved, with the twenty-four-hour prayer line channel on the television in the background. She seemed to see no conflict between the two. She just happened to be every bit as entertained by the despair and brokenness in the lives of famous people as she was by con artists offering to pray on someone's behalf in exchange for a modest donation and a promise of ongoing financial support.

But she wasn't in her study. I set my handbag down in the foyer and locked the front door behind me. I stepped over stacks of records and magazines and picked up a couple of carryout food containers as I passed. I walked into the kitchen, which was the biggest travesty of all the travesties in her home. It was enormous. Gorgeous. A marvel of marble and stainless steel and perfectly situated islands (yes . . . plural). It looked like something straight out of *Better Homes and Gardens*. At least, it *would,* if the marble countertops weren't hidden under stacks of papers and the islands didn't serve as my grandmother's makeshift office. And if all those shiny new stainless-steel appliances weren't being wasted in the home of a woman who hadn't cooked in thirty years.

A lot of chefs—especially the Southern ones—probably got their start in the family kitchen, testing out recipes passed down from generation to generation with more reverence applied to them than actual physical heirlooms. I hadn't experienced any of that. At least not with her. My dad liked to cook, but he had been no master. We'd had fun together in the kitchen, and he had passed on some impressive skills with the barbecue grill, but that had pretty much been the extent of it. Well, apart from the hours and hours he and I spent watching cooking shows together.

My own mastery had actually come about *because* my grandmother preferred takeout. My mother was only occasionally around—and couldn't hard-boil an egg when she was—and my dad was often working or, during the bookends of my life with him, incapacitated—either by bad choices or, later, the illness caused by those earlier bad choices. I'd learned out of desperation, and in the process, I'd discovered the great love of my life.

"Where are you?" I called out, once I had

peeked into all of the rooms and come up empty.

"In the attic."

The attic? She'd been living in the house in Belle Meade for five years, and my apartment was only ten miles away. I was at her house a lot. And yet I'd had no idea she had an attic.

I followed her voice, and it didn't take me long to realize why I hadn't been aware. It wasn't really so much an attic as a glorified crawl space in which the previous owner had seen fit to lay carpeting. It stretched almost the length of the house and had to be accessed by a set of hidden stairs that you pulled down from the ceiling with a hook through a cord—as seen in many of the coolest movies and TV shows of my childhood. And the access was from a spare bedroom, which was only used for storage.

I crawled up there to join her and laughed at the sight. She was sitting on the floor, leaning against a tiny window—don't ask me why I'd never questioned the location of that window from the outside—with her legs crossed in front of her. Bent over almost at the waist, I went and sat beside her.

"I didn't know this was here," I said, still laughing. "Do you come up here often?"

She shrugged. "Sometimes. It's quiet."

"You live alone, Meemaw."

"I know, but this is a different type of quiet. Here, I'm choosing it."

I pulled my knees up against my chest and spoke softly. "You okay?"

She laughed and brushed off my concern. "Of course I'm okay. Did you just get back into town?"

"A couple hours ago."

"Good week of taping?"

I nodded. "I think so. I don't know. Sometimes I bore myself, you know? I don't understand why anyone would want to listen to me prattle on about food, or anything else."

"It's funny what entertains people, isn't it?"

She didn't intend to insult me, I knew. It just wasn't in her nature to think about how her words might make someone feel before she said them. I think she thought she'd earned the right to not have to bother with stuff like that.

"The network sent me an enormous bouquet of flowers. They were waiting for me when I got home. That was nice, I thought."

"What kind of flowers?"

"I don't know. A mixture. There are some roses, for sure. Lilies, I think. Then there are some that look like tulips, but I've never seen tulips that color." Flowers were always nice, but as little time as I spent at home, I couldn't help but think I would have appreciated the gesture even more if they'd sent me some fresh herbs. Some rosemary or sage around the apartment would be lovely. "Oh, and they sent chocolates too." Now *that* was useful.

My grandmother began laughing. Cackling, more like. It was an unsettling sound that transported me a little too quickly to thoughts of Margaret Hamilton threatening Judy Garland, and her little dog too.

"What?" I asked, more than a little worried that her cackling was caused by the thought of me trying to fit into my bridesmaid's dress for my cousin Mandy's wedding in two weeks, after I'd eaten a box of truffles.

"This is perfect!" She squealed in a way that didn't at all help put my Wicked Witch trepidation to rest. "Was there a note?"

A note? What were we even talking about here? "You mean with the flowers and chocolates?"

"Yes."

I looked at her in confusion. "Yes. I told you. It was from the network."

"But did it say anything else?" she asked impatiently.

I guess I hadn't paid too much attention to anything else. Once I knew the chocolates were from a trusted source and therefore could be ingested without fear of poison, it hadn't really occurred to me that anything else mattered.

"Um . . . let's see." I closed my eyes and tried to picture the card in my mind. "It was pretty basic stuff, I think. Something like, 'With affection from your grateful and devoted Culinary Channel family.' Or something of that sort."

She stood from her spot against the window and began pacing across the space—something she could get away with, with her tiny five-foot-nothin' stature. I'd have been decapitated. "Grateful . . . grateful . . . yeah, okay," she muttered. "Grateful in the long term? In the short term? Both, most likely. And devoted, did you say?"

She'd transformed from Margaret Hamilton to Nicolas Cage, trying to interpret the card—a less fragile, rose-scented stand-in for a treasure map on the back of the Declaration of Independence. My grandmother's version of the Wicked Witch of the West somehow came across as less unhinged than her version of Nicolas Cage.

Well, *any* version of Nicolas Cage, really.

"This is perfect, darlin'. Don't you see what they're doing?"

I instinctively knew that she was not looking for the answer I wanted to give—that they were expressing their affection, gratitude, and devotion.

"Why don't you tell me, Meemaw?"

She stopped on the spot and turned to face me. "They're bribing you!" She cackled again. "We've got 'em exactly where we want 'em."

"And where do we want them?"

"They think you're going to take your show somewhere else. Maybe even file a lawsuit, I would bet."

I gasped. "A lawsuit? I would *never*—"

She shushed me. "Nope. Never say never. And you definitely never say never to *them*."

"I don't even understand. You mean because of *America's Fiercest Chef*?" I turned it over in my mind, trying to figure out how she possibly could have gotten all of that out of a few words on a card, which were no doubt actually written out by the florist, transcribed during a call from a network receptionist I'd never met. "Chef Cavanagh never touched me. I wouldn't even have grounds for a lawsuit."

"Wake up, hon. What world are you living in? Clearly not this one. He didn't have to touch you. He made you feel uncomfortable and created a hostile work environment, didn't he?"

"Well, yes. But it's not the network's fault that Max Cavanagh is a certifiable maniac."

In the past three months, I'd played the whole thing over in my mind approximately seven hundred times. I'd tried to look at it from all sorts of angles—even angles that didn't portray me in such a positive light. And I don't just mean that awful camera shot cooking competition shows seem to love, where you have to cross your arms and look down at the camera operator who's kneeling on the floor about four feet in front of you. Why do they *ever* have us look down? It's like taking a selfie with someone half your height. It's *never* going to be flattering for the tall girl who, every single time, suddenly possesses about sixteen double chins and the neck width of a linebacker.

But no angle, not a single one, had presented a viewpoint compelling enough to dissuade me from my determination that Max was ultimately to blame. Sure, the network had kept up his liquor intake and let him get away with it all, and I fully understood and was frustrated by all the things they could have and should have done differently. Nevertheless, the blame began and ended with Max. I'd even created justification to blame him for the double chins.

"You're missing the point, Hadley."

"And what is the point, Meemaw?"

"The point is that your *At Home with Hadley* contract is up for renewal, and I finally have some negotiating chips I can cash in."

"Because my ratings weren't negotiating chips? Or the fact that I won *America's Fiercest Chef*? Or the magazine? Or . . . or . . . hey, how about the fact that when I was on the *Today* show last month, there was that whole group of fans out on the Plaza, who had camped out all night to see me?"

"There were about ten of them."

"But they were there to see *me!* They were wearing Team Hadley shirts and everything."

She chuckled, and heat rose to my cheeks. I could face my *America's Fiercest Chef* victory being undermined by my curry dish being flung at the lead judge, and I was willing to accept that I would most likely be the number-two show again, if they ever put *To the Max* back on the air. I'd even keep on crossing my arms and looking down at the floor for unflattering photos, if that was what I had to do. But there was no way I was going to let her take away my ten groupies on the Plaza.

I wanted to jump up, ready to defend myself, but all the height of the ceiling allowed me to do was slowly and awkwardly rise to a hunched-over position. Just like Dale Carnegie taught us in *How to Win Friends and Influence People*.

"Do you even believe in me, Meemaw?" I asked—with more vulnerability in my tone than I had intended. "I mean, why are you even working with me if you think so little of my career?"

She placed her fists on her hips and planted her feet. "Hadley Jolene Beckett, what in the world are you talking about?"

I hated when she used my middle name. Especially when we were having a business conversation. It was unprofessional. And maybe I would have had a leg to stand on with that argument if I hadn't just called her Meemaw.

But actually, I've just always hated my middle name, period. I get it. My family owed a lot to Dolly Parton. But Jolene was "the other woman," right? Wasn't it sort of like naming your little girl Bathsheba? Or Anne Boleyn?

"You know I'm not desperate for clients, Hadley. I was perfectly happy in my retirement, and I'm not exactly going to build an addition onto the house with my measly commission on your take."

Wow. I wasn't sure which hurtful words to react to first.

Silly me, thinking I'd be allowed time to react to any of them.

"I'm doing this because I love you. And because you need me. If it weren't for me, you'd still be a line cook down at the Cracker Barrel."

I groaned. "How many times do I have to tell you? I was never a line cook at Cracker Barrel. I waited tables there for about two months when I was seventeen. And by the time you started managing me, I was the executive chef at one of the top restaurants in Nashville. Not only that, I was already writing a regular column for *Southern Living*."

"Oh. I see. Pardon me."

Her inflection indicated the arrival of my worst nightmare. The road-worn country music star-maker was tough to deal with, and I walked on eggshells around the matriarch who seemed to think she was doing me a favor by pretending I was left on her doorstep in a basket. Like she was the only hope I had of living any life at all, rather than ever acknowledging my dead father, whom she had loved like a son, or my mother—her daughter—whom she had stopped referencing at all. Probably because it was easier for her to pretend my mother had never existed. But the approaching persona was my least favorite of all. Half Georgia peach, half Jewish mother from 1930s Brooklyn—or at least from 1930s Brooklyn in a Neil Simon play—this version of my grandmother could, if you didn't have your defenses up, lure you in and devour you whole before you had time to say, "How did Dolly put up with this?"

"Well, sweetheart," she continued, laying it on thick, her voice feeble. Feeble! The woman hadn't had a feeble moment in her life! "You just need to allow me to apologize. I guess I've gotten it all wrong in my head. But please don't think for even a second that I don't think you're capable of making it all on your own."

She brushed off her corduroy pants before effortlessly turning her tiny frame around and making her way down the dangling steps, leaving me to follow. Neither of us said a word until we had completed our descent—her gracefully, me like a giraffe doing . . . well, doing exactly what I was doing. I joined her in the living room, where she was already sitting, holding a glass of sweet tea.

"Stop it, Meemaw. Seriously. Do you think

we'll ever get to a point where we can just be real with each other? Is that too much to ask?" I walked into the kitchen and opened the refrigerator—the only appliance she used, I figured, apart from the microwave—intending to help myself to a glass of that iced tea she was sipping. But there was no tea. "Do you seriously just have the one glass of tea? Do you make it by the glass?" I grabbed a bottle of pop instead and took it back to the living room, where I sat down across from her and continued.

"I am grateful—so grateful—for all you have done for me. As my manager, yes. You bet. I know you don't make much money off of me, and it's probably time we rework our arrangement, to make it more beneficial for you. I know you didn't plan on ever managing anyone ever again, and I know that you're helping me out because you love me. No matter what games we play with each other, or how tough you like to be, I know you love me more than probably anyone else on earth."

I paused to allow her time to comment. Confirmation would have been lovely, but I was really just expecting a snarky retort. When I received neither, I decided to push my luck and continue.

"More than anything, Meemaw, I'm grateful for all you've done for me in *life*. Truth be told, I love *you* more than anyone else on earth too.

But I need you to understand some things. I'm a thirty-three-year-old woman who has already achieved more than most people achieve in a lifetime. And I'm not done. I have big dreams. Big plans."

She set her glass on the coffee table—from what I could tell, for the sole purpose of freeing her hands so she could throw them in the air in exasperation. "So do I, darlin'! For you, I mean. That's what I'm talking about." She sighed as she reached out and squeezed my knee. "Can I be your grandma for a minute? I mean, *just* your grandma. No business talk."

I don't know. Can *you?*

"Umm . . . sure . . . I guess." I had no idea what that was going to look like, but I was willing to give it a shot if she was.

"I'm proud of you," she said in a tone I hardly recognized. It was . . . kind. Comforting. One might even say grandmotherly. "I'm proud of the way you held your head high through that whole competition. Lesser women would have crumbled."

I decided just to take the compliment rather than argue over semantics, but there was a part of me that wanted to point out that lesser men would have crumbled as well. In fact, they had. I wasn't sure I'd ever forget the sight of Chef Norman crying and telling Chef Max he was a "meanie-pants" on the first day of taping.

"Thanks, Meemaw." I smiled and savored the tenderness I had only witnessed from my grandmother on rare, isolated occasions throughout my life.

"But now it's time to put on your big girl pants and get ready to deal with these bloodsuckers in a way that will *really* make me proud."

Well, okay then. Grandma mode had lasted longer than it usually did, at least.

"You need to warn me before you step into your phone booth and transform back into Super Manager. A girl's liable to get whiplash."

She chuckled—tenderly—and I was confronted with the terrifying thought that maybe she was *still* in grandma mode. If that was the case, the rest of my life was destined to be an anxiety-ridden vortex of uncertainty.

"The thing is, Meemaw, that just doesn't feel like *me*. You know? I'm sure we can find ways to move my career forward and still let me stay true to who I am through it all."

Let Hadley be Hadley.

What would that even look like?

"This guy stopped by the studio," I began hesitantly. I didn't really know why I was telling her. Probably just to get it out of my mind so I could stop thinking about it—since it was pretty much the *only* thing I had thought about for most of the week. "At first I thought he was a sniper."

"A sniper?"

"Yeah. Like, an assassin or something." She looked at me with confusion and I added, "He wasn't though."

"Well, no." She laughed. "I didn't figure."

"Anyway, he was actually a manager. Interested in *me,* if you can believe that." I paused, probably expecting her to reply in a way that I'd pretend wasn't hurtful. Thankfully she just kept listening, so I kept talking. "He only manages people like me."

"What do you mean, people like you?"

"Chefs, I guess. Food personalities, anyway. He seemed pretty interested in me—I mean, in managing me—and of course I told him I wasn't interested—"

"What's his name?"

"Um, Leo."

"Leo *Landry?*" she asked, with a whole new level of interest, I noticed.

"Yeah. Leo Landry. You know him?"

"Honey, everybody knows him."

Well, not everybody, clearly. "Why? Is he good?"

"Leo Landry's the best. Leo Landry *manages* the best. If he wants to represent you, he sees something. Something I don't see." My eyes darted to my lap so as not to reveal how stung I was, but she quickly remedied my understanding. "Because I don't know what I'm looking for, darlin'. Don't you think for a second that I don't see your potential. I do. But potential for what? I don't have the faintest idea."

"Well, I already told him I was perfectly happy where I was, and that I wasn't the least bit interested. So we don't need to give another second of thought to any of that."

"You want to sing at the Opry? Great. Let me make some calls. But if your dreams include anything other than that, you need to sign with Leo Landry. When you have an opportunity like this, you jump on it. And that's my final word on the matter."

She stopped squeezing my knee, patted it quickly, and then stood from the couch and walked into the kitchen. Golly, she was difficult. My entire life, she'd been the thorn in my side. The woman I was always trying to please, who would *never* be pleased. And the thought of working with someone else was exciting. Terrifying. Exhausting. Learning someone new, letting them learn me. Working out a routine. Giving up more of my money—but maybe having more money to give up? Possibly an end to the New York commutes? Could I actually film in Nashville or had Leo just been blowing smoke?

"Are you going to take me to dinner, or do I have to heat up this lo mein from the other day?" Meemaw asked as she stared into the nearly bare fridge.

I stood and attempted to shake away the conflicting thoughts and emotions flooding my senses. "Why don't you let me make something?"

In response, she turned to face me. "Are you kidding me? Look at this place. This kitchen ain't fit for cooking in."

3. Prepare stock in large pot.

HADLEY

A couple hours later I walked into my apartment and collapsed on the couch. My bags still sat by the door where I had dropped them. I knew I needed to begin the process of unpacking, doing my laundry, and making sure there was no spoiled food stinking up my fridge, but travel, time with Meemaw, and fried catfish for dinner had left me exhausted.

Apart from the commute to Brooklyn, I really did love my *At Home with Hadley* schedule. At various times throughout the year we'd spend a solid week filming what felt at the time like a million episodes. That week was always difficult—the days were long, I was on my feet for hours on end, and I had to change clothes frequently, so that viewers believed they were really joining me in my home a week later, and not just minutes later, after dishes were quickly scrubbed.

The winter episodes were especially tedious as fall decorations morphed into Thanksgiving, which seamlessly morphed into Christmas. It was enough to mess with the senses and rob a person of the joys of the holidays.

But it meant my time was freed up to focus

on the magazine and my restaurants—not that they needed a lot of help these days. They were each finely tuned machines, and I had great management and chefs in place. Even with the increased business, my staff was more than capable.

I couldn't believe the boost that business had received from the victory on *America's Fiercest Chef*. Well, I *wish* the boost had come from the victory. The comments I received from patrons as I passed by their tables made it pretty clear what had actually caused the boost.

"You go, girl." I hated that one.

"It's about time someone stood up to that chauvinist pig!" I always figured the people who said that hadn't watched the show. In actuality I hadn't stood up to him all that much—but headlines about it always seemed to make it sound as if I had.

"Good for you, Hadley." That comment was usually accompanied by a somewhat patronizing expression that made me feel like they actually thought there was much more I should have done to stand up to Max Cavanagh.

And then, of course, my personal favorite: "I know he's a creep and all, but you have to tell me . . . is he as sexy in real life as he looks on TV?"

Seriously? You're asking *me* if Maxwell Cavanagh is sexy? No! Maxwell Cavanagh is not sexy. Maybe before I met him I would have agreed that he wasn't horrible to look at, but no man can be considered sexy while flinging chutney. No matter how good he looks in black. Maxwell Cavanagh was the least sexy man I'd ever met in my life. I always thought the people who asked me that were so misguided, buying into that "Playboy Gourmet" persona, and I wished I could tag a "Use your brain!" up-charge onto their bills.

But it had all been good for business, nonetheless. Even without the up-charge.

I sat up and pulled my phone out of my pocket and Leo Landry's business card out of my handbag. I stared at it and ran my finger over the high-quality gold lettering.

"Okay, Hadley," I muttered aloud, jumping to my feet in an attempt to manufacture energy and courage. "Just get it over with."

With trembling fingers, I dialed the number on the card and then I waited . . . through one ring and then another, and then one more. I hadn't thought about having to leave a message, so as panic filled my brain, I tried to come up with something adequately clever to say.

Leo, it's Hadley. Let's do this. No, that was far too bold.

Mr. Landry, this is Hadley Beckett. If you were serious about wanting to work with me . . . No. That was not nearly bold enough.

"Do you really think I'll get a new kitchen out

of the deal? If so, where do I sign?" I giggled at myself, having practiced that last message aloud.

"I can meet you with paperwork in the morning," he replied.

My eyes flew open and my mouth sealed shut. I toyed with the idea of hanging up or saying, "Sorry. Wrong number." But there was no point.

"This *is* Hadley, isn't it?" Leo asked, amusement in his voice. "I don't *think* I've told anyone else lately that I think I can get them a new kitchen. Never can say for sure, though." I was still mortified and couldn't bring myself to speak, but he filled the silence. "A few months ago, I might have thought it was my now-ex-wife. But she already signed. And her lawyer definitely got her enough for a new kitchen."

"I'm so sorry," I stated softly.

"Eh, it's okay. I got to keep the vacation home."

I giggled again. "I meant about my awkward greeting. I was talking to myself and didn't realize you had picked up."

"Ah! Well, no need to apologize about that. It was a very good question. And to answer it, yes, I think you'll get a new kitchen. I meant everything I said to you, Hadley. I see the gold mine the Culinary Channel is sitting on with you. To be honest, I don't even think *they* see it. Not fully. I mean, they love you, I'm sure. You're getting good ratings, and there's not a doubt in my mind that they don't want to lose you. But in my opinion, they haven't done all they can to take advantage of the boost from *Fiercest Chef*."

First my head dropped, and then my entire body collapsed back onto the couch. *Of course. Well, that had been nice for the moment it had lasted.*

I sighed heavily. "Okay, Mr. Landry. I appreciate your interest. I really am flattered, and I was thinking it might work. But I'm ready to put all of that Max Cavanagh stuff in my rearview mirror. I won't lie . . . I'm happy we got that ratings boost, and sure, it's helped my restaurants out too."

"And the magazine, I would assume."

"Yes, and the magazine. It is what it is, and I'm grateful for the blessings. But I'm not going to take advantage of it. I mean, not any more than is just happening naturally. I'm not wanting to build it all up, just to play the victim and get some sympathy viewers."

There was silence on the other end of the line, giving me an opportunity to think through it all for a moment. My grandmother said this guy was the best, and I really did want to film in Nashville. But with each passing moment of silence, I was even more confident that I was prepared to stand behind what I'd said. More than I wanted any of the dreams I had for my career, I really just wanted to never be forced to think or talk about Chef Cavanagh again.

When Leo finally spoke, his voice was soft and gentle, and full of more emotion than I had been prepared for. "You think you're getting *sympathy* viewers? Oh, Hadley. It really makes me sad to think you haven't had someone by your side encouraging you but also helping you see what you're unable to see."

My defenses rose to the surface, but faced with his unexpectedly emotional slant on it, I found it all very confusing. I wanted to be professional, but I *had* to defend Meemaw, right? Not just because she was my grandmother but because she had done so much for my career. She'd believed in my dream—even if she wasn't the most overtly gushy and supportive person in the world—when no one else had.

But what Leo was saying—even though he hadn't actually said much, so far—was somehow grabbing onto my heart. Not in a feeling-like-I'd-just-been-slapped kind of way, but as if something or someone was tenderly saying, "Shh. Don't talk for a minute. Just listen."

I still talked, of course.

"It's not been so bad," I croaked out through the unexpected frog forming in the back of my throat.

He sighed. "Hadley, how many times have you been the only woman in the room? As a chef, I mean."

"More than I can count."

"And how many times has some other chef—let's not even count Cavanagh for a moment—called you doll or sweetheart or sugar?"

Again, more than I could count, but I knew I had to stop him. I didn't like where the conversation was heading. "Look, Leo, I know what you're saying. And I appreciate it. I do. But the fact is, I'm not called to be an activist. I'm kinda old-fashioned, actually, and I know so many great men—men who are respectful of me and what I do. And me being a woman doesn't matter to them in the least."

"But all I'm saying, Hadley—"

"And you know what else? Sometimes I like being called sweetheart. I like when a guy holds the door open for me and lets me order first . . . just because I'm a lady. When done properly, sometimes I even like it when a guy orders *for* me." I quickly realized I'd never actually seen that done properly, except in the movies, so I guess I just liked the *idea* of that one. "And yes, I'm quite often the only woman in the room. I'm proud of that while also being incredibly frustrated that it is sometimes so difficult for women to get up there alongside the boys. But also, most of the time, I love being the only woman in the room. Not because it means I was successful and others weren't, but because most of the guys—most of the good, nice, respectful guys I know—treat me like a queen. See? I'm not the girl to carry this flag. I agree that men and women are meant to be equal, but I also think they're meant to be different. That's just how I feel."

The instant I ended my rant, he said, "You don't listen very well, do you?"

Maybe being managed by Leo would resemble being managed by Meemaw more than I had thought.

He continued. "I told you in Brooklyn—I think our absolute best play is to let you be you. We're all ready for a change. Those of us in the business, sure, but I really mean the viewers, Hadley. Chef Cavanagh will always have his fans. He will always have an incredibly loyal following. That's undeniable. He certainly has something that no one else has. But—"

"Sorry to interrupt, but can you tell me *what?*"

"Excuse me?"

"What does Max have that no one else has? I'm always hearing that, and I have been for years. Max has *something*. That's fine and dandy, but now that I've had the pleasure of his company, I have to admit . . . I'm at a loss. Why does he have this incredibly loyal following?" *Incredibly looney, more like, if they've really stuck with him this long.* "What is it about him? I want nothing more than to be the anti–Max Cavanagh, and I think you're saying that's what *you* want me to be too, but you're also saying he's got something special that no one else has.

I'm just trying to understand what people see in him, and how in the world you think *I,* of all people, can ever be a substitute in viewers' minds."

"I've been in this business a long time, and I've carefully watched the career of every chef that's come and gone. Believe me when I tell you, Chef Beckett, that you *are* the anti-Max. You don't have to do a thing. What I'm trying to tell you is I don't *want* to turn you into something or someone different." He exhaled into the phone as the thought passed through my head that after all of this, I was probably going to *have* to sign with him—just for putting up with my questions and uncertainty as long as he had.

But he still hadn't given me the answer I was looking for.

"Okay, great, but that still doesn't tell me—"

"What Max has going for him?"

I grunted my acknowledgment and he sighed.

"When he first started out, he was very, very different. He's always been passionate. Determined. Obsessive. Driven. And I believe he still possesses all of those characteristics, but they used to be positive traits. All of those characteristics helped get him to the top. And, sure, they've also always been at least a little tinged by a negative side of the coin. He's always had a bit of a temper—"

"Oh, do you think?" I asked, my voice dripping

with sarcasm. I didn't mean to. It just jumped out of me. "Sorry."

"No apology necessary. You know that better than anyone, I suppose."

I still couldn't say for sure why that whole experience had affected me the way it had. After all, Leo was right. I *was* accustomed to being the only woman in the kitchen. Lots of guys had called me doll and talked down to me, and more guys than I could count had been absolutely convinced I couldn't keep up. But I *had* kept up, and that had always had more impact on me than their doubt and dismissal ever could have.

Max Cavanagh's doubt and dismissal were sticking with me in a different sort of way.

"The network sent me flowers, Leo. And chocolate." I reached out and grabbed the card from the enormous bouquet on the coffee table in front of me. *With much affection and gratitude from your devoted family at the Culinary Channel.* I'd gotten it pretty close. "Why do you think they did that?"

Without a moment's hesitation he said, "Well, that depends. When was this, exactly?"

"Today."

He clicked his tongue. "Then I'd imagine it has something to do with the fact that your friend Chef Cavanagh's suspension officially ended today."

I didn't have much wind left in my sails for

the day, but that took care of the pesky little remainder that had been trying to hang in there. Meemaw hadn't gotten it exactly right, but she was closer than I had imagined. It wasn't so much a plea of "Don't sue us!" as it was "We hope you enjoyed your time at the top, and very much hope you'll stick around to once again collect *To the Max*'s dust in your face."

"That explains it," I whispered. Then I cleared my throat and jokingly added, "Maybe we need to hurry up and get the ball rolling on my kitchen." When he neither laughed, agreed, nor argued with me, I tagged on, "You know, while I still have the top show."

"Oh, I see," he replied softly but with heaviness. "You really do think you only took the number-one spot because the reigning number one was . . . what? Unable to fulfill his duties?"

That made it all sound a little too beauty pageant-ish, but I suppose that was the gist.

"Sure," I replied matter-of-factly.

"Hadley, Max committed career suicide on the set that day. It's one thing to be seen as the bad boy of the culinary world. It's another thing entirely to be seen as the bad guy. You've been looking at this as if you're just a placeholder while he's gone, and once he's back, he'll regain his position. And if he had gone away to work on something new, or to spend time with an ailing parent, or to feed impoverished orphans in third-world countries, maybe that would be the case. You would have maintained, and his fans would have been right there waiting for him—and yes, many of them still will be. But you don't even realize, do you? He hand-delivered them to you. In droves. You didn't just maintain your audience, Hadley. You stole his." He sighed, and it was mingled with a gratified chuckle. "Yes, you have such different audiences, but both audiences think he's a jerk. And what's more, he was a jerk to *you,* while you remained kind and graceful under pressure."

"So the flowers and the chocolate—"

"The network sent you the flowers and the chocolate for the same reason they're going to give you a new kitchen when we ask for it."

It was beginning to sink in, though it was still difficult to grasp. "Because I'm kind of filling the gap he's leaving behind?"

I could hear the smile in his voice as he said, "No. Because you're filling the gap he has *always* left behind."

4. Steep for one month.

HADLEY

"Be sure to join me next week, y'all. I'm having a special guest from the neighborhood stop by, and this girl . . . well, you're just gonna love her. I sure do. Not only is she an absolute sweetheart and an inspiration in about a million-and-one ways, she also knows how to cook up a mean Kentucky hot brown."

Stuart held up three fingers on his right hand and made a fist with his left, to let me know I had thirty seconds left.

"If you don't know what a hot brown is, let me just put it this way: it takes the perfection of bread, turkey, and bacon, and then sends it all into a different dimension with a Mornay sauce worth trading your waistline for. Good thing too. Because that's exactly what happens." I smiled at the camera as Stuart's finger began making the "wrap it up" signal. "Thanks for spending some time at home with me today. Let's do it again real soon."

"And that's a wrap! Great show, everyone," Stuart called out. He removed his headphones and set them on the stand beside the camera, then walked toward me. "So, this girl you're having on the show . . ."

"Lacey."

"Yeah, Lacey. She's really seven years old?"

I nodded. "She is."

"And she's going to be able to handle the stress of all of this?"

He gestured around him, and I couldn't help but laugh. I looked around at our oh-so-stressful temporary set—my grandmother's kitchen—and then back at him.

"I think she can handle it. She and I made cookies in here last night."

"But with the cameras and the retakes and—"

I placed my hand on his forearm. "Stuart, this girl makes the best Mornay sauce I've ever tasted in my life, bar none. I mean, I make a world-class Mornay myself—"

"I know you do."

"And compared to hers, mine deserves nothing more than a proper burial via garbage disposal. Any girl who can cook like that can handle Jerry operating a boom mic."

He laughed. "Say no more."

Stuart walked away and I began my cleanup. I didn't miss my Brooklyn studio by any stretch of the imagination, but I did look forward to the completion of my new kitchen—in my new house. Well, it wasn't *mine,* of course. The network owned it. But I got to live in it for the foreseeable future, rent-free.

When Leo first told me about the deal he had

worked out, these awful thoughts ran through my head. For instance, I imagined that "the network is providing you with a house" actually meant I was scheduled to be a contestant on the first chefs-only season of *Big Brother*. I just wasn't sure I'd be able to live in a house where Emeril was always waking everyone up in the morning by shouting "Bam!" and Bobby Flay was constantly challenging us all to household chore throw downs.

Thankfully, the reality was a three thousand square foot home on three acres in Brentwood, about ten miles outside of Nashville. And I was going to get to live there all alone. Without a Rachael Ray in sight.

In the meantime, Meemaw's kitchen had been a nice stand-in. It had taken a whole lot of convincing—not to mention a whole lot of cleaning—to get it to happen. I had told Leo I would be okay filming in New York a little bit longer, but he seemed to think it was imperative that letting Hadley be Hadley begin right away.

Ultimately Leo had offered to send Meemaw to Branson for three weeks so she didn't have to be displaced. That had done the trick. It really had been like a dream come true, getting to cook in her kitchen. The first time felt to me like a scene from *Seabiscuit*. Or *Secretariat*. Or basically any horse movie I'd ever seen. There's always that moment when they let the horse run for the first time—unbridled or at full speed or across the wide-open countryside—and the horse comes alive. Finally, the horse is allowed to do what it has always been meant to do.

I imagined my grandmother's kitchen that way. The stacks of papers had been cleared away and the burners had been fired up, and finally that kitchen was allowed to run.

Unfortunately for Jerry and his giant boom mic, however, that kitchen was not meant to be a television set.

Stuart walked back over to me, clipboard in hand. "We'll film two episodes tomorrow, starting with Lacey and her legendary Mornay, and wrapping up with your sweet tea episode. Then that will be a wrap for the Meemaw's Kitchen set. Thank goodness. When does Twyla get back from Branson?"

"Thursday. It was going to be tomorrow, but she decided to squeeze in one more Oak Ridge Boys concert." I smiled as I wrung out my rag over the sink. Leo had really nailed it.

He jotted a few more production details on the paper and then set down the clipboard. "Need a hand?"

"Nah, thanks. I'm basically done. Or done enough for now, anyway." I'd been staying in the house too, having already given up my apartment. I'd have time to spit polish before everyone got back to the house in the morning. I draped the rag over the faucet. "I can't wait for you to see the new house, Stu. It's gonna be a dream."

He pulled out a barstool and sat across the island from me. "I googled it this morning and was able to pull up some photos, from when it was last on the market. Before the network bought it. It's unbelievable."

I squealed. "I know!"

The whole thing was so weird to me. When does that actually happen? How often does someone say, "Hey, here's a house that's five times the size of your apartment. Go live in it for free." It was crazy. I actually felt a little bit guilty about it, in a way. I mean, not guilty enough that I wasn't going to take them up on the offer, of course, but guilty enough that I was very businesslike about it all when talking to the crew. I didn't want to rub it in or anything.

I had no problem rubbing it in to Stuart.

"There's a whole shower room. A *room,* Stuart. Like, you walk in—"

"Don't you walk into most showers?"

"Yes, but this is different! There's enough room to film the show in that thing. All three cameras, Jerry and his boom . . . the whole shebang."

He laughed. "All three cameras! That's all I need, Had. I don't care if we film in the kitchen or the shower, or that three-car garage. I just want to get back to all three cameras!"

I laughed with him and followed him as he

began walking toward the door. "You've been a good sport through all of this. I know how much you hate filming here, but I really appreciate it."

"I'm excited about the new place. It will be good to get to stay in Nashville most of the time."

"Right?" I leaned in and pointed my finger in his face. "All the same, you have to tell me if filming here gets in the way of too much other work stuff for you."

He was the director and executive producer of my show, of course, and whenever I appeared on other programs, such as *America's Fiercest Chef*, I usually worked it out to bring him with me. He loved that—getting more and more credits for his résumé. And filming in New York, he'd also been able to pick up some nice side jobs on other shows when we weren't filming.

With the move to the Let Hadley Be Hadley era, he'd insisted there was nowhere else he wanted to be. And I really couldn't imagine doing it without him.

Stuart had been with me since the very beginning of the show. Since before the beginning, actually. Truth be told, it had started out as his show. We were part of the same group of friends all through college at Belmont, and when he needed a final project for his degree in video production, we pulled together a cooking show. It was called *Belmont Brunch* back then, but there was no doubt it laid all the groundwork for *At Home with Hadley*.

He smiled before leaning in to kiss me on the cheek. "Didn't I promise I'd never leave you?"

"No, as a matter of fact, you didn't. I believe the promise was that you'd never leave me unless you got a better offer."

"Same thing. Besides, I've gotten better offers, and I'm still here."

"What better offers have you gotten?" I asked in mock horror.

"Well, not recently. I mean, now you're a hit. There *aren't* better offers at the moment. But not all that long ago, an offer to work for some kid filming YouTube videos of him playing Call of Duty might have been intriguing." I elbowed him in the ribs, and he laughed. "You've come a long way, baby. No doubt about it."

"*We've* come a long way."

We stopped at the door and he grabbed the doorknob, but I placed my hand on his shoulder to stop him before he could turn it.

"Stu, can I ask you something?"

"What's up?"

"Was I . . ." I took a deep breath and tried to figure out how to say what I wanted to say. "Did I come across okay? On the show, I mean?"

"You mean apart from your continual two-syllable mispronunciation of the word *mayonnaise?*"

"Hey!" I fired back. "I know you're from Baltimore, but you've been in Nashville more than a decade now. *You're* the one mispronouncing it. But that isn't what I'm talking about. I mean on *America's Fiercest Chef.*"

He did a double take and his hand fell from the doorknob, and his arms quickly crossed.

"What are you talking about?"

I shrugged and began regretting I had brought it up. Stuart had been witness to it all, and he was protective and defensive of me—always. He wasn't the right one to ask. But at the same time, he was the only one. Since college, there hadn't been anyone else I trusted as much—with my emotions and for the truth.

"How could you not come across very well?" he pushed. "No security guards had to forcibly remove *you* from the premises that day, to my knowledge."

I chuckled. "No. Not that day." Not *any* day, of course. I was the good girl. But I was worried that on that day, I hadn't been quite good enough.

"I don't know," I continued with a sigh. "I just worry I may have missed an opportunity."

"What kind of opportunity?"

"Never mind. This is stupid."

"Seriously, what's going on, Had?" He leaned back against the door, arms still crossed. "Why are you thinking about this?"

"I just . . . well, I watched it."

An exasperated groan escaped his lips. "Why did you do that? What happened to doing everything in your power to never lay eyes on Chef Cava-nasty, ever again?"

I laughed. "Cava-nasty? That's what you landed on?"

"Do you have something better?"

"I liked Cava-gnarly."

Stuart pondered that for a moment. "Yeah. That's better. So what happened? Why did you watch it?"

I leaned my back against the door next to him. "It's just been bugging me, you know? All this time I've been getting credit for the way I handled it, but it was all such a blur. I didn't really know *how* I handled it."

"Then you should have asked me." He stood up straight and faced me. "You were strong, Had. That was the thing that stood out for me more than anything else. You held your own. Under unfair, cruel pressure, you still managed to make a dish no one else would have thought to make, and that you had never made in your life, and you won. I'd like to know how you think you could have handled that any better. How you think *anyone* could have."

He stared me down, having had lots of practice waiting out my obstinacy.

I smiled. "Thanks, Stu."

"You're welcome." He nodded, and his arms finally relaxed to his sides.

We stood in silence for a moment, each of us

staring goofily at the other. Me trying to decide whether to voice the unspoken part of my worry; him, no doubt, waiting to see if I was actually going to let it go—since I was never very good at letting things go.

He tilted his head and studied me. "Do you think maybe you should talk to somebody?"

"About what?"

"You know . . ." He wagged his head back and forth. "About all of this."

"Oh, gosh, Stu! No! It's not worth all that. I'm fine." And I meant it. "I just shouldn't have watched the stupid episode." I meant that too.

"Yes. That's the moral of the story."

My eyebrow rose. "What? Always listen to you?"

"Well, that goes without saying. But, no." He placed his hand on the doorknob once again and prepared to finally head out. "The moral of the story is everything will be fine as long as you never have to see Chef Cad-anagh ever again."

I scrunched up my nose and shook my head. That one wasn't my favorite. He laughed and pulled me in for a quick hug.

"See you tomorrow."

He turned the knob and opened the door, and we each took an involuntary step back in response to the surprise of finding someone standing just on the other side of the doorway. But the involuntary quickly became extremely deliberate, at least for

Stuart, as he stepped forward and to the right, so that he was standing directly between me and the unexpected guest.

It was none other than the cad himself, live and in the flesh.

5. *Season generously.*

MAX

It was a mistake. He'd known it was a mistake long before he threw a pair of jeans, two T-shirts, some socks, underwear, a phone charger, deodorant, toothpaste, and his toothbrush into his trusty backpack that had traveled around the globe with him more times than he could remember. He'd certainly known before hopping in his Range Rover and navigating through Manhattan, on to the interstate, and toward Nashville. In fact, it had been about the time he crossed into Pennsylvania that he'd realized there was probably no good whatsoever that would come from the endeavor.

But by then he was enjoying the solitude of the open road, and there was no way he was going to head right back into the city.

His hand had been frozen in place, poised to ring the doorbell, for probably a solid thirty seconds, and it stayed in place as the door opened.

"What do you think you're doing here?" the man on the other side of the door asked, stepping in front of Hadley as if she was the president and he was Gerard Butler in one of those movies. That would make Max pretty much every outlandish action movie threat that could be conceived, he figured. Seemed about right.

He was thrown off by the abruptness of the door being opened—not that he'd been cool and collected prior to that happening—and for the life of him, he didn't know what he should say.

"I asked you what you're doing here," the man repeated.

Seeing Hadley peek out from behind her protector—looking almost like a little kid, curious about the Santa Claus at the mall but not quite ready to walk up to him and present her list—jarred him into action.

"Um, I'm sorry," Max said, pulling himself together. "I didn't mean to startle you."

"We're not startled," he replied tersely. "What do you want?"

"Hadley," Max said quietly, maintaining the eye contact he'd finally acquired from her. "Chef Beckett," he corrected himself. "I was hoping we could talk."

The man in front of Hadley rolled his eyes and crossed his arms, and in response Max lost Hadley's focus. She looked instead up at her bodyguard—Friend? Boyfriend? Husband? Secret Service agent?—and placed her hand on his arm. Max looked at the man then, and realized for the first time that he looked familiar.

"We've met, haven't we?"

"Yes, Chef. We've met," he replied with disgust

in his voice. "It was my job to keep you well hydrated on the set of *America's Fiercest Chef*, if you recall."

Again, seemed about right. Two people who hated him for the price of one.

"Sorry," Max said as he stuffed his hands in his pockets. "I know I should remember your name." He waited for the man to tell it to him, but he didn't say a word. "But I don't." Still nothing. Was he thinking if he waited long enough, Max would remember? That really wasn't going to happen. "Maybe you can remind me?"

"His name is Stuart Bain," Hadley said, darting a glance up at Stuart's face as she stepped in front of him. "He was the assistant director on *America's Fiercest Chef* and he's the director of my show. And if you'll excuse us, Chef, we're going to talk for just a moment. Be right back."

With that, the door closed and they were gone, and Max was left to awkwardly stand there and act like he couldn't hear the elevated voices on the other side of the door. He turned around, his hands still in his pockets, and rolled up on the balls of his feet—up and down, up and down.

At Tranquility Peaks, a treatment center in Malibu where he'd spent thirty corporate mediation–ordered days in the aftermath of his very public crash-and-burn, they'd taught him that the only way to waste a moment in life was to *choose* to waste a moment in life. Sure, it was

New Age hooey, but he'd noticed that choosing not to waste moments was actually helpful. In that moment, for instance, he didn't just stand on the porch and stew in his frustration at driving for thirteen hours and then being made to wait outside like the kid who's been splashing around in mud puddles and can't go in the house until his mom grabs a towel. No, instead he used that moment to decide it had been a lovely drive, and the best possible thing he could do next was get back on the road.

The discussion inside had subsided—or at least they'd stepped further away from the door—and still no one appeared. That was a pretty clear indication that Hadley didn't want to speak with him—as if it hadn't already been clear.

"You're leaving?" she asked from the doorway, just as he reached his vehicle.

He nodded. "I think this was a mistake."

"Probably."

"I do think it's best if I just go."

She again said, "Probably."

Max smiled at her as genuinely as he could, considering he was the most uncomfortable he'd ever been in his life. "Well . . . bye." He waved. Idiotically.

She just nodded again.

There was no doubt these moments would go down as wasted, and he couldn't deny that was entirely of his choosing. It was too late to do anything about that. But he still had the opportunity to make sure his entire drive back to New York wasn't wasted on regret.

"I just wanted to apologize," he said, taking one small step back toward the porch. "I was really awful to you that day—"

"Two days!" Stuart called from inside the house. "You were awful to her for two days."

Max cleared his throat and nodded. "I was really awful to you those two days, and you deserved better. Sorry."

Awkward silence filled the air, even as relief began to fill Max's heart. When he'd set out from Manhattan, he hadn't had any clue as to how an apology would be received. He'd been so busy focusing on the reception of it that he hadn't given any thought to how good it might feel just to say it.

Hadley hadn't moved or said a word, but she stared at him intently. Max knew he would appreciate her telling him his apology was accepted, but it wasn't necessary. But he also didn't want to just hop in the car and go, if she *was* planning to say something. His eyes began to twitch with uncertainty, from Hadley to the Range Rover and back again, as he tried to decide what to do. And still she stared.

"Okay, well . . . I think I'll go," he declared, gesturing with his thumb toward the vehicle. "Unless . . ." He raised his eyebrows, but she didn't respond. "Nope. Okay. I'm going." He walked to the driver's side and opened the door. He waved again—just as idiotically as before—as he climbed in, and then he had a thought. He pulled his wallet from the glove compartment and reached inside for a business card, then he jumped out and hurried back around to the porch. "If you want to talk, here's how you can reach me. You know . . . if there's anything you want to say. Anything at all." He held it out for her, but she made no attempt to grab it. "I'll just, um . . . I'll just set it here." He placed it on the railing beside her, but the breeze made it flutter instantly, and he had to grab it before it flew away. "I guess that won't work. Um . . . here . . ." He rushed again to the driveway, this time to grab a large stone from the collection that lined the path of minuscule gravel. He ran back over to her and set the card down in the same spot, but secured by the stone. He returned to the driver's seat and climbed inside, but not before calling out, "Sorry again." Then he shut the door, fired up the ignition, and drove away—pretty sure he'd just proven that sometimes you had no control whatsoever over the most wasteful moments of all.

6. *Marinate.*

HADLEY

Everything felt deceptively normal as I walked back into my grandmother's house. Stuart left for home about a minute later, after neither of us had known what to say, really, apart from "That was weird," with a commitment to talk more about it later. There was something about the comfort of the place that could almost trick me into believing I hadn't just experienced the closest thing to a parallel universe I would ever feel.

I headed into the kitchen, a little bit zombie-like. I didn't know what I was going to cook, and I certainly wasn't hungry, but I pulled out a bowl and pie pan and a whisk, and then instinctively opened the refrigerator and grabbed eggs and cream, as well as some of the bacon and Gruyère that had been set aside for Lacey's Mornay sauce and hot brown. I fumbled around the kitchen, grabbing everything else I needed to make a quick, easy quiche, although there was a part of me that thought it was the perfect time to tackle turducken or some equally arduous and ridiculous recipe that I'd always thought would be fun to have in my repertoire.

What in the world was *that?*

I set down the bowl of eggs I had begun

whisking and looked toward the door—as if making sure the door Max and I had just stood on the other side of was still there would help it all make more sense. And then I realized I was asking the wrong question. *Who* in the world was that?

I sunk down gradually onto the stool beside the island and picked up his business card from the marble in front of me. It was one of those cool cards reserved for either the most successful or the most pretentious of people—only a name and a phone number. No job title, no company name, no website encouraging you to go learn more on your own. No . . . people with this sort of card were aware that you knew *exactly* who they were. What's more, they were doing you a favor by gracing you with their phone number—but they certainly couldn't be bothered to stand there and exchange digits with you, or to wait while you put each other's information in your phones.

The card indicated the man on my porch had, in fact, been Maxwell Cavanagh, but nothing in my mind was doing much to confirm that. And it wasn't just that he had said he was sorry, although that had certainly sent my senses into a topsy-turvy freefall. No, what was really causing sensory overload was the humility that had been evident in his eyes.

And how much that humility conflicted with the eyes—full of pomposity and anger—that were evident every time I remembered the image of him that was seared in my brain.

I groaned as I watched a single tear splatter into the eggs. I stood and carried the bowl over to the sink, prepared to pour the mixture down the garbage disposal—out of habit, I guess. The rules of presentational cooking had taken over my instincts. Thankfully I remembered, just before I tilted the bowl, that the rules of stress relief cooking, for only myself, were very different. You didn't have to start over on a quiche simply because a tear dropped in. You just had to add less salt.

I flipped the bacon in the frying pan, standing back to avoid the hot, splattering grease, and tried to think about anything other than the way I had been completely disarmed by Max's surprise appearance—and even more so by the apparent purpose of the appearance. And the way I had just stood there, silent and numb. For *months* I had thought of all the things I should have said to him on the set that day, and those things varied widely from, "Clearly something is bothering you. If you need to talk, I'm here," to "If you call me Hayley one more time, I'm going to shove your special 'secret ingredient' somewhere that you'll *never* have to worry about anyone figuring out what it is." But I hadn't said any of it then, and I'd said even less during our surprise reunion.

Quiche was not nearly distracting enough.

It had clearly been a mistake not to pull out a turkey, a duck, and a chicken and begin the arduous turducken process.

I shifted gradually from shock into a deliberate attempt to try and focus on the good things I'd heard about him through the years. If I was going to have any luck whatsoever reconciling the eyes of the two Maxes in my mind, maybe that was a good place to start.

He was a genius. Clearly. I'd watched him enough to know that was true. I'd eaten some of his food from time to time—in his restaurants or on *Fiercest Chef*, of course—and he was undeniably a genius. Each bite was much more pretentious than I preferred, but boy was it good. I'd always heard that he could be charming— only when he wasn't drinking, according to some; only when he was, according to others. He'd apparently donated a whole bunch of money through the years to help stamp out hunger in America's inner cities, but none of it had been done discreetly. From what I could tell, Chef Cavanagh did not believe in letting his good deeds fly under the radar. Not when he could become the poster boy for some cause or other, and he could list his uppity restaurants—where each side of risotto cost more than a week's wages in those inner cities he was helping—as sponsors of his initiatives.

Okay . . . the good things weren't helping very much.

When my phone rang and I saw Leo's name, I instantly knew I'd never been more grateful for a manager who had no respect whatsoever for his clients' desires not to be bothered late at night.

"Hey, Leo."

"Good evening. Sorry to bother you so late."

I glanced at the clock on the microwave: 9:34. Okay, so it wasn't quite as late as I had thought. I would have sworn it was 2:00 a.m. in the year 2070 or so. I definitely felt like an octogenarian at the moment.

"No problem. What's up?"

"You doing okay? All ready for the big move? I bet you're exhausted."

"I *am,* actually," I replied with a yawn. I hadn't realized just *how* exhausted until that moment. I speared the bacon with my fork, pulled it out of the pan, and placed it on the paper-towel-covered plate on the counter. I turned off the stovetop and looked around with exasperation at the mess I'd made for a quiche I no longer had any desire to make. "But everything is going well. We're all set for tomorrow's show"—*Or we would be, if I hadn't broken into Lacey's Kentucky Derby ingredients*—"and we'll also tape one extra, just as security in case there are any unexpected delays with the move. And then Stuart and the guys will immediately break down the set—"

"The network will be sending over an additional crew to help."

"Great. Yeah, so, I guess that's all good. They'll get everything moved over and set up at the new place, and then we'll start taping there on Monday."

"Good. Good. This is a positive thing, Hadley. An exciting thing. There's already been such an impact, just from being in Nashville. Don't you think?"

"Yep. Definitely." I covered my mouth to try and stifle a second yawn, but it was to no avail.

Never one for silence of any kind in conversation, I'd already discovered, Leo jumped in again. My half-hearted, sleepy affirmation and acknowledgment that he had been right to move the show to Nashville was all he sought, I guess.

"And there are some other things in the pipeline too. Exciting things."

"Oh really?" I asked, hopeful that my tone expressed interest. Because there *was* interest. I was greatly interested. I just also happened to suddenly feel like *I'd* run the Kentucky Derby.

If I had any hope of staying awake while Leo wrapped up the conversation, I knew I needed to keep moving. Clearly I wasn't going to follow through on a quiche. As much as I wanted to dump it all down the garbage disposal and be done with it, I couldn't ignore the guilt that had been instilled in me throughout my childhood and all thoughts of how a starving child in a third-world country would have benefitted from my egg pie. I begrudgingly began rifling around for plastic containers to store the mess I had created for myself.

"They want you on *Renowned*, Hadley."

I froze, bacon-grease-splattered pot holder in hand. Surely my emotional and physical exhaustion had transported me to a dream-like state where I only *thought* my manager had just told me that the single greatest establishment in the history of culinary entertainment—with the possible exception of Dan Aykroyd's Julia Child sketch on *Saturday Night Live*—wanted me as a guest. *Me.*

Renowned is the Hollywood Walk of Fame. No, that's not big enough. Mary-Kate and Ashley Olsen have a star on the Hollywood Walk of Fame. *Renowned* is an all-star game. Careers were forever cemented as legendary on *Renowned* and, on a few disastrous occasions, careers came to a close on *Renowned*.

In my world, there was nothing else quite like it.

"You there?" Leo asked, after a little too much stunned silence.

"Yeah, I'm here. Did I hear you right? Did you just say—"

He laughed. "They want you on *Renowned*. You heard me right. Now, look . . . if you want to do this, things are going to move fast. Mario Borjomi was scheduled for this season, but he came down with tuberculosis or something while filming his National Geographic special."

"Oh my gosh, Leo! Is he okay?"

"I'm sure he'll be fine. But they'll want to be out in Nashville soon—I'm talking next week—to scope out the house and some locations, and start filming some promos." He gave me a moment to process before saying, "We'll sort out the details over the next couple days, but congratulations, Hadley. You deserve every bit of this."

I put my arm out behind me to feel around for the stool I desperately needed to sit down on. I found it and pulled it a little closer and collapsed onto it. I nearly biffed it, but I righted my position and settled in. *Renowned.* I had watched *Renowned* with my dad from the time I was a little girl, and I'd never missed an episode in the years since his death. It wasn't like any other show. It wasn't like the current state of entertainment—not even the current state of entertainment I was a part of. Now we worked hard and we worked fast to try and keep up. Constant content. Constant publicity. Constant attempts to somehow stand apart.

Renowned stood apart by maintaining the same slow, methodical pace it had employed since the 70s. It was a relic from a different time.

One season of eight episodes ran each year, and each year a different chef was the subject of all eight of those episodes. Joël Robuchon, Nobu

Matsuhisa, Jacques Pépin, Wolfgang Puck . . . Julia! The best of the best. My heroes. They'd all been the subject of a season of *Renowned*, and I'd read quotes from each of them about how it had been one of the greatest honors of their ludicrously distinguished careers.

And now Marshall Simons—who had created the show and hosted every single episode since—was going to be in the kitchen with *me*. Hadley Beckett from Nashville, Tennessee, who had a Bachelor of Business Administration degree but had dropped out of culinary school. Lover of fried okra and hot chicken and sweet tea. Henceforth those things wouldn't be used against me as insults. Henceforth other chefs—of the too-big-for-their-britches variety—wouldn't look down their noses at me for calling it powdered sugar rather than confectioners sugar.

Henceforth I would be important enough to get away with using words like *henceforth*.

"I'm really at a loss for words here, Leo. I have so many questions, but . . ."

"I get it, kid. This is big."

I shook myself out of my stupor. "You made this possible." My eyes began to burn as I thought back through the past several months—and really, everything that had ever happened in my entire life—leading up to the moment. "I just don't know how I'll ever be able to thank you enough for—"

"You're welcome." He interrupted my moment of appreciation, which was no doubt about to get sappy. "But you need to also remember to give credit where credit is due. Clearly, I'm not the only one who sees the special qualities that come to life just by letting Hadley be Hadley. Now, as for all those questions you have . . . don't worry about them. Not yet. I can fly out tomorrow and we can sit down and—"

"To Nashville? Oh, there's no need to go to all that trouble. We can talk on the phone. Or I can fly to New York if that would be easier."

He laughed. "When are you going to stop acting like you don't want to inconvenience me?"

"Well, I *don't* want to inconvenience you . . ."

"And I appreciate that. But this is my job, Hadley. *You're* my job. And any client of mine who is appearing on *Renowned* is, quite frankly, my most important job. Besides . . ." He cleared his throat and his tone shifted completely—from "easy breezy" to "I am gravely vexed!" "I'm afraid there's one part of all of this that you may not be too crazy about."

I scoffed. That was difficult to imagine. Unless Marshall Simons was going to expect me to make turducken . . . I smiled at the thought and then without thinking glanced again at the clock. It should only take, what? Thirteen, fourteen hours? I could still squeeze one in tonight if I needed to.

"Leo, it's *really* difficult to think of anything

that could ruin this for me, so you might as well just go ahead and—"

"The invitation is for you and Max Cavanagh, Hadley." He took a deep breath. "Together."

A pounding began to reverberate inside my head. No. No, no, no. That didn't make any sense. *Renowned* featured one chef each season. One. I mean, there was that one married couple that had appeared together, but they were famous for their partnership as much as they were famous for their ramen (which I'd had the opportunity to try once while passing through the East Village in New York, and which was legitimately *Renowned-worthy*), so that made sense. Jacques Pépin and Julia Child had been featured jointly around the time their first series together began taking off, but that also made sense. Besides, they had already been featured individually.

But Max and me? That just seemed, I don't know . . . exploitative, I guess. Cheap. Mean.

"I saw him tonight," I muttered softly, sort of into the phone but sort of to myself.

"Who?" Leo asked calmly, before more urgently adding, "Hang on. Max? You saw Max tonight?"

I nodded and then quietly said, "Yes," when I realized Leo couldn't see me nod. "He came to apologize."

"He—he—you're saying he came—" I'd never heard Leo sound flustered before. It made me feel better about the relative levelheadedness with which I had handled it all. "To Nashville? Max Cavanagh is in Nashville?"

I nodded again and added a shrug to the silent mix. "He said he was sorry he had treated me so horribly. He actually seemed surprisingly sincere about—"

I was interrupted by Leo's laughter. "Of course. Of *course!* Oh, Hadley, I'm sorry I didn't anticipate this sooner. I should have seen it coming so I could have warned you."

"Warned me about what?"

"He must have already gotten the call about *Renowned*."

I didn't understand what that had to do with anything. Unless . . . "You're saying he just wanted to clear the air before we had to work together."

"Something like that. I imagine he isn't entirely sure you'll agree to work with him again." He laughed again, this time more quietly. "He didn't mention *Renowned* at all?"

"No," I whispered. "Not a word."

"Smart."

I saw his eyes in my memory again—not the cruel, unfeeling eyes but the pair that had caused me to question my initial perception. Did he really have the ability to manipulate the very fiber of his being that way, all so he could manipulate *me?* Well, I wasn't going to allow him to play those games with me. But I also knew I wouldn't allow him to cheat me out of the greatest opportunity to ever come along in my career. Neither set of eyes got to have that kind of power over me.

I picked up a sponge and resumed my cleanup. "Don't come to Nashville, Leo. I appreciate it, but I'm fine. The next few days are going to be pretty busy anyway. Just give me a call when you're ready to fill me in on all the details, and we'll go from there. Sound good?"

"Sounds good. Get some rest and we'll talk soon. And Hadley . . . this is it, kid. This is the big time. Don't get bogged down in the details. You're going to be on *Renowned*! That's all you need to think about for the time being."

I smiled. "Thanks, Leo. Good night."

I hung up the call but didn't set down my phone. Rather, I wiped the drop of splattered bacon grease off of Max's pretentious card and dialed.

"Chef Cavanagh? Yeah, this is Hadley Beckett. If you're sticking around Nashville for a bit, I was wondering if you might have time for breakfast in the morning."

7. *Chill overnight.*

MAX

Max was awake with the sun, as he usually was. Admittedly, Tennessee sun felt different from New York sun. At the very least, it seemed like there was so much more of it. He sat on the edge of the bed and stretched his arms over his head, and then reached down to touch his toes. His custom-made Range Rover was more comfortable than at least the first four homes he'd lived in in his life, but it had still been an awfully long time to sit in one position. Of course, that vehicle had been designed for him with just that purpose in mind. During filming of *To the Max*, he spent more time on the road than in any one location. For months that Range Rover had sat in a parking garage, wasting away, probably wondering (if machines were susceptible to such thoughts) if its entire purpose in life had been undermined.

Max knew the feeling.

He clicked the remote on the bedside table, meaning to turn on the television. Instead the curtains opened, and the rising sun very nearly blinded him. He was a morning person, but that was a bit much.

He picked up the phone and was greeted by

a perky voice from the front desk. "Yes, Mr. Cavanagh? How can I assist you this morning? Do you need a ride, sir? Or some coffee perhaps?"

With a grunt and a stretch, he responded. "Coffee. Black. Strong. And bacon."

"Absolutely, Mr. Cavanagh. And how would you like—"

"Black. Strong. That's it."

"No, sir, I'm sorry . . . I was referring to your bacon."

It was a little too early for the perkiness, but the attention to detail won him over. "As crispy as possible without burning it. And one egg. Poached." He caught himself. He just wasn't in the mood for a bad food experience, and there was nothing worse than a chef who didn't know how to properly poach an egg. "Actually, how is your breakfast chef here?"

"He is excellent, Mr. Cav—" She gasped. "Oh, forgive me, sir. I didn't realize that you are . . . I mean, I'm sorry. It just clicked." She cleared her throat. "All of our chefs are excellent, Chef Cavanagh. I wouldn't necessarily recommend the poached eggs, but they are delicious, in my opinion."

This was far more conversation than he had ever wanted pre-coffee. "But you wouldn't recommend them?" He knew he didn't really require breakfast, since he was meeting Hadley in less than an hour, but he hadn't had the opportunity to go to the gym for four days now, and he just wasn't sure he would be able to find anything remotely healthy to eat at a place called Pancake Pantry.

"I just meant, sir, that I'm sure my taste is not as, um . . . *discerning* as yours. I've had them and I like them. But I don't know if my standard is up to your—"

"Yeah, I get it," he replied, rubbing his eyes. When he ordered food, he often felt like a police officer, minding his own business, frustrated that everyone on the road was driving 35 in a 65, just because he was in the lane behind them. "Let's just go with the bacon. And the coffee. Definitely the coffee."

"Yes, sir. Black, strong coffee is on the way to your room right now, and the bacon—extra crisp—should be to you in just a few minutes. If you change your mind on the egg, just let me—"

"Yes, yes, it's fine." He prepared to hang up the phone, the conversation coming to its conclusion, finally, but he had thoughts of Hadley—or, rather, thoughts of Hadley's perception of him— running through his head. He took a deep breath and added, "Thank you for your help. Sorry if I'm a little cranky this morning. I'm sure that coffee will do the trick."

"Oh no, sir. Not at all. And I'm happy to assist,

however I can. Please don't hesitate to call if there's anything else I can do for you."

With that he hung up the phone, satisfied by how much better he felt about it all.

It wasn't that he thought about Chef Hadley all that often. Not the woman herself, anyway. But very early on at Tranquility Peaks, once he'd allowed himself to settle in and become somewhat open to it all—having gotten used to not being able to go to the bathroom without Martin, the yoga instructor, saying "Namaste" as he passed his studio—they'd taught him that one of the best ways to tackle his anger was to personalize it. Not just the anger itself, but the results of losing control of the anger in unhealthy ways. For him, that would always look like Hadley Beckett—dark circles under bloodshot eyes, complete shock written across her face— being robbed of what should have been one of the proudest moments of her career. As much as it pained him to admit it, that sight was one of the very few things he actually remembered from that day.

Thirty seconds later there was a knock on the door, and Max rushed to receive his coffee, not certain he would survive another moment without it. He was forced to slow things down just a bit, however, as he realized, once his hand was on the doorknob, that he was only wearing his underwear. He groaned, threw open the closet door, and was relieved to find a hotel-provided bathrobe inside. He slipped it on and cinched the tie around his waist as he pulled open the door.

A man in full hotel uniform greeted him and began rolling a cart into the room. He was instantly about his business of performing each step of the process—pushing down the little brake on the cart wheels, assuring that the presentation was flawless, talking to Max in a way that made it evident he, unlike the sane people of the world, had been up for hours and had already consumed unfathomable quantities of caffeine. Max appreciated the effort but still decided to cut to the chase and pour the coffee for himself.

"My apologies, sir. Allow me to pour that for you."

Max shook his head emphatically but gently —so as not to spill—as he lifted the cup to his lips and gulped down as much of the steaming black gold as his throat could stand. When he came up for air he said, "No apology necessary. The coffee is just desperately needed this morning."

The man in uniform nodded and walked toward the door, but stopped and turned, just short of his exit. Ah. Of course. The internationally recognized symbol for, "Aren't you going to tip me, you doofus?" Before Max could scramble for his wallet, a second uniformed man—boy, really—

showed up in the open doorway with a covered plate of what was hopefully very crispy bacon.

"Good morning, Mr. Cavanagh," he said in greeting. "I hope everything meets your approval."

Max gestured that he could set the plate down on the cart, as he took another gulp of coffee and then poured himself a refill. As he drank, he fumbled around for his wallet, only to discover he didn't have any cash.

"Thanks for your prompt service," he said to both of the uniformed gentlemen, who were still awkwardly standing there. "Please add a 30 percent tip to each of the bills and charge it to the room." They both nodded and smiled and took their leave, but he quickly realized that his attempt at a fairly generous tip only amounted to about a dollar or two for each of them. "Eighty percent!" he called out down the hallway. "Sorry! Too early for math."

He walked back into the room and shut the door behind him. He yanked the cover off the plate and took a bite of crispy, delicious bacon. *Well done, Chef. Even if I wouldn't trust you with a poached egg.*

Once the caffeine began washing over his brain, the conversation that awaited him came into clearer focus. He sat on the edge of the bed— coffee in one hand, bacon in the other—and wished he knew how to prepare himself. When he'd gotten her call, he was halfway to Knoxville, with no plans to stop until at least somewhere in Virginia. But he'd turned around immediately, knowing she deserved at least that from him.

"It's about *Renowned*," he muttered aloud. "It has to be."

But what, exactly? He figured he could live with whatever it was, as long as she hadn't decided not to do it. And he didn't think that was very likely. She probably wanted it just as much as he did.

Well, maybe not quite that much. He had no doubt whatsoever that she wanted it—he'd never met a chef in his entire life who didn't—but Max was fairly certain no one wanted it as much as he did. He'd been passed over for years—when he won the James Beard Award, when new restaurants opened, even when a major network that *didn't* normally focus on food began airing his annual Christmas special. And when chefs he'd grown up watching and looking up to got their season on *Renowned*, he was primarily a viewer: excited for it to come on each Sunday evening, anxious to see if he could learn anything new, and yes, wanting his turn so desperately he could taste it.

But for the past few seasons, he'd mostly just been furious with the show's choices. Chefs he'd gone to culinary school with. Chefs he consistently defeated in the ratings. Chefs who had absolutely no right to appear before Max Cavanagh did.

If the circumstances were different, he would have certainly been grouping Hadley Beckett into that classification. Actually, who was he kidding? Circumstances were what they were, and that was still the case. But mostly he was just disappointed in *Renowned*. As an institution. Not for choosing Hadley—or at least not *just* for choosing Hadley—but for wanting the two of them to appear together.

It was a tabloid media choice, and Max was disappointed that they'd broken from their tradition of excellence for nothing more than the pursuit of ratings and headlines.

That didn't change the fact that he wasn't sure if his mouth would even be capable of forming the words to turn down the offer.

Stuffing the last of the bacon into his mouth, he stood from the bed, took a last swig of coffee, wiped his hands on a cloth napkin, and began searching for his clothes—more grateful than ever that he'd actually thought to pull some things together before hitting the road. This meeting was far too important to be wearing yesterday's socks.

About forty minutes later he was walking into an old brick building. An old brick building with a line of people down the block, it bears mentioning. "What is this place?" he wondered aloud, looking back at the line snaking through the door. He walked immediately to the front, without really thinking. Without a doubt, never having to wait for a table at a restaurant was one of the most appreciated perks of being, quite possibly, the most famous chef in the world. But he was clearly out of his element at Pancake Pantry, and he didn't know if the usual rules applied. And it sure hadn't occurred to him that he should call ahead.

He lowered his Ray-Ban aviator sunglasses on his nose and prepared to greet the hostess, but he spotted Hadley instantly. Hmm. Interesting. No corner booth, no hat or sunglasses specifically designed to help her blend in, no sitting with her back to everybody. There she sat at a small wooden table, right in the middle of the room, unobstructed face in plain view of the door. She lifted a hand in greeting as he thought again, this time aloud, "Interesting."

He pushed the glasses back up the bridge of his nose and turned to the hostess. "My party is already seated. Thank you."

He watched Hadley fidget—first with her napkin, then with her straw—as he approached, but he didn't give any thought to the cause of the fidgeting. He was still too caught up in how different her approach to dining in public was from his.

"Good morning, Chef," he greeted her. He put his hand out to shake hers, and after a moment she offered her hand in response.

"Good morning."

"I'm surprised you can just sit here in the open like this and not worry about being recognized," he said as he sat down across from her.

She cleared her throat. "I guess some of us haven't quite reached your level of stardom yet, Chef." Cynicism and hostility were gushing from every syllable. "Thank you for deigning to appear in public with me."

Uh-oh.

"No, I didn't mean . . ." It's funny how words can sound so nice and polite in your head, and then those exact same words can come across like a Catskills comedian confronting a heckler by the time they make it out of your mouth. "My surprise—and, truthfully, my admiration—is at the not worrying part. I wasn't meaning to comment on whether or not you're recognized. I think . . ." He sighed, already having talked so much more than he preferred to in any given day. "I think I tend to overreact some in that way. I assume everyone's going to recognize me, when more often than not, they don't want to mess with it. They just want to enjoy their meal, same as me."

Max knew he'd never been very good in certain social situations—well, *most* social situations, really—but in Hadley Beckett's presence he seemed to possess all the etiquette and social grace of a kitten chasing a laser light.

"Sorry," she said softly, shaking her head. "I just assumed you were insulting me." She let out a deep breath and rolled her eyes. "Sorry again. I didn't mean to say that . . . at least not that way."

He smiled at her discomfort—not because he was glad she was uncomfortable, but because even in the midst of it, she was undeniably genuine. That wasn't something he saw very often.

"No, it was a reasonable assumption to make. Most of my words to you *have* been insulting."

That was it. He didn't follow up with another apology, or act as if there were more to say, and that seemed to, for some reason, put her at ease. Her fidgeting, of which he had become increasingly aware, seemed to dissipate in an instant.

And then awkward silence permeated the air.

The only thing permeating the air more intensely was the delectable aroma Max suddenly caught a whiff of. He looked around at nearby tables and spotted bacon . . . eggs . . . even grits, a food everyone in the South seemed to have been jointly hypnotized into believing had flavor. But none of that was what he smelled.

The waitress appeared beside their table and Max ordered coffee, while Hadley went with sweet tea and something called apricot-lemon delight. The waitress—Holly, according to her name tag—jotted it all down in her memo pad and assured them she would be right back with their beverages.

"Actually, excuse me, Holly," Max said, stopping her just as she turned to head to the kitchen. "Can you tell me what that smell is?" Holly—twenty-two years old if she was a day—was overtaken by an expression of panic and looked around as if the smell he was questioning could only be a gas leak or a busted sewage line. "No, it smells fantastic," Max clarified in response to her reaction. *It smells like four thousand calories.* "It's food. I may order it. I just don't know what it is."

Holly seemed flabbergasted, and *far* out of her element. "Sorry, it's only my second week . . ."

We can talk all day about arts education and whether or not kids should be learning cursive, but why aren't schools teaching the lost art of customer service? Max thought, frustration beginning to boil up inside of him.

He turned his chair to face Holly full-on. "Well, it's definitely banana. What banana dishes do you have?"

"Do the bananas smell ripe?" Hadley interjected, grabbing Max's attention.

He turned in his chair. "Yes, but not overly so."

"So not mashed up and cooked in?"

115

He thought for a moment. "No, I don't think so."

She nodded. "Pecans or walnuts?"

Max closed his eyes and brought the earthy smell of the dish to the forefront of his mind. "Pecans. And . . . coconut, maybe?"

"Oh!" Holly exclaimed with excitement. "That's the Caribbean pancakes!"

Max smiled first at Holly and then at Hadley, and was surprised to discover both ladies were smiling back at him. "Thank you! I'd like an order of the Caribbean pancakes, please."

Hey, he thought. *I could always* walk *back to New York. That would burn* most *of the calories.*

He sat there, satisfied, until Hadley said, "You're a lot, you know."

Max tilted his head. "What do you mean?"

"Well, for one thing, why do you still have your sunglasses on?"

He removed them from his face, and hung them on the V-neck of his T-shirt. "I guess I'm just used to—"

"Do you really think no one recognizes you as long as you keep your sunglasses on? I promise you that poor thing knew who you were." Max started to argue but Hadley continued. "So there you are, the great Max Cavanagh, asking her to reverse engineer a pancake with you in her second week of work. Yeah. That's a lot."

Max wasn't sure what he should do. Should

116

he dispute what she was saying? Apologize for being . . . a lot? Whatever that meant. He stared at Hadley and attempted to interpret her mood, but he quickly discovered he didn't know the first thing about her or her moods. And then he reached the point when he knew he shouldn't still be staring, but he wasn't sure what else to do. She seemed to grow uncomfortable under his gaze, but he had no clue what to say. He wanted to ask her if she had done something different with her hair, but he knew that would most likely get him into trouble. He liked it the way it was—long, blonde layers—but to ask if the hairstyle was new would be to admit he hadn't paid much attention before. Not to her hair, certainly.

"What?" she finally asked, breaking the silence as she squirmed beneath his attention.

An amused smile crept across his face. "That's not normal what we just did."

"What do you mean? What did we do?"

And then he laughed. He just couldn't help it. "Figure out what I wanted to order for breakfast by breaking down whether or not the bananas smelled ripe." He tapped his nose. "Every chef's greatest tool."

It took a moment, but slowly she joined him in his laughter. Hers was more subdued. Much quieter. A little more uncertain. But they were laughing together, and that was certainly something Max hadn't counted on.

8. *Bring to boil over high heat.*

HADLEY

The good humor found in our "particular set of skills," as Max had said with his best Liam Neeson impression, carried the conversation up until the time our food came. And then our mouths were full and we didn't speak, apart from the occasional proclamation that what we were eating was amazing. But awkwardness started making its way in again, the longer we sat without talking. We were each nearly done with our pancakes, and I realized we still hadn't talked about anything of substance.

"You knew about *Renowned*, right?" I asked, blunt as could be.

He had been chewing, eyes focused downward on his plate, but the muscles in his jaw stopped moving and his eyes slowly made their way upward. His Adam's apple bounced as he swallowed. For a moment I began anticipating his next moves. I started playing it out in my mind—the way he was going to set his fork down slowly, look around the room to avoid my eyes, cross his legs in an attempt to act as if he were relaxed, and then, most likely, play dumb.

I really wasn't expecting him to reply, "Sure,"

118

and then look back down at his plate and fork off another bite of pancake.

I suppose there was nothing else to say. At least in his opinion.

"That's it? Not even an apology? No, 'You caught that, did you?' "

He looked back up at me and tilted his head. He stared at me for a moment, and then he brought his napkin to his mouth and wiped. When he had removed the lingering powdered sugar from his top lip, he set the napkin beside his plate and cleared his throat.

"What should I be apologizing for?"

Ah. *There* he was. There was the cocky, ego-centric Max Cavanagh with the special "something" no one quite knew how to define. Well, I could define it. Not with any words a Southern lady would use, but I could define it all right.

I smiled at Holly as she dropped off our bill and asked us if we needed anything else. Once we had assured her we didn't, and that everything was excellent, she walked away and the displeased expression immediately returned to my face.

"You should be apologizing for the fact that you showed up at my door under false—"

He held up a finger to silence me, and it worked. Although I didn't really quit talking as much because of the finger as the fact that he wasn't looking at me, and he didn't appear to be listening either. He was watching Holly go, and as soon as I stopped talking, he stood up and hurried toward her. He offered a quick, "Be right back," over his shoulder, but that was it.

"Pretenses," I completed my sentence aloud, stunned as he walked away from me in the middle of the very important thing I had been trying to say.

Holly turned to him as he approached. She appeared startled—nervous, maybe. She was probably worried he was going to give her a customer service lesson. Or at least a sense of smell lesson. And for that matter, maybe he was. I figured you couldn't put it past him. But before long, Holly's cheeks, which had been drained of all color, began to turn rosy. A smile overtook her lips and a sparkle overtook her eyes.

"Oh, come on!" I whispered emphatically. "She's practically a child!"

Okay, so she was probably a college student. Not *actually* a child. But Max was far too old to be hitting on her. And yet there she was, soaking it all up. Hook, line, and sinker.

I turned my attention from Holly to Max and tried to figure out what in the world women saw in him. Confidence, most likely. There was no doubt that the right amount of confidence could be very attractive in a man. Not that Max had the right amount. Not even close. But poor Holly hadn't had a chance to realize that yet.

And maybe that was the key.

I squinted my eyes and bit my lip as I studied him more closely. He had good hair. I'd give him that. It had been a little too floppy in the past, but now he had more of a side-swept Ivy League style, with a bit of deliberately tousled personality. Less Hugh Grant in *Four Weddings and a Funeral*, more David Beckham on a Tuesday. It worked.

I'd seen him wear glasses on TV, I knew, but I wasn't sure if they were prescription or pretentious. Either way, when he went without, as he did today, you could see just how blue his eyes were. And then there were his arms. I couldn't remember many times—in person or on television—that I had seen him wear anything other than his trademark black V-neck T-shirt and jeans, apart from the occasional apron, of course. A leather racer jacket sometimes. Maybe a down parka when he was hunting waterfowl or something in Alaska on *To the Max*. But it all stayed basically the same. And it all seemed designed to accentuate his arms as much as possible. Even the parka, somehow.

I felt heat rise up my neck as I allowed myself to survey him objectively, and I suddenly realized that Max wasn't as accustomed to eating pancakes as I was. The T-shirt sleeves strained just slightly to their resting point midway down his bicep, and with his arms crossed over his chest, as they were now, you could almost hear an audible sigh from the front of the shirt, as it was allowed a moment to relax from the tightness that Max's well-toned chest and shoulders usually created. *He probably eats just as many pancakes as I do,* I thought defensively, but also with admiration as I remembered how much more physical activity was involved in an episode of *To the Max* than *At Home with Hadley*. I'd been too scared to mount Marigold, while I'd seen Max ride Arabian stallions through the deserts of the Middle East. He'd earned those pancakes, and he'd earned that muscular build.

And yeah, looking at it all objectively . . . if you didn't know Max, you could almost think he was attractive.

He glanced over his shoulder and looked straight at me—at the worst possible moment. I could feel the pink splotches spreading. When he caught my eyes, he smiled at me. Pretty instantly he looked back at Holly, who was giggling at whatever he was saying. Had he said something about *me?* Probably. They were probably making plans to meet up somewhere as soon as he could ditch me. Well, I sure didn't want to stand in the way of that.

I stood from my chair, grabbed my handbag and the bill, and went up front to pay. While I signed the debit card slip, he noticed I was leaving. He quickly placed his hand on Holly's arm, and she pulled her memo pad from her apron and jotted something down on a piece of paper, which she tore out and handed to him.

Oh, good grief.

I rolled my eyes and walked to the exit. Pretty instantly he was right behind me.

"What's wrong?"

He held open the door for me and we pushed our way out through the line of people waiting— many of whom seemed to realize Hadley Beckett and Max Cavanagh were squeezing past them, together. I'd been too caught up in my own thoughts to prepare myself for that, but Max seemed instinctively aware of the whispering and pointing that had begun to take place.

Of course he was. I doubted that man ever missed an opportunity to enjoy some attention— good or bad. During his hiatus, while laying low out of the public limelight, he had probably developed a vitamin D deficiency. He hadn't had nearly enough chances to soak in the rays of his own majestic light.

I was used to being recognized myself, of course, but it was Nashville. And I was just *me*. I had my fans, no doubt, but I wasn't used to the level of interest that I was currently in the center of. And I sort of understood. Seeing Max and me together had to be a little like catching Rocky Balboa and Ivan Drago—or maybe Nancy Kerrigan and Tonya Harding—walking together after sharing pancakes.

I felt bad once I realized I'd been ignoring everyone, so I stopped at the end of the line and turned to face them. I offered a smile and a wave, and then a couple girls asked if they could take a selfie with me. *Where is Max?* Intending to tell him I'd be just a second, I instead saw for the first time that he was no longer with me. He'd probably gone back in for a curtain call.

"Hey, y'all," I called out as I waved, and the line of people cheered for me. "Well, aren't y'all so sweet?" I walked over to the girls asking for a selfie and smiled for their camera, and then the next person wanted a selfie too. An autograph, another selfie, a hug, three more selfies—each person kinder and more appreciative than the last.

"Whenever you're done with your fan club meeting, let me know," Max's frustrated voice muttered behind me.

"Is that Max Cavanagh?" The whispers grew in intensity until finally all I saw was a row of cell phones, snapping pictures, and all I could hear was a loud buzz of questions and commands—for us to turn or smile or pose with them.

They hadn't noticed him before?

"Don't act like you don't live for all of this atten—"

"Come on," he ordered, cutting me off and grabbing my elbow. His head was down and he had his sunglasses back on. He was so rude. He kept pulling on my arm, leading me away from the building, but I turned to face everyone one more time.

"Thanks, y'all! Enjoy your breakfast!"

At least that was what I tried to say. I got as far as "Thanks, y'all! Enjoy," before I tripped over my own feet and tumbled forward. Max pretty much caught me—not enough to keep me from scraping up my knee pretty good, but enough to keep me from face-planting on the pavement. And the way he caught me . . . golly, it was awkward. I mean, don't get me wrong. I was grateful I didn't break my nose or bust my lip, but he had caught me under one of my arms, and across to the other shoulder, facing him. My face was temporarily pinned against his chest as he wrapped his other arm around my back to pull me up to my feet.

"Are you okay?" he asked.

"Are people watching?" I mumbled into his chest, ignoring his inquiry. And then I realized I was still pressed up against his chest, and that I really could have waited a few more seconds before beginning to talk.

With one final hoist, I was on my feet again and free of him. I guess he'd heard my question though.

"Of course they are. You told them to enjoy. Why would they have turned away?"

My attention flashed from my torn jeans and

bloody knee as I glared at him. "I was going to tell them to enjoy their breakfast!"

He laughed. "Oh. Well, I'm sure they will. And they'll also enjoy their breakfast conversation, as they all talk about . . ." He looked over my head, back toward the restaurant. "Never mind. They won't have to talk about it. I think they all recorded it, so they'll probably be busy during breakfast, getting it uploaded on YouTube." The corner of his mouth continued to twitch just a bit as he looked down at my leg and surveyed the damage. "Really, though, are you all right?"

"Are you okay, Hadley?" I heard some people call out.

There was no way for the situation not to be humiliating, but I wasn't going to also allow it to be uncivil.

Facing back toward the concerned voices, I shrugged and smiled. "I'm fine. Hope y'all enjoyed your dining entertainment!" They laughed, I waved again, and then I turned to Max.

Obviously, the smile went away as soon as I was looking at him. And it turned into a full-blown scowl when I saw the obnoxious smile on *his* face.

"What?" I asked sharply.

He shook his head and smiled more. "Come on," he said for the second time, and then he led me around the corner, to the back of a shopping complex. There was no one in sight so we stopped, and I leaned back down to further inspect the damage to my knee.

"Why do you do that?" he asked.

I pulled a tissue from my pocket and dabbed at the scrape. "Do what? Fall? I don't usually. If you hadn't been pulling my arm—"

He laughed again. "You're going to blame that on me?"

I stood up straight and threw my hands into the air. "Of course I blame it on you! You were walking too fast, and you shouldn't have been pulling me in the first place."

"I only pulled you because you were about five seconds away from becoming tabloid fodder! I had no idea you were so vain."

"What? Me? You think *I'm* vain?" I was nearly choking over all the words that were trying to make their way out, as the heat flooded my head. "I was just being polite! You, on the other hand . . ."

"What are you talking about? I hate this stuff."

I scoffed. "Don't give me that. You love the attention."

"What are you even talking about?" he repeated, his voice growing more elevated. "I was just trying to walk out unnoticed. Meanwhile you're all, 'Hey y'all!' "

I put my hands on my hips and stomped toward him. "Are you making fun of me? Because I'm Southern?"

He shook his head. "Of course not. But I do

find it interesting that you get *more* Southern when you have a crowd to entertain."

"Well . . . but . . . well . . . sure, but . . . it's like . . . what . . ." I couldn't make anything come out apart from random, disjointed words.

Max, on the other hand, had no trouble at all using *all* the words, and forming *all* the sentences.

"And you only fell because you turned back. That's the sort of thing that sometimes tends to happen when you don't watch where you're going. And *why* did you turn back? Because you're vain. Because you had to look back and take one more bow. You're perfectly content letting them get the picture, get the autograph, get the story to tell all their friends and quite possibly the highest bidding scum magazine. It's all a small price to pay for—"

He stopped abruptly and his face fell. The volume and intensity of his voice had been continually growing, and then . . . silence. I looked behind me to see what could possibly be causing the reaction, but there was nothing.

"What's wrong?"

"I'm doing it again."

"Doing what?"

His eyes bore into me—they looked exasperated and incredulous—as he said, "I don't know." He sighed. "Attacking you?"

I was so taken aback by the questioning nature

of it. In an instant, vulnerability had washed over him.

"You weren't attacking me," I said softly but confidently. "We're just arguing. Fighting, maybe. But I don't feel attacked."

"This time," he added softly, I think only for his own benefit. He kept his head down, his eyes directed toward his feet, as he nodded and said words to himself that I couldn't hear.

He cleared his throat and said, "I'm sorry I called you vain."

I didn't understand what was happening. "No, you're not."

The shadow of a smile spread across his lips and he pulled off his sunglasses. He tilted his head and squinted to help those brilliant blue eyes avoid the sun. "No, I'm not. But I think I'm supposed to be."

I laughed. "Well, then . . ." I stopped myself from speaking aloud the rest of the thought. *That's progress.* I cleared my throat. "I shouldn't have stormed out back there. Sorry about that."

"Why did you?"

I walked a few steps past him and leaned against the brick wall. "The truth is, Max, I was in the middle of saying something pretty important— important to me, anyway—and you left me hanging, midsentence, to go hit on a waitress." I thought he would respond right away, but he didn't. He stared at me, and that was more uncomfortable than any of the awkward conversation that had taken place between us. "I mean, you can do what you want," I continued, needing to fill the silence. "I would recommend you make sure you have her home by curfew, but other than that . . . your life." *Don't be catty, Hadley,* I lectured myself. "I just . . . I just think it was rude. To me. That's all. Still, I shouldn't have—"

"You thought I was hitting on her?"

I laughed again. "Oh, come on! Call it what you want, but there was obviously some flirting happening there. And I saw her write down her phone number. And I don't care. Really." How many times was I going to tell him I didn't care? "It makes no difference to me." A few more, apparently. "But at least treat me with enough dignity to be honest about it, Max."

He shrugged. "Okay. The truth is I was apologizing."

Oh, come on! "You're just an apologizing machine lately, aren't you? Did you apologize to everyone in New York, so you had to take your little one-man band of apologies on the road?" *What? What was that even supposed to mean?* I laughed uncomfortably.

"It's going to take me a while to get to everyone I owe an apology to in New York. It was easier to start in Nashville."

He didn't laugh or even smile, and my discomfort grew. He looked down at the pavement as he stuffed his hands in his pockets, and I *really* hated that I noticed that was perhaps the most flattering position of all for his arms.

"I'm not going to do the show, Hadley," he said, mercifully snapping my attention back to his face.

"What show?"

"*Renowned.*"

I did a double take. "What? What are you talking about? Why wouldn't you do it?"

He turned his face away from the street until a couple walking by had passed. He was so much more adept at the celebrity thing than I was. That was evident.

"When I was a kid, I used to tape every episode. Every single one. Except we didn't have a VCR. We just had this old, beat-up Betamax camcorder that my parents had gotten as a wedding gift. So I'd sit there, holding that camera, through the whole episode, every week." He chuckled. "As if that weren't bad enough, I didn't have any way of playing back what I'd taped. The Betamax didn't have a playback function. That's probably why the Betamax didn't last very long. Anyway . . . I had this friend down the street who had a Beta player. Well, he was sort of a friend. I was really just using him for his Beta. I'd take my tapes down to his house all the time. Whatever the chefs were cooking that week, we'd try to make it. Did you do that?"

"Yeah. I'd make the dishes with my dad."

Max nodded and smiled. "I don't think my friend really cared too much about the show, but the more *Renowned* I watched, the better I got. I could cook pretty much anything by the time I was fourteen, and by that time his parents were the ones who actually let me go over there to watch the tapes. They got to benefit from the meals, and my friend just did his own thing."

"It sounds like you've been dreaming of being on *Renowned* as long as I have."

"Yeah. Sounds that way."

I took a deep breath. "From what I understand, the offer is for both of us. I'm not sure that's negotiable." I bit my lip and looked down at my bloody knee to distract myself from the flood of emotions I was feeling.

"That's what I understand too," he said softly. "But you're the hottest thing around right now." He leaned in closer to me and whispered, "You're welcome for that, by the way."

I glanced at him, prepared to be offended, but he winked at me and smiled—just a little bit sadly—and I understood the humility and regret within the statement.

"I've been meaning to send you a thank-you note."

He chuckled—again, sadly. "I think if I refuse to do it, they'll still invite you. I do. They'd be stupid not to. And there's not much time left to find anyone else, anyway. But if we do it together . . . I don't know." With one fluid motion he pulled his hands out of his pockets and put his sunglasses back on, as a European tour group walked past us, on their way to Pancake Pantry. "Don't you think it cheapens things?"

"What things?"

He absentmindedly kicked some small rocks into the street. "*Renowned*, mostly. But also . . . *us,* I guess. What we do."

I pulled myself away from the wall I had been leaning against and joined him in his rock-kicking. "*Renowned*, maybe. But I can't blame them, really. Ratings are ratings, I guess. But *us?*" Another tour group approached our stretch of pavement and I caught myself subtly turning my shoulders away—though that wasn't something I had knowingly ever done before. "You've made s'mores with the Dalai Lama, and I've decorated a sound stage for the holidays, as if that was where I was going to wake up on Christmas morning. And let's not forget that on *America's Fiercest Chef* we each threw a fit about whether or not we were described as 'legendary.' " I regretted adding that last part when I saw the expression—which I had to interpret as pain—that fleetingly consumed his face.

I don't know if I was more impacted by his regret or my own.

"Although I was just throwing a fit in my head,"

I added with a laugh, doing my best to defuse the weight of the moment. "Anyway, the point is, where's the line there? What 'cheapens' and what entertains? And when it comes to that, I have to admit, *Renowned* is probably on to something. Getting us back in the kitchen together? That could probably be pretty entertaining."

"Well, of course it would be entertaining," he agreed with a smile. "In the same way disaster movies are entertaining. But . . ." He cut his words off with a groan, and then he shook his head and turned away from me. "Never mind."

"What?"

He turned back. "They *want* us to fight, you know."

I considered that for a moment and then scoffed. "Now I don't think *that's* true."

He threw his hands in the air. "That's *exactly* what they want, Hadley! They're counting on you being the sweet and sassy belle of the Southern kitchen, and me being the troubled— 'but brilliant!'—jerk with a short fuse." The air quotes he put around the words made it very clear he'd been hearing it all for a very long time. "They want us both because we hate each other. Don't you see that?"

The air had been knocked out of me, so I could only *just* get the words out. "I don't hate you, Max. I don't . . . I mean, I don't *hate* anyone."

He sighed and took a step closer to me. "And I don't hate you. Sorry. I didn't mean . . ."

My eyes began to sting, and I suddenly wished I had Max's sunglasses. "No, I get it." And I did. Maybe for the first time. "Um, so I think I'm going to go." I began heading back toward the lot where my car was parked. He had not seen me cry even once during two of the most horrible days of my career, and there was no way he was going to see me cry now.

"Hadley, I just meant that's what *they* think. And that's what they *want*." He was following after me and we were almost back to the Pancake Pantry line—a line of *new* observers to humiliate myself in front of.

I stopped suddenly and turned around to face him—not realizing how closely he had been following. I took a couple steps back, so that I didn't have to look up at him. Beyond that, I wasn't sure how to handle the situation. Tiny little battles were taking place in my head. My Southern manners were trying to hold down the fort against the desire to lash out at him for ever having hurt me in the first place, just to get it out of my system. The idea he had planted—that maybe there was a chance I could get *Renowned* to myself after all—was firing cannonballs at the resolve I'd already established to do the show as a duo. And my self-confidence was threatening to retreat with the approach of the battalion crying out, "We *really* like you when Max thinks your name is Hayley."

"You . . . you . . ." I groaned in frustration. *Egg separator. Fish scaler. Garlic press. Hot plate.* "You frustrate me!"

He blinked rapidly several times before the corners of his mouth began turning upward. "I bet I do."

"Mainly just because you confuse me."

Nodding—and still smiling—he said, "I'm not trying to frustrate you. Or confuse you. If that counts for anything."

"You knew about *Renowned,*" I said, finally resuming the very important thing I had been trying to discuss in Pancake Pantry. "When you showed up last night, you already knew."

"I did."

"And you . . . what? Thought you could get on my good side so I'd agree to do it?"

"My goals were not so lofty as to think I could get on your good side, but I guess that was the general idea."

"Oh." Honesty. Hadn't expected *that.* "But what if I hadn't called you? And . . ." *Hang on a minute.* "You're the one saying you aren't going to do the show."

He shrugged. "I'll just say this, Chef Beckett: Not a single moment between us, since the very first moment we met, has gone according to plan."

What was that supposed to mean? And whatever it meant, why were the words, combined with the sly half-smile on his face, putting me at ease and also issuing a danger warning, all at the same time? Not to mention causing the pink splotches to start making their way back up my neck.

Definitely time to go.

"Look, you're doing *Renowned*," I stated, arms crossed in front of me. "You know it and I know it. Because it's *Renowned*, and you just don't say no, but also because *they,* whoever they are, don't get to decide what we're known for. We decide that. At least we try. They sure don't get to pigeonhole us. So, you're doing it. *We're* doing it. And that's that." I spun on my heel and began hurrying to my car in a desperate need to get away. A desperate need I didn't understand. But of course, I also felt a desperate need to be polite. "And thank you for the pancakes," I tagged on, turning back quickly.

"I think you paid!" he called out with a laugh. "At least . . . I *hope* you did. I didn't!"

I nodded my head and, without facing him again, stuck two thumbs-up in the air—which caused him to laugh a deep, genuine laugh that resonated all the way to my vehicle.

"Thank you!" he shouted.

I reached my car and climbed in as quickly as I could, turned the key in the ignition, and got the air conditioner pumping. *Oregano. Parsley.*

Quinoa. I fastened my seat belt and checked my mirrors, knowing nothing was going to stop me from getting away from him before I was forced to consider, one more time, whether it was actually possible that he wasn't the scum of the earth. Or at least that he was sincerely trying not to be.

And before I was forced to acknowledge to myself that a relatively decent human being—with that smile and those eyes . . . and those arms—could pose more threat to me than the old Maxwell Cavanagh ever had.

9. *Reduce to simmer.*

MAX

What was that?

Max attempted to process it all the way back to his Range Rover, and all the way back to the interstate. He was so glad he packed light, and that he'd thrown everything into his backpack before breakfast. He was ready to get out of Nashville and begin the process of getting everything back to normal.

Normal.

What was normal? He didn't have a normal work schedule anymore, that was for sure. Yes, his suspension had ended, but so far, the Culinary Channel had made no official moves to get *To the Max* back on the air. He didn't doubt that would happen—probably sooner rather than later—but for the moment, he wasn't filming or even making plans to film. For the first time in years.

And then there were his restaurants. Business was solid. Business was *always* solid. When you could consistently serve patrons one of the best meals they've ever eaten and do it with the best customer service they've ever experienced, there would always be plenty of people willing to pay exorbitant prices and make reservations months in advance. The problem was, they didn't need him. They needed him to check in on occasion and to stay in touch with the manager and the executive chef; they needed him to introduce new dishes every so often. They needed his name—still a mark of excellence, even if people weren't thrilled with his behavior. But they did not need *him*. He may have had the right to walk into any of his kitchens and take over anytime he wanted, but it wasn't a good way to do business.

And if he didn't have work, what did his life look like?

He clicked two buttons on the console, and a call began dialing out.

"Hey, Candace! It's Max. Max Cava—"

"Hey there, stranger! Long time no talk. What have you been up to?"

Max gave her a couple seconds to become aware and answer her own question, but there was nothing but silence coming across his vehicle's speakers.

"Um . . . rehab."

Candace gasped. "Oh, Max, I'm so sorry. That was stupid of me."

He forced a chuckle. "No, no. It's fine. Anyway, it's good to be back. I'm anxious to get back to work, actually. Is he in?"

She paused, and all he heard were computer keyboard clicks on the other end of the line.

"No. Sorry. He . . . he just stepped out."

"Okay, no problem. Should I just try him on his cell?"

"You know what? He's in meetings all day today, Max. Why don't I just give him a message, and I'm sure he'll call you just as soon as he gets a break."

He shifted into higher gear and felt the power swell beneath him as he floored the gas pedal. "Sure. That's fine," he lied. No longer being his manager's most important client was apparently part of the new normal. "Just tell him I'm leaving Nashville now, *Renowned* is a go, and I'm ready to get *To the Max* back on the air. This Range Rover needs to be given more to do than making me speed trap bait in Tennessee."

She chuckled. "I'll give him the message. Talk to you later, hon."

"Thanks, Candace."

He ended the call and pushed play on his "Standards" playlist. The soulful sounds of Sinatra began filling the air, and he settled in. He firmly believed that if you wanted to truly feel like a man, the two most important components were a great car and Ol' Blue Eyes. But the latter was stripped from him as quickly as it was given, as his phone began to ring. He clicked to answer the call.

"This is Max."

"Hey, hon. It's Candace again. He had a quick second between meetings, so I was able to get him the message."

Well, that was pretty speedy. Maybe he still had some clout after all.

"Great. What did he say?"

"He said, 'Don't tell people you were in rehab. Say anger management.' "

Max squeezed the steering wheel tightly and tried to remember the techniques they'd taught him at Tranquility Peaks. It was all about deep breaths and not wasting moments. Discovering new things about himself. Putting things in perspective.

And the best way he knew to put things in perspective at that moment was to remember how frustrated he had been at Tranquility Peaks every time Buzz, his counselor, had called him Maxim—which he insisted upon doing at least twenty-five of Max's thirty days. Despite his recurring insistence that unlike the Russian hockey player down the hall and the twenty-one-year-old model upstairs, his name was Maxwell. Not Maxim.

A little perspective can be a wonderful thing. At least Candace knew his name.

"I'll try to remember that," he finally replied. He hadn't lessened his grip on the wheel—or his desire to see just how quickly the Range Rover could get him across Virginia—but he had managed not to shoot the messenger.

Progress.

"Take care, Max," Candace concluded just

before a click indicated she had no further chastisements to pass along.

He had walked—or, rather, driven like a madman—into an impossible situation, and he was driving away the very next day having pulled off a miracle. Where was his credit for that? Not that it was *about* credit. No, it was about *Renowned*. But, still. Would one congratulatory comment—passed through Candace, even—have killed him?

"Don't act like you knew what you were doing back there," he muttered to himself with a groan.

Hadley hadn't been what he'd expected her to be. All he'd heard for the past four months or so was how she'd handled everything perfectly that day on the set, and he'd handled everything exactly wrong. That she was strong and generous and kind, and that she had suffered through his antics with grace and charm.

He didn't doubt that was true. He didn't remember any of it, per se, but he could imagine. She seemed to have the brassy, sassy Georgia—or Tennessee, rather—peach thing perfected on her *At Home* show, and he had no trouble at all piecing together in his mind the way it all played out.

Seeing her sheltered behind that guy, the director from the show, as soon as Max was spotted on the other side of the door, the evening before, had thrown his assumptions into instant chaos. Add to that the vulnerability that appeared in her eyes at the most unexpected moments—not to mention the healing that seemed to happen inside of him when she laughed—and he'd been left with intentions and plans in a tailspin.

He lifted his hips and tilted slightly so he could reach into the front pocket of his jeans, and then he took his eyes off the road just long enough to confirm he had fished out the correct scrap of paper. He sighed as he wadded up and threw in the backseat a half-sheet from a server's order book, with Holly's name and ten digits written on it.

All he knew for certain was that the same old Max he was used to being wasn't going to cut it with Hadley Beckett.

10. Cover and remove from heat.

HADLEY

"And with that," I concluded as I dusted powdered sugar across the plate, "you've created a dessert the entire family will go crazy over. And if you really want to make them go crazy, serve these little ditties for breakfast, and wash them down with that sweet tea we made earlier. But only on school days, or days when the sun is shining and the kiddos can be sent outside to play. Seriously, y'all, these vanilla donut drops have enough sugar in them to upset the apple cart of behavior in your house in a way it may never recover from." I smiled into the camera as Stuart gave me the "wrap it up" cue. "And while that apple cart is lying over on its side, pick up a few of those apples—preferably Granny Smiths— and set them aside for next time. I'm going to be sharing my delicious apple fritter recipe with y'all. What's more, we're gonna be getting the new place all gussied up for fall, and I may or may not have plans to jump into a big ol' pile of leaves. I guess you'll just have to tune in and see! Thanks for spending some time at home with me today, friends. Until next time."

"And that's that," Stuart called out. "That was a good day, everybody. Great work! Now, you should have all received your relocation assignments. Let's get it going—the network crew will be waiting for us at the new house. If all goes well, we'll have this place packed up before Hadley comes down from her sugar rush." He walked over to me and began speaking in conversational tones. "You know, it's always a good day when you can find an opportunity to use the word 'gussied.' "

I laughed as I washed my hands in the sink at the island. "I couldn't agree more."

"You're not actually going to jump into a pile of leaves though, are you?"

I scrunched up my nose. "Well, considering it's technically still summer, probably not." Filming ahead really created a weird sensation sometimes. "But I was thinking maybe I'd make some pumpkin spice lattes for everybody, since, as we all know, that's the only thing that screams fall *more* than jumping into dead foliage."

Various crew members, many of whom I was fairly certain I had never seen in my life, passed by, asking Stuart various questions and giving various reports. "Good shows, Hadley," they called out to me, one after another, and I just smiled and said generically nice things until they had all cleared the room.

"Is it just me," I whispered once Stuart and I were alone in the kitchen, "or do we have a few more people around now than we did in Brooklyn?"

He tapped the tip of his nose. "You're a sharp one, aren't you?"

"I can't always see!" I protested his attack of my observational skills as I placed my hands on my hips and followed him over to his chair, where his trusty clipboard sat. "The lights are on me, and it's harder than you think to . . ." I groaned. "Besides, I've just spent most of my time making sure no one walks into random rooms in my grandmother's house, looking for the bathroom."

He chuckled as he jotted things down, but he didn't provide the insight I had been hoping for.

It felt like such a light day, having already filmed two episodes by 3:00—Lacey's Kentucky Derby episode, which had been every bit the success I'd known it would be, and then the extra one, which might as well have been subtitled "The one in which Hadley enters the sugar trade"— with no more on the slate for the day. Not that there wasn't plenty of work still to do, of course. But in the moment—and with talk of all things autumn—it was feeling like a short day at school before being let out for Thanksgiving break.

"So . . . why are there so many more people?"

I stepped back out of the way as a burly man— who looked like the stereotypical version of a merchant marine in a soap opera—walked across the room with what I figured had to be about ten yards of cable wrapped around his arm.

"Hi there," I said to him.

He nodded and smiled, and I think he actually winked.

"Like that guy," I whispered to Stuart when Flint or Huck, as I imagined his name to be, had left the room. "Who *is* that guy?"

"Your agent got you more people."

"He *what?*"

Stuart looked up from his clipboard. "You have more people. A bigger crew." He leaned in and guilefully added, "And two more cameras."

I slapped his arm in genuine surprise. "We have *five* cameras now?"

"I feel like it's your birthday, but your new manager bought *me* all the gifts. Although I suppose all of my gifts will be put to use in *your* gift, so . . ."

"Did I tell you my new house has a shower room?"

"You did mention it, yes." He smiled as he gently bonked me on the head with his clipboard, then he walked away from me to get busy on his relocation assignments.

I followed after him like a puppy dog.

"My new manager got me another gift."

Stuart quickly glanced over his shoulder at me. "Are we going to let Hadley be Hadley on her own private island now?"

"No!" I chuckled nervously.

Why was I nervous? Because I knew *Renowned* had its own static crew, and Stuart wouldn't be able to film with me on this one? Or maybe because I knew I was in store for a lecture? That could definitely be it. There was no way he was going to learn I had agreed to work with Max again *without* making sure I heard his thoughts on the matter. Or was it just because once I said the words aloud, all of the good and all of the bad would become reality?

I lowered my voice and leaned in discreetly. "Guess which chef is being featured on the next season of *Renowned*."

He froze, and I knew that in an instant he had begun to process all of the emotions I had experienced the evening before when Leo told me the news. Well, the *first* set of emotions, anyway. But Stuart being Stuart, he had to handle his emotions—pride in me and all we had created together being chief among them, I was sure—in his own way.

"Norman Salverno?" he teased, and I couldn't contain my giggles at the thought—or at the memory of Chef Norman throwing his pesto on the floor during the first day on *America's Fiercest Chef*, after Max said it looked like baby poo.

"No, shockingly. Guess again."

"Um . . . Lacey? No, I suppose she's a little

149

young. But I bet they'll ask her before they ask Norman. Let's see. Oh, I know!" His eyes flew open wide with humor as he crossed in front of me and began packing up the crew's headsets. "Max Cavanagh!" he exclaimed. "Because he's definitely the guy all of America wants to invite into their home each week." He set down everything he was holding and turned to face me with an enormous smile on his face. "Congrats, Had! I'm so proud of you!" He threw his arms open wide and pulled me in for a hug. "This is huge," he said into my ear before grabbing my shoulders and pushing me to arm's length. "I mean, this is your dream! And you totally deserve it. No one deserves it more. Except Norman, of course."

He laughed but I didn't, and for the first time he seemed to detect that his wisecracking playfulness had left me behind.

"What's wrong? Aren't you happy about it?" He scowled. "I don't have this all wrong, do I? You weren't just really excited to tell me the next season of *Renowned* is going to be all about the Barefoot Contessa, were you?"

I shook my head and smiled. "Ina really is overdue, but no. It's me." The excitement returned to his face, and he pulled me back into the embrace. But the excitement was short-lived. "And Max."

Again, he froze, but this time he had his arms

150

wrapped around me, so I was left to awkwardly wait for everything to process.

"What do you mean, 'and Max'?" he asked through clenched teeth. Actually, I could vouch for the fact that Stuart was clenched from head to toe.

I extracted myself from his stunned death grip. "They want us both." He opened his mouth to speak, but I put my hand up to stop him. "And before you say everything I'm sure you want to say, just know that I'm okay with it. Would I rather have my own season? Of course I would. And I hope I still will someday. But I'm going to be on Renowned, Stu! I'm not going to pass up this opportunity just because my co-star and I aren't best friends. I mean, think of all the movies that would never have been made if everyone did that."

He considered that a moment. "*The Tourist.* Angelina Jolie and Johnny Depp."

"Um . . . okay. Sure. And I bet there are some we even would have missed. You know I'm right. And besides, I really think Max is trying to be a better person."

"Ha!" He returned to his headset packing. "Look, Had . . . you want to do it, do it. You know I've got your back, no matter what. But don't try to sugarcoat this."

"But that's what I do. I coat things with sugar." I reached behind me and grabbed the plate of vanilla doughnut drops, then held them in front of me with an innocent smile. "That's how I make friends."

He eyed me warily but eventually broke and stuffed a doughnut in his mouth. "Just be careful, okay?" he muttered, mouth full. "The guy showed up last night and apologized. Great. Hopefully he meant it. But you don't know him. And you certainly don't have any more reason to trust him than you did twenty-four hours ago."

I wasn't sure if that was true or not, but I didn't feel like right then was the best time to tell Stuart that Max and I had gotten to know each other a little better over breakfast—or during some post-breakfast drama on the street, rather.

"I'll be careful," I assured him, and popped another doughnut in his mouth.

We each got back to work—him boxing things up and calling out instructions, me scrubbing Meemaw's kitchen so she would at least have a clean surface for her Chinese takeout when she got home—but I had one final thing that needed to be discussed.

"Hey, Stu?" I shouted at him over the noise of the bustling crew.

"Yeah?"

"Will other directors know how to use that really flattering light filter that I like?"

"So *that's* why you keep me around!"

I laughed. "Don't act so surprised. I don't even remember your name half the time. With the other crew members, I just refer to you as 'The Guy with the Flattering Light Filter.' "

11. *Preheat oven to desired temperature.*

MAX

"Hey, man. I'm back. Just walking into my place right now. Sorry to call so late." He looked at his watch: 1:14 a.m. Max's calls had been ignored all day, but this one was justified. "Hopefully you got my messages. Call me tomorrow. Or today, I mean." He pulled the phone away from his ear to end the call but rushed it back as he thought of one more thing he needed to say. "I'm feeling good. I want to get back to work. *Renowned* will be great"—he still wasn't completely sure that was true—"but I can handle more. If the network's lost interest in *To the Max*, I've got some other ideas." None of them as good as *To the Max*, but he didn't figure it was necessary to include that disclaimer in his pitch. "Let's talk." He fumbled around in his mind for what else he needed to say, but with all of that now having been added to the countless thoughts he'd left with Candace throughout the day, he figured there really wasn't anything else.

That done, he jammed his phone into the back pocket of his jeans and pulled his key from the front pocket. He steeled himself and turned the key, and then walked inside and felt the familiar emotion of . . . nothing.

He set his backpack down by the door and looked around. Everything was the same. Of course it was. Just like it had been the same when he'd walked back in for the first time, a month earlier, after returning from Tranquility Peaks. He'd picked up a few habits at Tranquility Peaks and he'd hopefully kicked a few, but *life* had not changed.

He closed the door behind him and immediately removed his shoes. There were few things Max loved more than being on the road, but after his two-day round trip to Nashville, he was ready to be home. At least for a little while.

He reached down, picked up his backpack, and hoisted it onto the farmhouse table in the dining room. He wondered, as he often did when he looked around his apartment, how many other people bought homes they didn't really love, in locations that weren't the most convenient, simply because they fell in love with a kitchen. Max had never been much of a romantic, but his SoHo kitchen had made him believe that love at first sight was actually possible.

He unzipped and prepared to unload the bag of clothes, but his eyes stopped on the wall of his beloved kitchen, and then *everything* stopped. Without a doubt, the built-in wine rack and full bar setup had been among the most appealing traits of the apartment. Those, along with the perfectly positioned eight-foot skylight.

He walked to the wall of liquids a bit zombie-like.

At Tranquility Peaks, Buzz had helped him realize he didn't *need* alcohol; he only *wanted* alcohol. Buzz had also taught him that he could avoid a lot of his anger by being okay with other people receiving credit for their accomplishments. Even if their accomplishments were actually Max's accomplishments. Even if their accomplishments were stupid. Even if their accomplishments weren't actually accomplishments at all.

So he was okay with giving Buzz credit for helping him realize that he didn't need alcohol, despite the fact that he'd told everyone—including Buzz—that from the very beginning.

Buzz had advised him to remove all the alcohol from his home—not because Max thought he needed it, but because, at certain times, he knew he'd want it. In four months, he hadn't had a drink, and he'd been fine. But throughout most of that four months, the most stressful thing about each day had been the relaxation everyone kept trying to force upon him. Once he got back to filming—existing on four hours of sleep a night and losing track of time zones over the course of a week—would he really be okay saying goodbye to a nice relaxing bourbon at the end of a long day?

He didn't even bother looking at the wine bottles—those were easy enough to dispose of. The midlevel bottles could be served at one of his restaurants, or maybe even just kept on the rack for decoration. Wine had never been his temptation anyway. It was a miracle worker when it came to complementing a meal, but on its own . . . no thanks. The big-ticket wines, kept in climate-controlled (and keypad-protected) storage in his bedroom? Well, those were mostly just investments. Maybe one lucky network executive would receive an 1811 Chateau d'Yquem for Christmas this year. Regardless, he had no plans to ever drink the elite bottles anyway. He'd sooner drink his Apple stocks.

Now the hard liquors were another thing entirely.

He threw down the socks he had just pulled from the backpack and marched over to the bar. He grabbed the bottle of Macallan, quickly removed the top, and in one fluid motion poured the expensive brown whiskey into the sink. He reached up and to the left to grab a bottle of Grey Goose, and soon it was chasing the Macallan down the drain.

Max held the two empty glass bottles in his hands and felt extremely proud of himself. So proud that he figured the twenty-five or so other bottles of liquor could hang out a little longer. He'd emptied enough into the New York sewer system for one day.

He'd also unpacked enough for one day, he decided, looking at the used socks—the only clothing he had removed from the bag—which now lay on his kitchen floor. He dug into the backpack and pulled out the brown leather-bound journal he'd taken away as his one physical memento from Tranquility Peaks. Each of his thirty days there, and then continuing for another two months as he met with Buzz on an outpatient basis, he'd been required to write a journal entry detailing something new he had learned about himself that day.

Today, in my ongoing adventure of discovering who I truly am—the parts I like and should celebrate, as well as the parts I hope to improve—I discovered . . .

He had been strongly encouraged to continue with the daily journal entries once he returned to his normal life, and to find a licensed therapist to discuss them with on a regular basis. He had no idea if he was going to follow through on all of that, but he had intended to keep up with the discovery journal, at the very least. But he hadn't even cracked the thing open since leaving Malibu. Not because he had stopped caring about improving, but because he hadn't learned a single new thing about himself.

At least not until that day. That day had been full of discoveries. For instance, he'd never known just how much he enjoyed really good pancakes—or how slowly his body digested really good pancakes when he did nothing but sit in a vehicle for the rest of the day.

He grabbed a pen from the coffee table and sat down on the couch in his living room—just feet away from the kitchen in his open floor plan apartment.

Today, in my ongoing adventure of discovering who I truly am—the parts I like and should celebrate, as well as the parts I hope to improve—I discovered I'm not always the most important person in the room.

He sat back against the cushions and chuckled—at *what* he wasn't exactly sure. The wording, maybe. Possibly just the fact that it had taken him thirty-six years to "discover" something about himself that most people learned from *Sesame Street*. Most likely, the chuckling was caused by the memory of Hadley storming to her car with her thumbs hoisted in the air.

The chuckle morphed into full-blown laughter for no reason at all, really, except it had been a couple of really long days. He just kept picturing her shouting "Thank you for the pancakes!" And every time he saw it replay in his mind, he laughed harder. It wasn't funny. Not really. Although there was just the slightest touch of the ridiculous about her which he found incredibly entertaining. All of that—all he had done and all she *thought* he had done—and she still thanked him for pancakes *she* had paid for.

The laughter went away with a sigh and a quick swipe of moisture from his eyes. And then another sigh—the second one much weightier than the first. He opened the discovery journal again and ran a line through a few words before scribbling some new ones.

Today, in my ongoing adventure of discovering who I truly am—the parts I like and should celebrate, as well as the parts I hope to improve—I discovered it's nice to not always be the most important person in the room.

Max took another glance at his watch: 1:36. But only 12:36 in Nashville. "That's still too late," he said aloud. He walked back over to the bar, grabbed a bottle of cognac, and attempted to distract himself with the gurgling noise it made as it rushed down the drain. 12:37. A call would be rude, but a text . . . A text wasn't rude. If a text woke someone up, they needed to learn to turn on their "Do Not Disturb" function. One single late-night text would always be met with the understanding that a reply wasn't expected until after the sun was up. Everyone knew that.

Hi Hadley. It's Max. Just wanted to say thanks for

taking the time to chat today.
Glad you thought of it. I'm
looking forward to working
with you and getting to know
you better. And I wanted to
again say how sorry I am for
everything.

He studied what he had typed and then let out
a disgusted groan as he deleted every word. He
thought for a moment and then chuckled again.

Next time, breakfast is on me.

With a satisfied grin he hit send, and then set
his phone on the dining room table. He reached
down to pick up his backpack—determined to at
least get it into his bedroom, even if he got no
further anytime soon. He grabbed the socks in the
other hand and took a few steps before stopping
in his tracks. The vibration of the phone against
the table filled the big, silent space.

He dropped everything into a dining room chair
and grabbed his phone.

Now would be good. I'm
starving.

Max read Hadley's text at least five times, and
then a couple more for good measure. "What?"

he asked aloud with a laugh. Maybe he shouldn't have deleted the "It's Max" part. He scratched the three-day stubble on his cheek and tried to decide how to respond, while also being fairly certain that if he gave her a few more seconds, he'd receive a "New phone. Who dis?" text.

> Don't think I could get there before lunch. You may succumb to starvation by then.

He hit send but instantly regretted it. That one felt too casual. Yes, she had set the casual tone, but he still wasn't entirely sure she wasn't sleep-texting. He added:

> Sorry to text so late, by the way. I hope I didn't wake you.

He stared at his phone, but nothing happened. He looked at his watch again. 1:40.

1:41.

1:42.

Either she'd fallen asleep, which would be totally understandable, or she'd realized she was texting with Max Cavanagh, rather than someone who *wasn't* her sworn enemy. Either way, he knew his best play was to call it a night and hope that this confusingly friendly and familiar text exchange would result in less awkwardness the next time they saw each other, and not more.

He hadn't accounted for a third option: she was texting him a book.

> It's my first night in a new house. And that's great. But weird. It's bigger than my old place, which was about the size of a canoe. I've been hearing every single noise. I'm hearing the water heater right now. I didn't know water heaters made noise. And worst of all, I didn't think to buy any groceries. The loudest noise of all is my stomach growling. You are correct . . . by lunch I will be nothing but bones heaped in a corner, where I had been hiding from the water heater.

A smile covered Max's face, but he was no less bewildered—and, really, still not certain Hadley knew who she was talking to. Well, it was time to make sure.

> Are you saying now wouldn't be the best time to tell you (in excruciatingly appetizing

detail) about the dishes
I intend to prepare on
Renowned?

1:45.
1:46.
1:47.

You're free to do as you like,
Chef.

And then instantly:

At your own risk, of course.

With a laugh, Max dumped his backpack and socks out of the chair, plopped himself down, and settled in for . . . well . . . whatever this was.

12. *Stir until just combined.*

HADLEY

"Good morning, Meemaw," I greeted her as I let myself in to her house and spotted her on the couch, already settled back in after her early morning flight, reading one of her tabloids. "Welcome home."

"Hey there, darlin'." She didn't get up, but she did look up at me with a smile. If she cared enough to pull herself away from her reading, I could be assured she had missed me.

I set the box I had brought in down on the counter and then leaned in from behind the couch and kissed her on the cheek. I kept my chin on her shoulder to sneak a peek at what she was reading.

"Of all the great literary journals you read, this one makes the least sense to me. Nothing but gossip about country music stars? We live in Nashville. I see Faith and Tim at Kroger at least twice a month. Miranda Lambert cut me off in traffic on the drive here. These are real people, Meemaw." Not that the other celebrities she read about weren't, but it just felt weird to think about reading that much gossip about someone you might bump into at Whole Foods.

"How is this any different than neighbors

standing around at the county fair, swapping stories about their other neighbors who aren't there?"

I kissed her again and stood up. "It isn't!" I walked into the newly usable kitchen and grabbed a couple plates. "I brought donuts from Five Daughters. Want one?" I didn't wait for an answer. I just began plating.

"You and your trendy hotspots. Whatever happened to good ol' Dunkin' Donuts?"

I handed her the plate, to which I'd added the flourish of a raspberry syrup base and a sprinkle of powdered sugar. "When Dunkin' Donuts starts describing their filling as a 'brownie batter buttercream infusion,' we'll talk. Until then, you're welcome."

I carried my own decked-out plate into the living room and sat down in the chair across from her. And yawned. I suspected it was going to be a day full of yawns.

"How was Branson?" I asked.

"Unseasonably warm."

I waited, but that was apparently all she had to say about her free three-week trip, which she had chosen to extend twice.

Good talk.

"I have something big to tell you, Meemaw."

Her eyebrow indicated she had heard me and was ready to receive, but she didn't stop reading.

"Seriously," I added. "This is big. Can you

maybe take a quick breather from your pictures of Jason Aldean filling up his truck?"

It was clearly a burden to her, but she did as I asked.

"Thank you." I took a deep breath. "I'm going to be on *Renowned*, Meemaw." I couldn't imagine those words would ever be less surreal.

"What's that?" she asked.

Spoon. Turmeric. Utensils.

"You know *Renowned*. It's the show Dad and I used to watch—"

"You watched lots of shows, as I recall."

"Well, yeah." I sighed. "But *Renowned* was our favorite. Remember? That's the one where the entire season is all about one chef?" Usually, at least. "And it's not just cooking. I mean, a lot of it is cooking, but it's also kind of an in-depth profile of the chef." She was still staring at me somewhat blankly, so with a sigh I concluded, "Just . . . trust me. It's a pretty big deal."

"That's great, sugar. Really great." She took a bite out of her donut and then quickly attempted to clear away the appreciative expression from her face before I caught it. She failed.

"I know it's no Dunkin' Donuts . . ." I smirked.

Her face was once again captured by complete nonchalance. "Why didn't you ever tell me you wanted to be on there?" she asked. "I would have gotten you on this . . . what is it again? Redeemed?"

"*Renowned*. And I *did*—" I cleared my throat to cut myself off. There was no point. It would just start a fight. "I thought about telling you I wanted on, but I don't think I had a wide enough base to even be considered, before all the *America's Fiercest Chef* stuff."

That part was true. *Renowned* had always been a "someday" dream. Maybe after I opened another restaurant, or once my flagship restaurant, Scratch, was upgraded from a two- to three-starred Michelin restaurant. But why hadn't I ever told her? I had. More times than I could count, from the time I was a teenager, just cooking for the family. When Marshall Simons, the creator and host of *Renowned*, chose one of my dishes as his 2018 Taste of the Year, I had told my grandmother it was a great open door, and it would be the perfect time to start a conversation about *Renowned*. She had told me she was on it.

She had also told me to stop telling her how to do her job. She hadn't taken that from Dolly, and she wasn't going to take it from me. But apparently, I had never even mentioned any of it to her. Okay. Sure. And then Leo had gotten it done in a little over a month.

Don't be bitter, Hadley, I reminded myself. *Leo had some help.*

"There is one thing a little different about this season of *Renowned*, Meemaw. It's still going to be great, and it actually feels really special to be part of something new, when they're trying it for the first time."

That was my newest emotional justification. It was actually working pretty well.

She kept eating so I continued on. "Do you remember that guy, from *America's Fiercest Chef*?" That seemed like a silly question, but at that particular moment I was half-inclined to ask her if she remembered my name. "Max Cavanagh. Remember?"

She laughed. "Of course I remember. What about him?"

"He and I are doing the show together." I forced a smile, stood from my seat, and carried our empty plates into the kitchen.

A minute or so later I had the plates washed and was ready to dry them, and I still hadn't heard a word from her. I glanced back over and saw she was right back into her tabloids, as if neither the donuts nor the announcement of the biggest opportunity in my career had ever happened.

Moving on, I guess.

"You should come see the new house later," I called out as I opened the cabinet door and stowed the plates away. "It's pretty spectacular. I can't wait to get busy in that kitchen. It's going to be nice to—"

"Here!" she shouted.

"No, that's fine," I muttered under my breath. "I was basically done talking."

She bolted up from the couch and walked into the kitchen, carrying one of her magazines. "If the *Celeb Scoop* is to be believed, he'd just gotten dumped by Miss Fancy Pants Kitty Cat."

So many things to say. The one thing I knew wasn't worth saying was that no . . . *Celeb Scoop* was most assuredly not to be believed. I'd tried to convince her of that one, but I was just wasting my breath.

"Miss Fancy Pants Kitty Cat?"

"You know. That girl group that always wears summer clothes on TV. Tube tops and hot pants, no matter how cold it is outside. She's the one who's a judge on that singing show, though if you ask me, none of those Meow Meow Girls, or whatever they're called, know singing from moonshine."

"Meemaw, I honest to goodness didn't understand a word you just said."

She turned the magazine around so I could see it. "Max Cavanagh. That's why he was drinking a little too much that day."

Again, *so* much to say.

"First of all, he wasn't 'drinking a little too much.' He was hammered. Two, it doesn't matter if he *had* just gotten dumped. That's no excuse to . . ."

My voice trailed off as I snatched the magazine out of her hands. It was strange to look at a photo of him from before. *Before* he showed up at my door to apologize. *Before* breakfast. *Before* a texting marathon that had kept me up until nearly 3:00 a.m.

In the paparazzi shot, he looked more like the Max I remembered from the set, all those months ago. The surroundings were certainly different—the streets of New York rather than a studio kitchen—but the distance and disregard in his eyes could have been stolen directly from the way he looked when he called me "doll" and compared me to Colonel Sanders.

A breakup?

I rolled my eyes and handed the glossy pages back to her. I knew better than to believe those reports. There'd been a fair share written about *me,* for goodness' sake—usually about how I wasn't really as nice as I seemed on TV, or how my heart had been broken by Guy Fieri's hairstylist's refusal to cut my hair, or something equally absurd. More often than not it was all about chef "turf wars"—I guess we knew whose side Guy's hairstylist was supposedly on—and ridiculous battles we were all, apparently, having with each other nonstop. I'd never met Guy *or* his hairstylist, but publications like that weren't interested in the facts. They were just interested in whatever sold copies.

I had to admit, though, that those pictures looked legit. Max and Miss Fancy Pants Kitty Cat were clearly fighting about *something*. But to make the leap that a public argument on the Upper West Side was the cause of Max being on his worst behavior at work for those two days, to the point that he was suspended and his show was put on hiatus, was a bit extreme.

At least, I hoped so. I hated to admit to myself that a couple of days of conversation with him had me feeling cautiously optimistic, but I was. *Very* cautiously, but optimistic, nonetheless. If I found out he'd acted like a swine, treated me and the other chefs like underlings, and shown so little consideration for an entire studio of professionals for no better reason than girl problems, I was not going to be pleased.

"No, it's looking great, Leo. We'll definitely be ready to film on Monday." I squeezed my phone between my ear and shoulder so I could reach up and straighten the light fixture over my new huge, beautiful kitchen island. "This place is so perfect for the show. I really can't thank you enough for everything you did to make this possible."

"I did very little, but you're welcome. And we'll just leave it at that. If I tell you just how little convincing it took, you might decide I'm not earning my keep." He laughed on the other end of the line before adding, "I mean it. The network is firmly in your camp, and more than happy to do what it takes to keep you happy."

I looked around at my luxury Thermador appliances and the marble countertops, the gorgeous walnut floors under my feet, and the three acres of rolling Tennessee hills outside my window.

"I think this will do it."

"Good. And I'm glad the house is about ready to go. Do you think it will be ready for *two* film crews on Monday?"

My breath caught in my throat. "*Renowned*? Already? Monday?"

"Mostly just preproduction. Marshall Simons wants to fly out there next week and get acquainted with you."

"Well . . . su-su-sure," I stuttered. "I mean, if it's not a problem that it's a full day for *At Home with Hadley*." *And if it's not a problem that I may be busy breathing into a paper bag at the thought of Marshall Simons in my house.* I looked around again. Admittedly, it was going to be a lot easier to welcome a culinary icon into my home knowing my home looked like a spread in *Architectural Digest*. Previously, I'd always decorated according to the "Hadley would rather buy baking pans than wall art" school of thought, so I needed to shift my thinking a bit.

"No, it's not a problem," Leo replied. "His team knows what they're looking at. They want to see you in your natural habitat."

Hmm. I wasn't sure I could pull off "This is my

natural habitat" by Monday, but other than that, I figured I could make it work.

"Okay, no problem. Easy breezy lemon squeezy." *Note to self: never say that to Marshall Simons.* "Max will be here too, I presume?"

He sighed. "Afraid so. Sorry."

I crossed into my partial-turret dining room, where windows covered the walls, floor to ceiling, and watched the breeze pass through the trees. How strange. A few days prior, my response to hearing Max Cavanagh would soon be in my house would have been, "Somehow I'll find a way to get through it." Now I found myself wondering if he'd ever seen a red-flowering dogwood tree as beautiful as the ones in my backyard.

"It's fine," I said simply and dismissively.

"You're a trooper, Hadley. Thanks, kid. Talk to you soon."

I ended the call and then immediately went to Messages.

> I guess the problem with the network owning my house is I don't really have any say when brilliant, bold, groundbreaking chefs I look up to are invited over. Oh . . . and apparently you're coming over too?

I smiled as the three dots instantly appeared, indicating he was crafting his undoubtedly snarky reply.

A brilliant chef in your house?
Your house won't know what
to do.

I laughed out loud, and then my laughter grew when, within seconds, a second text confirmed Max was still working out the kinks on his new kinder, gentler personality.

That was a joke.

I yawned as I stepped out onto the veranda and settled into my new porch swing. As I had predicted, it had been a day full of yawns. But a lack of sleep wasn't going to stop me from having as much fun as possible at my suddenly friendly rival's expense.

13. *Coat evenly.*

MAX

"Knock, knock."

The front door was open and crew members were sweeping in and out, grabbing equipment from trucks and vans. No one seemed to care that Max was letting himself in, after his vocal knock had gone unacknowledged. That was one reason he'd never wanted to film anywhere he lived. How can you ever separate your life under those conditions?

Of course, from the look of it, Hadley had enough square footage to open up a small outlet mall and never be disturbed.

He stepped over cables and around lights and cameras all the way through the foyer and a living room roughly the size of his apartment. Finally, he heard Hadley's voice and began heading her way—although he would have walked that direction regardless. He would always be instinctively drawn to the kitchen.

"Thanks so much for spending some time at home with me today, friends," she was saying directly into a camera lens. "I hope you'll come back next time, because I'm going to be showing you how to make croquembouche. You're probably thinking to yourself, 'Now, Hadley, croquembouche sounds French and fancy and high falootin'.' And you're right. Croquembouche is *all* of those things. But you know what else it is? It's a tower of cream puffs, covered in caramel. And when you put it that way, I think it's a little more our speed. Don't you?"

Max let a snort escape and was finally acknowledged—by an entire production crew flashing him expressions of warning and gestures demanding silence. He raised his hands in apologetic surrender and nodded he understood, and then returned his attention to Hadley—who was the only person in the room smiling at him.

In a nearly indecipherable flash, she was looking back at the camera.

"We'll also be testing the best espresso drinks we can get our hands on, so if you notice I'm talking a bit speedier than usual, do not adjust your television set! In fact, I just recommend you're prepared and have some espresso of your own on hand, so you can keep up." She paused and smiled—with perfect timing, and a perfectly warm smile. "Until next time."

"And that's a wrap," her director called out. What was his name again? Steven? Sonny? "Good work. Great show, Hadley. Okay, *At Home* crew . . . we need to break down and clear out for the *Renowned* crew. Just minimal breakdown. Equipment can stay in place. Let's go!"

Everyone immediately snapped into action

and began working through their checklists efficiently and effectively. Max was impressed not only with how quickly they worked but also how happy they appeared to be while doing it.

The only person not moving was the star.

"You have hair on your face," she called out as Max approached the kitchen island where she stood.

He chuckled as he brought his hand to his chin and rubbed his week-old beard. "I do. Do you like it?"

Do you like it? Why would he ask something like that? In the context of his relationship with Hadley, it sounded incredibly vain. Or petty. Stupid, at the very least. Of course, even the thought that he and Hadley had any sort of relationship at all felt pretty vain to him. And stupid.

And yet, she smiled at him.

"That depends," she replied as she appeared to study him earnestly. "If you keep the beard, are you going to have it meticulously trimmed and manicured at some overpriced Tribeca salon?"

"Absolutely. By someone named Mystique."

She nodded and smiled. "Figured."

"Had?" The director—Sebastian?—got her attention and waved her over to him.

"Be right back," she said in response before bounding over to a row of cameras. Max turned and watched her go—and got caught watching her go by the director, who was shooting daggers out of his eyes.

At least, until Hadley reached him. Once he turned to her, his expression softened, and a smile overtook his face.

What's going on there? Max looked away and walked further into the kitchen. After a quick glance around him to figure out if he could expect to be fussed at for being where he shouldn't be, he stepped behind the island, and effectively onto the set of *At Home with Hadley*. The floor felt slick beneath him, and the dust of the white, bleached flour being stirred up by his shoes made it very evident as to why. There was flour *everywhere*. Not to mention a fair amount of sugar, what appeared to be cornmeal, and a little bit of Karo syrup.

"Are you kidding me?" he whispered under his breath, in utter disbelief. The woman was a professional chef. A successful one. How had she managed to get anywhere in the culinary world with less tidiness than one of those steakhouses where you throw peanut shells on the floor? If this were one of his kitchens, he'd fire her.

Do not tell her that.

He mentally thanked the voice of warning in his head, even as his fists curled and his feet shuffled uncomfortably—and then *stopped* shuffling when he realized flour clouds were starting to

179

leave remnants on the legs of his jeans, and his shuffling was just making it worse.

These were just *not* appropriate conditions for a professional kitchen. Not even close.

The old Max would have made sure Hadley knew that. The old Max would have made sure *everyone* knew that. And he wasn't proud to realize that. But he had high standards. He could acknowledge that the old way of dealing with those standards needed work. But the standards themselves? He wasn't going to apologize for that. He would just find less aggressive ways to meet those standards. Hopefully ways that didn't completely alienate the funny, forgiving chef who just happened to learn kitchen etiquette from the Swedish Chef.

He spotted a sponge in the deep farmhouse sink and wet it down with warm water. By the time Hadley made her way back over, Max had *almost* cleaned up all of the endlessly sticky corn syrup.

"You didn't have to do that," she said.

Yes. I did.

He shrugged as he scrubbed. "So . . . this house. You weren't kidding. It's a lot for one person."

She reached into a pantry and pulled out a broom and dustpan. Then she began cleaning up the mess on the floor, and Max felt tension release from his shoulders.

"Yeah. I keep having flashes in my mind of the entire crew living here, and each night we'd yell out 'good night' all across the house, like *The Waltons* or something. 'Good night, Hadley.' 'Good night, Jerry.' 'Good night, John Boy.' "

"Good night, Hadley," a member of the crew called out as she walked toward the door.

"Good night, Margo," she replied with a wave. "See you tomorrow." Then she winked at Max and said, "We've been practicing."

Max smiled and rinsed out his sponge. "This kitchen, though."

"Right? All these years, I think maybe I've just been working toward this kitchen." She let out a groan. "You know, though . . ." She lowered her voice and leaned in closer, to speak privately. "It's only been a few days, but I kind of hate the place."

"What?"

"I mean, I'm grateful. And I'll adjust. But at night, all alone with three thousand square feet . . . I don't know. It's weird. Playing the piano as late into the night as I wanted, with no concerns about disturbing the neighbors, was only fun for one night. Then I realized I didn't have any neighbors close enough to be *called* neighbors. I could hop in my car and drive to the grocery and back faster than I could walk to their houses to borrow a cup of sugar."

She swept and dumped what she had collected into the garbage, and then repeated the cycle. And through it all, she talked. And through it all,

Max watched. There was something so uniquely genuine about her. Just like it didn't make sense that she had achieved as much success as she had without learning to get the flour in the bowl rather than on the floor and countertop, it didn't make sense that she found a way to be more of a real person than any other celebrity he had ever met.

She abruptly cut off whatever she had been saying. Max had momentarily lost focus.

"I'm sorry." She groaned. "I must sound like the most pampered princess. I'm grateful. I am. And that's that."

He kept watching her as she returned her cleaning supplies to the pantry, but he didn't know what to say. He didn't know how to *be* around her. Texting was good. Texting was *easier*. In a text, he could be whoever he wanted to be. Not that he tried to be someone he wasn't, but he definitely tried to be a more presentational version of who he was. They'd exchanged countless texts back and forth, to the point that Max had walked into Hadley's house today feeling as if they knew each other. Maybe even liked each other. But suddenly without the ability to take an unobserved moment to think and calculate before he allowed his thumbs to do the talking, he felt destined for failure.

"It's fine."

You don't sound like a pampered princess. I

get it. Why do you think I'm always on the road? Maybe you could get a dog.

These were all thoughts he was having. Some more worth saying than others. All more worth saying than, "It's fine."

Max scratched the palm of his hand against his scruffy cheek. *I get it. Start with that.* He took a deep breath and opened his mouth to attempt *realness* with her. To attempt . . . what? Human connection, he supposed. It had been a while.

"Anyway," Hadley resumed. "I think this kitchen is going to be great for *Renowned*. Especially since we'll need room for both of us."

She kept talking about the best features of the kitchen and pointing out the aspects she thought Max would appreciate most, but he was only half-listening. She'd begun talking again before he'd had a chance to stumble his way through an attempt at realness, and he wasn't sure if he should take them back to the connection point or thank his lucky stars that she now seemed perfectly content to instead point out the telescopic racks of her Thermador range.

But he was unfortunately—mercifully—robbed of the decision. Max and Hadley both turned toward the commotion that was suddenly coming through the door. Marshall Simons and his entourage had arrived.

Max snapped to attention like a little boy who'd been caught yanking on a girl's braids. Marshall

Simons. In the flesh. Everything else was momentarily forgotten as he realized he couldn't remember the last time he'd felt starstruck. It hadn't happened many times in his life, that was for sure. He'd met Paul Bocuse once during his culinary school internship in Paris, and there was the time he and his dad bumped into Mr. Rogers at the hardware store when he was a kid. But that was about it. And now, Marshall Simons.

"Chef Simons," he said as he rushed across the room and put out his hand. "I'm Maxwell Cavanagh. It is such an honor to meet you, sir."

They shook hands and Chef Simons greeted him by saying, "Chef Cavanagh. What a tumultuous year you have had."

Max grimaced. "But it's led to this moment, so I'd say it's—"

"Ah! Chef Beckett!" Chef Simons's eyes widened. He pulled his hand away from Max's and rushed to where Hadley stood just outside the kitchen perimeter—pretty much where Max had left her without a second thought.

The elder statesman of the kitchen loosely grasped Hadley's elbows as he kissed each of her cheeks, in quick succession.

"Chef Simons, I want to echo what Chef Cavanagh said. It is *such* an honor to meet you. Thank you so much for inviting me to be a part of this. *Renowned* has played an important role in my life, and"—she glanced across the space at Max, who had been left behind with the entourage by the door—"and I know it's played a very important role in Chef Cavanagh's life too. Isn't that right, Chef?"

Max's eyes met Hadley's. *You just really aren't like the rest of us, are you?* He'd raced across the room to make sure *he* was the first one in Marshall Simons's path—and then Hadley . . .

Hadley, whose face got red the moment she felt any emotion whatsoever, it seemed. It didn't matter which one. He'd seen her turn red in anger and frustration, maybe a little bit of sadness. Embarrassment. Now what was this one? Excitement? Nervousness? Did she flush every bit as much due to the happy emotions as she did the unhappy?

Well, whatever emotion she was feeling, her hands—motioning subtly but urgently behind her back for him to join them—indicated there was at least a little bit of impatience wrapped up in it. Right. She'd provided him a perfect entrance back into the conversation. What had it been . . . ?

Max hurried over to join them. "It's true, Chef Simons—"

"Call me Marshall," he said, and for one split second Max and Hadley joined together in giddy disbelief. Their eyes met again, and he winked at her. Hadley allowed herself a brief, silent giggle in Max's direction as Chef Simons turned away, back to his entourage. It didn't even matter that

Max had been disregarded once again. He was on a first-name basis with Marshall Simons.

"Now," Chef Simons spoke again, instantly capturing the entire room's attention. "I assume you both know how this works. Are we ready to get started?"

Get started? Max had no idea what he meant by "get started." To his understanding, they were just going to be shooting some promos. Marshall wanted to get to know both of them before the shoot really began. But it sounded like he was ready to just dive right in. Max shrugged slightly in response to Hadley's questioning eyes, but there was no way he was going to allow himself to appear unprepared on his first day on *Renowned.* He'd figure it out as he went along.

"Excuse me, Chef Si—" Hadley went silent when Marshall pointed a finger in her direction. "Sorry. Marshall. But I don't think we *do* actually know how it works. I mean, I think we've both seen every episode *ever,* but as far as filming . . ."

Max stepped up behind her. "You always start in the kitchen, right, Marshall? The signature dish?"

"Very good, Chef Cavanagh. Someone has done their *Renowned* homework."

Hadley shot Max an expression of betrayal. He hadn't *meant* to show her up. He'd just . . . remembered. Pieced it together.

"Of course," Hadley said softly. She nodded

confidently, but her darting eyes and the way she was chewing on her lip gave Max the impression she was still confused. "I know the first episode of *Renowned* is always about the chef's signature dish. I just didn't realize we would be preparing them tonight."

Marshall's eyes flew open and he gasped in horror. With quick accusatory glances to various members of his entourage, he said, "Someone was supposed to make sure you knew. Did no one call?" He placed his hand over his heart. "My dear, I am so very sorry."

Yeah . . . Max wasn't buying it.

He had suddenly had a flash of Alain Ducasse claiming that Marshall Simons had not given him adequate time to mentally prepare to make the fish galantine for his signature cappon magro. Chef Ducasse had likely never watched an episode of *Renowned* in his life, but Max realized he and Hadley should have realized. The pressure, the lack of preparation, the element of surprise . . . those were probably *Renowned* trademarks as much as the sit-down interview at the end of the season. But only the sweating, unsuspecting chef was ever the wiser. Audiences just saw gripping television—the direct result of heightened emotions.

"You do have everything you need, don't you?" Marshall asked, his hand still over his heart.

Hadley thought quickly and then answered,

"Yes. I do. Not a problem." She turned to Max and opened her mouth, but before she could speak—presumably to ask him if the ingredients for his signature dish could likely be found in Hadley's show kitchen, Chef Simons continued.

"Fabulous. Then we'll film the signature dish tonight. That will give us some shots to work with for promotional purposes, as well as that traditional kickoff to the season that Chef Cavanagh mentioned. And then our regular production schedule will officially begin one week from today. As you know, the show is not live. There is far, *far* too much layered work involved for a live production. However, it will air relatively in real time. We will film Monday through Wednesday each week—again, beginning next week—and then Thursday through Saturday is for editing, postproduction . . . all of those things you don't need to worry yourselves with. Episodes will air on Sunday evenings, as I'm sure you are aware. That means our premiere is in thirteen days, in case you've lost count. We have Chef Borjomi to thank for the frantic preproduction schedule." He rolled his eyes, apparently unsympathetic to Chef Borjomi's tuberculosis plight. "Eight episodes and then we're done. Easy as that. Now, we'll let the crew finish setting up, and the two of you need to get a little powder on your noses. I'll meet you in the kitchen in about twenty minutes."

They both smiled at him and communicated their acknowledgment of the plan and then, as soon as Chef Simons was out of earshot, Hadley turned to face Max.

"Really?" she asked as she placed her hands on her hips. "Is this how it's gonna go? I get to look clueless while you swoop in with all the answers?"

"I'm sorry. I am." *Don't laugh. Do. Not. Laugh.* "That wasn't intentional. I didn't know at first, but then it clicked. Hadley, you and I know this show. I bet if we think back to every single disastrous moment we've ever seen on *Renowned*, it would come down to someone being taken off guard. I bet they count on that. I think you and I need to get together and think this through. Maybe even practice—"

"Practice?" She whispered through clenched teeth and looked around the room cautiously, as if they were conspiring to overthrow a small gourmet nation. "We don't need to practice. We just need to go back and watch old episodes."

"That won't do us any good."

"It might have done *me* some good, back there a minute ago!" she exclaimed, before once more looking around for the culinary despots against whom they were, apparently, staging a coup. Her voice was again calm and quiet as she said, "I'll just study up. It will be fine."

"But you're forgetting an important detail.

There hasn't been another season like this one. We don't have anything to study. Not really. At least not anything that will help us."

"I think what would help most of all is if you didn't show me up—"

"Good grief, woman!" he shouted. "I said it wasn't intentional!"

The room, which had been abuzz with the energy and sounds of diligent preparation, grew silent, and all eyes were on them. When neither of them said a word, and just stood there awkwardly—Max with his hands in his pockets, Hadley with eyes and a smile darting apologetically around the room—the buzz resumed. Max looked down and focused on his breathing. Their argument had been good-natured, but he couldn't afford even the misperception of being out of control.

Hadley, apparently, wasn't too worried about his reputation. He looked up at the sound of laughter erupting from her. "Sorry," she coughed out through the coughing fit.

He pulled his hands out of his pockets and crossed his arms across his chest. "It's not funny."

She nodded and tried to control her laughter, but she had completely lost it. Finally, she took a deep breath. Then another. The sound ceased but the overly amused look on her face made it clear *she* was the one out of control. She wiped the tears from the corners of her eyes and placed her hand on his arm. "Really. Sorry."

A new shade of pink made its way up her neck. He wasn't sure what that one represented, but he knew he liked it more than all the others combined.

Hadley cleared her throat and pulled her hand away. "Anyway, we'll be fine. It's not like this is a competition. It's not like they're going to try and use us against each other. *Renowned* isn't that kind of show."

Max wasn't too sure about that, but he was absolutely positive that he needed a moment alone to collect himself before he stood with her in front of any camera. "Go powder your nose like you were told."

She smiled and turned away, and once again he couldn't stop himself from watching her go—which didn't at all help him in his attempts to make himself cool and collected and ready for television.

"Oh, hey, Max?" she asked, poking her head around the corner he had just watched her disappear behind.

"Um, yeah? What's up?" he asked with forced nonchalance as he pretended his attention had been anywhere else.

"I like the beard. It makes you look much less like an uppity prep school bully."

She was gone before he could reply, which was good. Words were failing him.

14. Stew for two hours.

HADLEY

"For the last time," I seethed, "would you please get out of my way?"

Above the level of the island, where the camera was capturing every move Max and I made, I gently nudged him with my elbow. Below the camera line, I stomped on his toes, which caused him to shoot me a glare of surprise and frustration. But at least he acknowledged I was there. I'd barely been able to move my arms to prepare my signature dish. I'd never met such an insufferable kitchen hog in my entire life.

"Then you take your bouille mixture and stir in your sugar."

"*So* much sugar," Max added under his breath.

"Chef Hadley, darling, just a reminder," Chef Simons said kindly. "No need to look into the camera, or even walk us through the steps of your recipe. This isn't meant to be instructional so much as a look at your process. Most of this footage will just be used as background."

I nodded. "Right. Sorry. It's a habit, I guess."

"Not a problem. Just pretend the cameras aren't here."

Max leaned a hip against the island and crossed his arms. "You softened your butter too much."

"You've got it, Chef Simons. Thanks." I flashed him a smile. "Is it okay if I also pretend Chef Cavanagh isn't here?"

Max chuckled and raised his hands as he took a step away from my cooking space.

I didn't understand what had happened, but he was reminding me of an episode of *Beverly Hills, 90210*. He was like Jason Priestley, secretly getting along with Andrea, the smart nerdy girl, until his friends were around. Then he had to turn into Mr. Cool Guy.

"Chef Max," Chef Simons said, and instantly he had Max's attention. I'm not sure if Chef Simons was Luke Perry or Jennie Garth. "What are your observations thus far?"

"About Hadley's dish?" he asked, and Chef Simons nodded.

I stopped pouring my vanilla—just for a second—and looked up at him. "Yes, Chef Max," I said with a laugh. "What are your observations? I can only imagine."

Max smiled. "This looks delicious. Fattening, but delicious."

I groaned as I whipped my mixture. "Oh, don't do that."

"Do what?"

"You've been making snide comments this entire time. You've been questioning every single move I make." I slammed my spoon down into the bowl and faced him. "So if you have something to say, now's your chance. Don't stop now. Let's hear it." I crossed my arms and waited impatiently.

Fat separator. Grinder. Honing rod.

He tilted his head as his eyes connected with mine, and I saw his Adam's apple bounce up and down. I suppose I was beginning to build up a Maxwell Cavanagh research database in my mind, because I knew what that meant. It meant Max had a whole lot to say, but he was doing all he could to swallow the words down. I softened—just a little. At least he was going to make an attempt not to say every single insulting thing he could think of about my cooking. That was an improvement over the last time we shared a kitchen.

"Truthfully, Marshall," he began, but his eyes stayed on me. "I was just thinking that I'm beginning to understand why this is Chef Beckett's signature dish. I've eaten many a tarte à la bouille in my day, but usually in a Cajun setting. It is, after all, a Louisiana trademark. But watching Chef Beckett create her version is fascinating. She's managed to keep all the heart and tradition of the Cajun creation, while adding her own unmistakable Nashville flair."

Well, color me green and call me seaweed.

"What a perfect characterization," our host replied. "And having had the pleasure of being served Bouille Hadley on a previous occasion, I can assure you it is every bit as fascinating and delicious as it appears."

After all his words over the course of the past two hours—so, *so* many words—Max finally seemed to have run out of them. I stared at him and tried to interpret the strange expression on his face which, at first glance, I would have placed somewhere between him wanting to annihilate me and wanting to adopt me.

I didn't have time to figure out exactly where on the scale we stood, so I just got back to work.

"It's called Bouille Hadley?" he finally asked. Of me, I think. I didn't look up from my ingredients to verify.

I nodded. "Yes."

"Do you *mean* for it to sound like Boo Radley?"

I scrunched up my nose, prepared to make Max dig a bit. He probably thought the only thing we read in the South was *The Old Farmer's Almanac*. "Oh, does it? I mean, I guess if you pronounce Bouille properly."

"I know how to pronounce Bouille properly," he assured me, with an air of superiority that just came so naturally to him. "It's pretty close. And if you did it on purpose, that's . . . cute. What better way to draw out the distinct Southern characteristics of your cooking than by naming the dish after a character in *To Kill a Mockingbird*?"

What had I been thinking? What in the world

could I possibly have been thinking, agreeing to work with him again? I stirred as vigorously as I could without damaging the mixture.

"You think that would be *cute?*"

"Not in a demeaning way or anything."

I unceremoniously forced him out of the way as I reached for my tube pan.

"Hang on."

He placed his hand on my wrist and stopped me before I could set my pan down on the counter. Admittedly, when I'd touched him a couple hours earlier, I'd had a bit of a physical reaction I couldn't quite explain. It made no sense, I wasn't proud of it, and I didn't really want to give it any further thought aside from acknowledging, as I had prior, that the man had very nice arms. But with his hand on my wrist, I felt nothing but irritation.

"You're making tarte à la bouille as an angel food cake?"

Ah. He got it. And, if I wasn't mistaken, he was impressed. Or maybe he was just confused. I felt pretty gratified, either way.

I flipped my wrist to remove his hand and then went about my business. "Have you read *To Kill a Mockingbird*, Chef Cavanagh?"

"Yes. Of course I have."

"So you remember when Heck Tate told Atticus that they should keep the secret, about Boo Radley saving the kids. He told him that if the people of the town found out, they'd all use their appreciation as an excuse to meddle in Boo's life." I finished pouring my mix into the pan and then looked at him—probably a little more pleased with myself than good manners allowed for. "They'd all be showing up at Boo's door with angel food cake." He stared at me and I kept on staring right back. Even as I placed the pan in the oven. "What can I say? I thought it was cute."

A warm smile spread across his lips, and just like that he was back to looking like the guy I'd texted until way too far into the morning. And for the first time on the set of *Renowned*, I was nervous. I mean, apart from *every single moment,* basically since I'd first learned I was going to be on the show. Certainly all through preparing my dessert. Okay, so nervousness was nothing new. But not having any idea which Max Cavanagh was in the kitchen with me was very, very new.

"Um . . ." I fumbled around awkwardly, away from his eyes and away from that smile.

"Okay, cut," Chef Simons called out. He and Lowell, the director, were immediately speaking quietly to each other. Max and I stood there, awaiting instructions.

It was odd, filming *Renowned.* Already, it was odd. And I'm not just talking about all things Max. They captured so much film. We were told to just be natural—and I, of course, had to be told that a few more times than I was guessing most chefs did—but I didn't understand how any of this was going to shape up into a fascinating-as-always episode. So far, based on my signature dish preparation, I was pretty sure it was going to be the most boring season in history.

And yet I had no reason to think Marshall Simons had suddenly forgotten what he was doing. Only that he hadn't chosen the right chef. Or chefs, as the case may be.

I was yanked out of my thoughts by Max's hushed voice. "Nice job."

"With what?" I whispered back, so utterly annoyed by him.

"All of it. Your dish. Nice job."

I scoffed. "Really? Are you sure it was cute enough for you?"

I shook my head and turned back to face Marshall and Lowell, who were still discussing something amongst themselves—but looking at us in a way that made it very clear we were the topic of discussion.

"All right, you two," Lowell finally said as he walked toward us. "We're going to take a little break from the kitchen while Hadley's cake bakes. We'll use the next few minutes to get some B-roll outside, and then we'll run back in, cut a few quick promos, pull the cake out of the oven, and call it a night."

I put some additional distance between Max and me by heading over to the sink to wash my hands, and then I responded to Marshall's summons by following him and the crew outside.

"Max?" Lowell called into the house from the porch. "We don't have much time."

I blinked furiously to clear away the memories that had just barged in without an invitation. Back when Max had grown frustrated with me because I looked at the wrong camera on *America's Fiercest Chef*—as if I had been the one wasting time all along.

He was good. I'd give him that. I wasn't sure how he'd done it, but somehow he'd managed to convince me he'd turned into the nicer version of Oliver Warbucks. The one at the end who called in the cavalry to save Annie from Rooster, and gave her a locket and adopted her. But as soon as the cameras were on him, he turned into a more handsome version of the original Warbucks, who attacked photographers and hung the *Mona Lisa* in his bathroom. And just like I felt about Daddy Warbucks when I would rewatch *Annie* countless times as a little girl, I didn't entirely dislike Max Cavanagh, even when he wasn't very likable. Because I'd already learned that there were nicer qualities under there somewhere. But that didn't stop me from wishing he'd stop refusing to sing with FDR and Eleanor, and get to the part where he starts referring to Miss Farrell as Grace.

"We've got a path lit, down to the bottom of

the hill," Lowell explained. "All we want to do here is film the two of you talking."

"To each other?" I asked, and was instantly rewarded with laughter—from Max and no one else.

"Yes, to each other," Lowell replied, with a strained smile on his face. "Is that a problem?"

I shook my head. "Just clarifying."

"Is there anything in particular we should talk about?" I asked.

Marshall answered the question while grabbing my hand and squeezing it. "Not really for this one, my darling. We just want to see where it goes. You can talk about your shared history—"

"I'd really rather not," I interjected.

"—or not." Marshall darted his eyes Max's way, and then back to me with a smile. "Get to know each other a little better. Talk about your Bouille Hadley and how the idea came to you. Whatever you like. There is no script."

"Sounds good," Max said as he stepped off the porch, onto the lighted path.

It was a nice night. There was a crispness in the air that was undeniably a characteristic of summer coming to an end. It was cool enough to need a jacket but refreshing enough to be okay living on the edge without one. And the smell of the freshly cut lawn . . .

If I took time to savor it all, the sensory overload was almost enough to convince me I wouldn't rather be back at the orphanage with Miss Hannigan.

He followed after me, and we began our casual, unscripted, natural conversation—surrounded by cameras and boom mic operators and enough miserable tension to fill the cool Tennessee air.

15. Peel and mince.

MAX

"What was that about back there?" Max asked as soon as they were informed that film was rolling.

Her head snapped in his direction, and he knew he had taken her off guard. "What was what?"

" 'Are you sure it was cute enough for you,' and all of that."

She looked around and then back at him, and spoke quietly as she said, "I don't really think this is the right time to talk about this, do you?"

He jammed his hands in his pockets. He felt his phone in his pocket and briefly considered pulling it out to text her, but he figured with his luck he would probably trip over his feet and roll down the hill if he tried to walk and text. And *that* would be the memorable clip from their season of *Renowned*. Other chefs had created brilliant new recipes, had breakthroughs about their relationships with their parents, and even become parents themselves during filming. No doubt, Max would have an unfortunate texting accident.

"I do, actually," he replied. "That's why I asked."

Hadley turned on her heel toward him. "Look, Max. If you're about to try to embarrass me, can

I just ask that you . . ." It wasn't her face but her eyes that began turning red. She seemed to realize it and groaned as she continued on the path. "Can I just ask that you please *don't?*"

"Try to embarrass you?" They were walking side-by-side, but about as far away from each other as they could get. "What are you even—"

"We're going to talk about something else, or we're not going to talk at all."

He chuckled bitterly. "Okay. Whatever you say."

He could hardly wait to get back to the hotel and write in his Discovery Journal.

Today, in my ongoing adventure of discovering who I truly am—the parts I like and should celebrate, as well as the parts I hope to improve—I discovered Hadley Beckett was nicer to me back when we were sworn enemies.

Okay, let's get this back on track. The only way to waste a moment is to choose to waste a moment.

"Let's talk about the Bouille Hadley." The way her shoulders were up around her ears made him realize he should be a little bit proactive here. "*Not* how cute that is, although it is." She glared at him and he smiled. "But Chef Simons said he had tasted it before. When was that?"

Hadley released a slow, even breath. "He critiqued it once. In *Bon Appétit.*"

"Hang on!" Max stopped in his tracks, and

203

Hadley stopped as well, a couple feet further down the hill. He was flabbergasted. Absolutely flabbergasted. "Marshall Simons reviewed your cake in *Bon Appétit*? He only reviews . . . I mean, he *doesn't* review. Except for . . . that cake was a Marshall Simons Taste of the Year?"

She nodded. "2018."

He ran his hand through his hair. "Hadley, he only reviews one dish each year."

"I know."

"No, I don't think you do. He tries everything. He eats *everything*. And then each year he picks one dish as Taste of the Year. One. You're telling me . . ."

With a shrug she repeated, "2018," and then took off walking again.

How had he missed that? How had he missed that this infuriating, adorable, "aww shucks" chef whose name had been forcibly intertwined with his for months had been awarded Marshall Simons Taste of the Year?

While he never had.

He'd had it all wrong. He'd believed—his manager had even *told* him—that *Renowned* was his comeback. Hadley was likable, and Hadley by his side would make *him* more likable, but there was no doubt, it was Max's season, he'd said. Max wasn't sure he would take it that far, but that's what he'd been told. But he finally understood. He was only there to make her even more likable by contrast. It wasn't his season at all. It was Hadley's.

"That's really impressive, Hadley."

"Thanks," she replied curtly.

It wasn't her fault though. He knew she wasn't the orchestrator of the "Chef Beckett is good; Chef Cavanagh is bad" marketing campaign. There was just no way. He was being used—for ratings, to boost Hadley's career, no telling how else—but Hadley wasn't any more clued in to it than he had been.

And the thing was, he'd known he was being used. He'd known it all along. But not *just* him. *Both* of them. It was sensationalistic and the part of fame he hated more than anything, but he would suck it up and deal with it, because it was *Renowned.* He would still benefit. No harm, no foul. But now? Now that he saw it for what it was? Now that he realized they would reach the end of this season, and then they could finally be done with *him* once and for all? Because Hadley would have gotten that final boost she needed. *Hadley* would be firmly and irrevocably positioned to take control of the throne he'd occupied for years.

That changed things.

16. Bake at high heat
for several hours.

HADLEY

"It was awful, Leo. Just . . . awful."

"Now, that is *not* what I heard."

I looked around my kitchen at all the cleanup I needed to do and then walked into the living room and collapsed onto the couch. It would wait. I had absolutely nothing left to give right then.

"Well, unless Max is your source, they lied. I can't imagine that anyone else could possibly have been pleased with any of it."

"For your information, my source is Marshall Simons, so—"

I laughed dramatically. "Then he *definitely* lied to you."

"He said your dessert was perfect."

I couldn't laugh at that. My dessert *was* perfect. It had even gotten Max to shut up. Finally.

"That's nice to hear," I acknowledged with a sigh.

I heard Leo clicking his teeth on the other end of the line—either debating how to proceed or attempting to get a chunk of meat out of his teeth.

Debating, it turns out.

"Look, Hadley, I hate to even say this, but if

this is going to be too much for you, it's not too late to back out."

I shot up from my reclined position. "Back out? Are you kidding me? From *Renowned*? No. Of course I don't want to back out."

Pull it together, Hadley, I lectured myself. *Vent to Stuart—who will say "I told you so" about a million times, but who will listen nonetheless. Vent to Meemaw—who will* not *listen, and who will need to be reminded what* Renowned *is at least once, but who will still love you when you're done.* Do not *vent to your manager.*

"It's fine. Really, Leo. Thanks. I just needed to vent."

"Oh, I understand. Cavanagh is a lot to deal with, I'm sure. Everyone in the business is claiming he has it all together now—has things under control, got help, has dried out, all of that—but you never can tell. Try not to let him get to you. All this stuff . . . it's just for eight weeks. I suspect he's just grasping at straws at this point, pulling out all the stops."

I wanted to laugh at the thought. Max . . . desperate? Yeah, that didn't seem likely. I could more easily imagine his entire culinary dynasty reduced to nothing but a snow cone hut on the side of the road, where Max would still be wearing his sunglasses, proclaiming there was too much sugar in the syrup, and serving tiny little baby portions of crushed ice. Charging $100 a pop, no doubt.

I decided to keep my skepticism to myself.

"Yeah, maybe you're right."

"Okay, kid. Just get some rest and let me know if you need anything."

"I will. Thanks, Leo."

I laid back down and pulled the pillow out from underneath my head. I fiddled with the seam for a moment before pulling it up to my face, turning over, and screaming into it.

Coming up for air, I muttered to myself, "Why'd I ever notice his stupid, perfect arms?"

And his stupid blue eyes that were actually three separate shades that came together to look like the color of the sky as a thunderstorm rolls in. And his stupid, idiotic beard that I did actually like so, *so* much.

Not that it was just about his looks. His looks had always been there—except the beard. Oh, the beard. But I hadn't been able to see just how attractive he was through the pompous attitude, sexist tendencies, and nasty temper. When facing all those things, how is a person ever supposed to notice that someone's actually every bit as sexy as the rest of the world already seems to think they are? You just can't. So of course I was a little thrown off by seeing all of that for the first time.

But once I noticed his stupid, magnificent arms and all the rest, and I was forced to acknowledge that maybe I'd been wrong in thinking he wasn't all that attractive, well . . . in record time I'd had to acknowledge that maybe I'd been wrong about him in other ways too. Or at least that what I'd thought before didn't apply anymore.

It was much more disappointing to be wrong this time.

My phone buzzed and I raised it from the floor beside me, and then dropped it and screamed into my pillow once again.

I don't think we have anything to talk about.

No. I just didn't have it in me to face a chat with Sexy Texty Max. I threw the pillow across the room and sat up, taking my phone with me.

I don't think we have anything to talk about.

I studied my phone, awaiting his reply, but it came in the form of a knock at my door. It was him. I just knew it was him.

Are you at my door?

I need some more Bouille Hadley. I NEED IT!

Nope. Nope, nope, nope.
I stormed to my front door and threw it open.

"What is your problem? Seriously! Do you have some sort of texting alter ego? You don't get to be like *that* in the kitchen, and then like *that!*" I raised my phone in the air and shook it and, again, waited for his reply.

This time it came in the form of two self-assured steps into my house, both of his hands cupped around my jawline, his fingers tangled in the hair at the nape of my neck, and his lips pressed against mine.

There was no thought of protest. No breath left for words. There was only Max and his kiss—gentle but urgent. Growing more urgent as we ignored the need to breathe in favor of something we needed even more desperately. He grasped a fist of my hair and pulled my face away from his. Delicately so he didn't hurt me, but intensely, as if his hands were capable of doing what his mouth was not—separating, just long enough to gasp for air.

He panted. "Hadley, I'm—"

"Shut up," I whimpered as my arms locked around his neck and pulled him back to me.

He willingly complied, but the spell had been broken for us both. Or, more than the spell having been broken, reality set back in—and it was more powerful than the spell. We pulled away so awkwardly. Me as if I'd been burned, him as if he were one of those golden retrievers whose owner takes their picture with a chewed-up slipper and

210

a sign that says, "I'm a bad dog." I began to back away, and my mind began to transition into lecture mode, but before I could back completely away—and before my lips had even stopped tingling—he stopped me.

"Hey. Wait." He grabbed my wrist—so differently than he had touched my wrist earlier in the day—and then moved his fingers down to clasp my hand. "We'll talk. Or I'll go. Whatever you want. But . . ." His eyes did a pretty good job of communicating the intent behind the words that were failing him.

"Don't go," I whispered. "Let's talk."

He shut the door behind him and followed me into the dining room. I needed a table between us. We sat in silence not looking at each other for a few minutes. At least, I wasn't looking at him, so I don't have any idea what he was looking at. But I was choosing to believe he wasn't looking at me. I wouldn't have been able to bear it.

"Should I apologize?" he finally asked.

"I guess that depends. Are you sorry?"

He sighed. "Well, I guess *that* depends." I could hear his smile as he asked, "Did it make things better or worse?"

I chuckled softly and finally looked at him. That was probably a mistake. All I saw was the Max I liked. The one with the arms and the eyes, and good golly, the lips. The one who was surprisingly quiet and wonderfully funny.

"I don't know," I answered honestly. "Maybe a little bit of both."

"Then maybe I'm a little bit sorry. I think I'd have a pretty tough time being any more than that."

"Max, can we talk?"

"I think that would be—"

"No, I mean *really* talk."

He studied me and nodded. "Sure."

"I don't . . ." I took a deep breath. "You see, the thing is, I don't know what to make of you."

His eyebrow arched. "Go on . . ."

I stood from my seat and walked to one of the giant windows. It was too dark to see my dogwoods, but it was just nice knowing they were there.

"Okay, well, if we go all the way back to the beginning—"

"The beginning?"

"*America's Fiercest Chef.* You were . . . well . . . we know what you were then. Then you show up at my door months later with the most uncomfortable apology imaginable. The next day, you alternated between infuriating and charming. But then we start texting, and maybe it was naïve of me, but I thought we were becoming friends."

"We were. Weren't we?"

"See! That's the thing. I don't know! Because the minute the cameras started rolling today, you became the same cold, pompous, self-centered jerk from before." He looked as if I'd slapped him. "Okay, that's not fair. You weren't *that* bad. But it wasn't good, that's for sure."

I stopped talking so he could offer some justification. Maybe even an apology. Truth be told, if he wanted to swoop in for another kiss, I probably wasn't going to stop him.

"You're a really good kisser, by the way," I whispered sheepishly.

"Thanks. So are you."

"And this is why my head is a mess!" I shouted, returning to the table across from him. "Right there, I was waiting for you to say something to explain why you were a jerk to me earlier, and instead I complimented your kissing skills." I buried my head in my arms on the table. "I'm so confused."

I heard his chair scoot across the wood floor, and every muscle in my body tightened. I didn't know where he was going, or what he was doing.

"I'm sorry," he whispered against my hair as chills ran down my spine. I peeked my eyes above my bent elbow and was met with his face, just inches from mine. "I didn't mean to be a jerk today." He tucked my hair behind my ear, but it kept falling, so he kept his hand in place. "And truthfully, I really don't think I was so bad."

I laughed humorlessly and then stopped abruptly. I was going to give him some examples, but my Max confusion had consumed my brain again, and I couldn't fully remember what he had done that I had found so offensive earlier. Except *cute*. I remembered *cute*.

"No, I guess you weren't so bad," I conceded with a hesitant sigh. "But please understand I'm grading on the Cavanagh scale—not any sort of normal scale. By your standard, you weren't so bad."

His fingers fell away, releasing my hair to cover my eyes. I lifted my head and saw that he was sitting back in his chair, with the most ambiguous expression on his face.

"Remember when I said we should practice?" he asked, his voice low and raspy. "For *Renowned*, I mean."

"Yeah."

"They're pitting us against each other."

I scoffed. "I think we do a pretty good job of that on our own. Don't you? That's why we're both on this season. Remember?"

He shook his head and then stood and looked out the window, into my pitch-black backyard. I felt the strongest desire to stand behind him. Wrap my arms around him. Feel the muscles in his shoulders under my fingers. Maybe even invite myself into the comfort that I just knew would be found under the crook of his arm. Against his chest. What would he do if I did?

"When do I get to prepare *my* signature dish, Hadley?"

"What do you—"

"From the moment Marshall Simons got here tonight, he was pitting us against each other." He turned to face me. "Think about it. If you think about it, you'll realize I'm right."

I thought about it. Or I tried. But staring at Max, I wasn't going to be able to think about anything except how far away he was, there on the other side of the room, and how lonely my lips had gotten.

"What are you doing?" he asked.

"I can't look at you right now," I replied softly, with a quick peek through my fingers, which were covering my eyes.

A warm laugh filled the space between us. "Why? What did I do this time?"

I sighed and muttered, "You know what you did."

"No, I really don't." When my hands dropped from my eyes to my lap in exasperation, I spotted his mischievous grin. "You might need to remind me."

Uh-oh. My hands flew back to my eyes and I got up and turned away from him. I heard him chuckle lightly, but I decided I'd just have to ignore that too. There was something I was supposed to be thinking about. What was it . . . ?

Nope. Thinking wasn't going to happen.

I felt him before I heard him. He brushed

my hair away from my neck and over my left shoulder, as he began planting soft kisses where my neck and shoulder met on the right. His skilled, expert hands—that had climbed Kilimanjaro, caught scallops during a free-dive in Scotland, and prepared dinner for presidents and kings—wrapped around my waist.

"I'm supposed to be thinking," I whispered as I melted into him.

"So, think," he breathed against my skin.

Suddenly my eyes widened and I pulled away. "When are you going to prepare *your* signature dish?"

Max ran his hand through his hair. "Or maybe *don't* think . . ."

"No, you're right! They had me make mine. When are you supposed to make yours?" The thoughts were running wild and rampant all of a sudden—and in a decidedly less romantic direction. "What *is* your signature dish?"

"Beef Wellington. Well, and my wild mushroom risotto."

"Sheesh. Maybe they just didn't want us to be here all night. Maybe if your signature dish was meatloaf . . ."

"But no one even mentioned—"

"No one even mentioned it!" I exclaimed, every thought I was having totally original, of course. "And . . . hey! The way Chef Simons was practically ignoring you? I mean, I just thought he liked me better than you, and let's face it, he probably does—"

"Thanks for that."

"But it was a little weird, now that I think about it."

He nodded. "It was just pushing buttons. Wanting us to talk about our 'shared history,' two hours into this whole thing? I mean, c'mon. They definitely know how to push the right buttons to get us to act the way they think we need to, in order to get the show they want."

I decided to embrace the hopeful glimmer in my mind. "And that's why you were such a jerk?"

One corner of his mouth inched upward. "Doubt it. But it sure didn't help."

17. *Allow to cool.*

MAX

"So, what do we do?" Hadley asked as she walked into her dark kitchen and began rummaging through a drawer.

Max smiled at her as she fumbled around, unable to find what she was looking for in the drawer, but also unable to remember where the light switch was. Finally, she pulled her phone out of her pocket and turned on its light.

"Well, here's an idea. Just thought of this. We could practice."

She pulled two forks out and held them up, and Max went hurrying in to grab one of them. He hadn't been kidding about needing more Bouille Hadley. She had an uncanny way of making him throw self-control out the window.

He hadn't meant to kiss her, after all. And he hadn't even been thinking about it. But there was something about the sight of her in the open door, furious with him for reasons he didn't even understand, shaking her phone at him. He'd just needed her. That's all there was to it.

"Give me that," he insisted, pulling the plate of cake away from her.

"Okay," she began, cake still in her mouth.

"What do you mean? Practice *how?* Practice *what?*"

He stuffed another bite in before he had swallowed the last. The woman was a dessert genius. "Being in the kitchen together. I think if we refuse to let them manipulate the situation—"

Hadley pointed her fork at him. "See, that's the thing. Don't you think we can just agree to not let them manipulate the situation . . . and then they won't be able to manipulate the situation? Do you really think we need to practice that?"

The last crumb of the dessert was lingering on her bottom lip, and Max wasn't sure if it was a final taste of Bouille Hadley or its creator's mouth that he was more eager to capture. She licked the crumb away before he had the chance to attack, but when the eagerness didn't go away, he figured his question about preference had been answered.

For heaven's sake, Max. At least show enough self-control to get through this conversation.

He cleared his throat and scratched his neck at the spot where the beard began. "We walked into this kitchen as friends today. And it took . . . what? Ten minutes? We were at each other's throats in ten minutes."

"That's just because you turn into a jerk on air."

"And you turn into an episode of *Designing Women.*"

"Excuse me?"

Max looked into her eyes and saw the humor behind them, and he understood it was okay to tease.

He took on a dialect that was, admittedly, more *Deliverance* than *Designing Women*. "Let's see . . . a pinch of salt . . . a smidge of cream . . ."

She laughed a deep, throaty laugh. "I would never say a smidge of cream!"

"And more sugar than you can shake a stick at, y'all. Oh, that looks about right, I'd say . . ."

"I cook from the heart!"

"Oh, is *that* it?"

"Yes!" And then her laughter abruptly ended. "I guess we both have our on-air personas, don't we?"

Max let that register as he sank down onto a stool at the counter.

"Too bad mine isn't as nice as yours." All of the joviality was gone, but it was no less comfortable. At least, between the two of them. Within himself he was a *lot* less comfortable than he had been when they'd just been talking about Hadley. "I don't know when that started."

"When what started?"

He sighed. "My persona."

"Well, I don't know when it started, either, but it's not hard to figure out why it stuck around."

With a helpless shrug, he acknowledged, "Millions of people tuned in every week to see if I'd yell at a cook or curse at a fisherman."

"Did you ever curse at a fisherman?"

"Quite a few times, yes. But I knew what I was doing. I always knew. It was unscripted television, but I always knew exactly what I was supposed to say. Exactly what I was supposed to do."

"Same here, y'all. Same here." She stood behind him and wrapped her arms around his shoulders, and rested her head against his, and Max tensed up, just for a moment. He'd held her body tight to his and kissed her as passionately as he'd ever kissed any woman in his life, but none of it had felt as intimate as her comforting embrace.

He wasn't sure if he was ready for this. Ready for her. But he had to try.

"Can I be honest?" he asked, knowing that she would be fine with it. Maybe he needed to be asking himself.

"Of course."

"I did get that waitress's number."

Hadley tilted her face to look at him. "What waitress?"

"At the Pancake Pantry. The one I told you I was apologizing to. And I *did* apologize, by the way. That just . . . wasn't all."

She pulled away, and as much as he hated to admit it even to himself, he was glad. He could breathe again. And yet, at the same time, he wanted her arms back around him, making him uncomfortable again.

"I knew it! I . . . I mean, I didn't care. But I knew it!" She smiled. "Frankly, it just seemed like a very Max Cavanagh sort of move."

"It was. So was the fact that I never called her."

She took a deep breath and slowly—carefully, he thought—stepped around to the other side of the counter.

"I don't date, Max."

He laughed, until he realized she wasn't kidding. "What do you mean, you don't date?"

There wasn't a single trace of embarrassment or self-doubt on her face. "It's not that I ever intentionally chose my career over love or romance or any of that. It just kind of happened that way." She scrunched up her nose and added, "My last relationship was with Stuart."

"The director!" he exclaimed, proud of himself for remembering. But then understanding began to dawn. "Ah. That explains it."

"Explains what?"

"Why he hated me from the beginning."

She laughed so hard she had to hold on to the counter for support. "That wasn't because of *me!*" The laughter subsided a touch as she seemed to reconsider. "Well, not just because of me. He had to serve you drinks and clean up the Wagyu beef you threw on the floor!"

He'd thrown Wagyu beef on the floor?

"And sure," she continued, "he's protective of me. He's my closest friend. But we dated in college. For about two months. We weren't very good as a couple, but we worked together really well. And we're pretty great as friends."

Hang on. "You haven't dated since college?"

She shrugged. "I've dated. Not a ton. But no relationships. You, meanwhile . . ."

There it was. The whole "Playboy Gourmet" thing. How could he convince her it wasn't all as bad as the tabloids made it seem? Hadley hadn't been in a relationship since college. How many women had he dated and forgotten about since then?

"Ah. Yes. I've dated the US women's soccer team, if certain sources are to be believed."

"All at once?" she chimed in with a wink.

Max rolled his eyes. "I'm sure that's some magazine's version of it. I have been seen with a lot of women, I guess. But . . ." He stuffed his hands in his pockets, and his eyes darted downward, away from hers. What should he say? He was pretty sure he had never talked about his social life with anyone who was actually interested in hearing the truth.

As if reading his thoughts, or at least the uncertainty that was probably etched all over his face, Hadley leaned across the counter, so that her face was below his, and he couldn't avoid her eyes any longer. "You don't have to talk about this if you don't want to."

"It's not that. It's just . . . I don't know. It's just

part of this life. There's an expectation that I'll walk into an event with a beautiful woman on my arm, so I do. The truth is, nine times out of ten it's an unofficial business arrangement. They get their name and photo in *People* or on *Page Six*, and I get—"

"To be the Playboy Gourmet."

"Exactly. I usually don't know those women. I literally don't know their names sometimes. More often than not, I meet them when I step into the car my manager sends to pick me up. And then the minute we walk into whatever venue we're going to, they go talk to Leonardo DiCaprio or Andy Cohen, or one of the Desperate Housewives—"

"Do you mean the Real Housewives?" she asked as an impish smile overtook her face. "I mean, *maybe* they're snubbing you to go talk to Teri Hatcher . . ."

"Whatever!" He laughed. "The point is, they find someone who's more interesting than I am."

"Oh." She shook her head and waved her hands dismissively. "You are a lot of things, Max Cavanagh. But no one can say you aren't interesting."

"At a party, I'm not. I really hate going to those things."

"Then why do you go?"

Her blunt tone made it perfectly clear that she thought not going was the easy, obvious answer, and he'd just never considered it. And, while his gut reaction was to spurn her simplistic comprehension of it all, he quickly realized that maybe he never *had* considered it. That realization knocked the wind out of him and took away the certainty with which he'd been about to say, "It's just what I have to do."

Instead he murmured, "I don't know."

Hadley sighed. "Well, regardless, it's pretty obvious that we're very different, you and I."

He nodded. "We are."

"And the fact is, if you'd walked into my life and kissed me like that at pretty much any other time in my life, I probably would have been happy pursuing a career making lunches in a school cafeteria. But right now . . ."

He understood what she was saying, like it or not. "But right now, you're holding on to the brass ring. And everyone likes you better when you don't like me."

Hadley stood up straight. "That has nothing to do with it. I don't *care* what anyone thinks. It's just that I've worked too hard and come too far. And if I tried to live your type of life right now, Max . . . if I tried to keep up . . . I'm just not sure I could. I'm Nashville, through and through. I'm a homebody. I eat at home pretty much every night. You love adventure and travel." She chuckled. "You jumped in your car and drove here from New York on a whim. I don't do much of anything on a whim."

As if needing to prove her wrong—because something inside of him felt as if he did—Max stood up from his stool and walked around to her side of the counter. Slowly and deliberately. Waves of pink began rushing up her neck and he had a gratifying epiphany.

So I'm *the cause of that shade.*

Although, really, he knew he was the cause of all the shades. But he sure liked that one best.

"I don't know, Hadley. I think it's been a pretty whimsical night."

Her lips curled up in acknowledgment. "This has all been very unlike me. But that doesn't change the fact that down the road, beyond right now—"

He leaned down so they were eye-to-eye and whispered, "Who said anything about beyond right now?"

Max moved to kiss her again, but she placed her hands on his chest and stopped him before he could. She didn't push him away but rather clinched his T-shirt into her fists and took a deep breath. And released it with slow deliberation.

"That's what I mean, Max. I don't . . . I don't live in the moment. At least, I don't live *just* in the moment. And I can't be your next Miss Fancy Pants Kitty Cat."

"I'm sorry. My what?"

She closed her eyes tightly. "Forget I said that."

That would probably be easy to do, since it

had just sounded like a string of random words. Candle Bluetooth Winnebago artichoke dip.

"The point is," she continued as she rolled her eyes—at herself, he was pretty sure. "You confuse me. You distract me. And don't get me wrong . . ." She released his shirt from her fists and gently smoothed out the creases she had created. "You're a very nice distraction at the moment. But I'm on *Renowned*. We're on *Renowned*. I just launched a magazine, and I really want a third Michelin star. And yes, I want to be number one on the network. I just don't think I can afford to be any more confused than I already am."

She was driven. Competitive. Hardworking. Focused. Determined. If he was honest with himself, those weren't usually the personality traits he found attractive in a woman. Not that he had a problem with any of those things. They just hadn't ever been important. Very little had ever mattered beyond how the woman would look on his arm at a nightclub opening.

Hadley would look *strange* on his arm. Beautiful, no doubt. Absolutely breathtaking. But strange. She didn't seem to care about fashion—not that she wasn't stylish, but she wasn't trendy hotspot stylish. Max didn't care about fashion either. He'd found an outfit that worked for him and he'd stuck with it. But the women on his arm always cared. And Hadley barely wore any makeup. She didn't need to. But he'd dated women he knew he wouldn't even recognize on the street if he ever saw them with a natural face. For that matter, there were a lot of women he probably wouldn't recognize if they were wearing a "Hello, my name is . . ." badge. Even if the badge added helpful information like, "We went on three dates in 2015," or "You left me for that supermodel." Nope. Not specific enough.

"I'm sure you're right," Max finally said. He wasn't sure she was right, and he wasn't even sure what he was saying he thought she was right about. But he liked Hadley. He liked her a lot. Maybe he liked her a little too much. The more he thought about it, the more he realized he definitely liked her too much to date her.

He wouldn't do that to someone he actually cared about.

Her hands dropped from his chest. "So that's that, I guess." She stepped back from him.

"I guess so."

That was all that was needed. Now was the time when he could just calmly walk over to her, kiss her on the cheek, and say, "Tonight sure was fun, though," or something like that. He would be cool and distant, say goodbye, and then he'd head out to a bar for a drink. There he'd meet someone else and have a conversation that would probably be a lot less complicated than any he had ever had with Hadley Beckett.

Except he wasn't going to do any of that. Not a chance. Not this time.

"Hadley, I . . ." He chuckled uneasily and scratched his cheek. The facial hair was driving him nuts, but he knew he'd keep it awhile longer because she liked it. "I just want to say . . ." Cool and distant would be *so* much easier. "I probably said all the wrong things. I don't know. But I just need you to know that whatever we've got going here . . . being friends, or whatever . . . it . . . well, it matters to me. I'm not sorry I kissed you. But if it messed things up, well . . ." *Just end the blasted thought already.* "I just hope it didn't. Mess things up, I mean. That's all."

She looked at him for what felt like an eternity. Not moving. Not speaking. But finally, the trace of a smile appeared, and he breathed again.

"You know this whole *Renowned* thing? How they're pitting us against each other and setting us up to fail and all of that?"

He tilted his head and stared at her as if she'd lost her mind. "Um . . . yeah?"

"I just had a brilliant idea. Maybe we should practice." A wide, playful grin spread across her lips and he laughed harder than he'd laughed in a very long time.

18. Blanch all ingredients.

HADLEY

"What was I thinking? What was I thinking? What was I thinking?" I muttered to myself as I hurried through my ridiculously oversized house-for-one to the door. I looked down at my outfit one last time and smoothed it out and then took a deep breath before reaching for the knob.

"Hey, Max." I greeted him with a smile and moved out of the way so he could come inside.

"Hey, hey." He stepped past me with his canvas bags of groceries. "How are you today?"

"I'm good, thanks. You?"

Small talk. Nice, friendly small talk. It just didn't feel natural. The most common of all types of conversations was a complete anomaly between the two of us, who seemed to operate at only two levels with each other: friendly texts which had nothing to do with reality or shouting matches overflowing with disdain.

Well, there was that new third level: full-on making out in my living room. But of all the levels, that one—which, after a night of playing it over and over again in my mind, had been cemented as my favorite—was the one I was desperate to avoid.

"I'm good. You look rested."

I tilted my head. Really? I was *not* rested. I'd hardly slept a wink, thanks to him. "Rested?"

"I just mean . . . you looked tired yesterday." He shrugged. "Today you look rested."

Ah. Thanks for clearing that up.

I nodded and smiled. He was clearly feeling as uncomfortable as I was, so I decided to cut him a little slack. "Come on in. You know the kitchen, of course. Feel free to set everything down wherever."

With his full arms he gestured for me to lead the way, so I stepped in front of him and walked toward the kitchen.

"So how do you see this working?" he asked as all his bags came to rest on the island.

I crossed my arms and leaned up against the counter. "Practice, you mean?" *Because as for the other stuff, just as long as you don't grab me and kiss me, I think we'll be okay.*

"Yeah."

With a shrug I replied, "It was your idea."

"Thank you for finally acknowledging that."

I laughed and he smiled in response, and then the internal lecture began.

I'd meant everything I'd said. I wasn't going to take a chance on derailing my career, just when everything was going better than it ever had, to chase after the possibility of something developing with a boy. *A man, Hadley. Max Cavanagh is many things, but a boy is not one of them.*

231

Noted. The possibility of something developing with a *man*. A man I was now overwhelmingly, undeniably—and I feared irreversibly—attracted to. Funny how a guy taking your breath away and making your brain momentarily shut off for the first time in too long to remember can make you realize how good-looking he is.

But it was more than that. And the *more* was the part that had been even more difficult to admit to myself. I *liked* him. Moving past the pain between us had been one thing, and agreeing to work with him had been another thing entirely. But *liking* him? Enjoying his company? Respecting him for more than just his culinary acumen and his eye-opening, mind-blowing kissing skills? Where had *that* come from? Seemingly from nowhere. All I knew was I had climbed in bed the night before appreciating some of his individual characteristics and had climbed out the next morning appreciating the man himself.

The man who, without a word or even a glance in my direction, seemed to be inviting me back into his arms, just by standing in my kitchen. By caring about this joint venture of ours enough to practice just being in my presence. By involving me in his thoughts and strategy, rather than sabotaging me—as he no doubt could have, pretty easily. By trying to be *better*.

By standing across the kitchen from me, back turned, stretching those fabulous arms over his head and bowing his well-defined shoulders in deliberate warm-up and preparation. As if he were preparing to run a 5k, not cook lunch.

I exhaled a shaky breath. *Pull it together, Hadley.*

"Do you always warm up before you cook?"

He faced me. "Don't you?" He smiled in reaction to my "Are you crazy?" expression. "I guess I tend to be pretty physical in the kitchen." He seemed to consider his next words carefully, and once he spoke, I understood why. I wasn't about to hear anything his on-air persona would ever reveal to his audience. "It's not so much that cooking is a sport for me, although it probably comes across that way. I don't know. It's really more of a dance." He looked down at his feet. "There's a rhythm. A tempo. A give and take. Someone leads and someone follows." His eyes returned to mine, a little bit sheepishly. "And I don't mean you and me. Or anyone else I might be cooking with." A smirk overtook his lips. "Although, obviously, I will be leading."

I laughed. Or at least I meant to laugh. With defiance. I'm afraid it came out as nothing more than a pathetic whimper.

"But, really," he continued, "it's a dance I share with the kitchen. I have to lead, and it has to follow. There's no other way to do it. But, just like a man and woman dancing, the only way for it to really be something is if there's trust.

Respect. If I'm leading, I have to be in control at every turn, but that's not about power. It's about creating something special together. It's about sensing what my partner needs, and my partner knowing I've got her. That my hand on her back, directing her with such a gentle touch, is also strong enough to keep her from falling." He looked back down at his feet and chuckled. "That probably sounds really stupid."

"It doesn't sound stupid, Max. Not at all." How I wished it did. How I wished that friendly ridicule was how I wanted to respond. I cleared my throat and directed my eyes to his grocery bags. "So, what did you bring for us?"

He began to unpack his ingredients so I walked over to assist, but I stepped back as if I had been stung when I saw the superfluous amounts of produce being pulled from the bag.

"What's this?"

He looked at me and then back at all the produce—then back at me again, confusion in his eyes. "What's what?"

"All this green stuff."

"They're called vegetables, Hadley." His smile widened. "I can deep fry them if you like."

I scrunched up my nose and began digging through what remained in the bags. "It's not that I don't like vegetables. I'm just not a salad fan, really. And I've never seen that many vegetables go into anything that wasn't a salad."

"A-ha! I'm not making salad. We're still on track to reach my goal for the day!"

"Which is?"

"For you to admit, at the end of the meal, that I'm the greatest chef of all time."

Laughter exploded from me. "Yeah, good luck with that, flyboy."

"Flyboy?" He chuckled as he opened a container of cleaned and prepared freshwater chestnuts and took one out and popped it in his mouth. "Where did you learn your insults? A USO slang instructional manual from 1942?" He held the water chestnuts out for me and I took one, and slowly took a bite.

"See? I like vegetables." I took another nibble as I questioned myself. Were they vegetables or nuts? I wasn't sure. And I wasn't sure if I should carry on in confidence or wink, as if to say, "Just kidding. What kind of chef wouldn't know that water chestnuts aren't vegetables?"

Thankfully he saved me.

"I thought they were some sort of legume for the longest time. For vegetables, they seem so . . . nothing."

"So, um . . . what is this fabulous non-salad dish you'll be preparing, Chef?"

"Chicken lettuce wraps."

"Great. Salad you eat with your hands. That's much better."

He threw his hands up in the air. "Are you even going to give me a chance here?"

235

"A chance? Sure." I smiled at his agitation. He was playing it up for comedic effect, but I had no doubt I was also pushing his buttons, just a tad. "But you set the bar awfully high. If you said your goal was for me to say, 'Hey, Max, that was pretty good,' then I'd be going a lot easier on you. You asked for this. Besides, do you really expect me to think you're the greatest chef in all the world after you prepare a dish that is included in most cookbooks for the beginning chef, aged five to eight years old?"

He and I were already looking at each other, right in each other's eyes, but in that moment—that lighthearted moment accompanied by smiles on both our faces—it was as if our eyes locked into place. As if the gears had been just a bit off—close enough, but not secure—and everything had been loose and flexible. That changed in an inexplicable instant and we both knew it.

"Hadley, I really am sorry about how I acted during filming yesterday."

I shook my head. "It's fine. You apologized last night—"

"But I didn't mean it then." My mouth dropped open in shock and he shrugged. "Just trying to be honest. Last night I would have . . . well, I probably would have said *you* were the greatest chef of all time, if that's what I had to say to keep kissing you."

I matched his dangerous smile with my own. "I

don't know if I should be insulted or flattered."

"Be flattered. And, for the record, Bouille Hadley is the best dessert I've ever tasted."

My eyes flew open—flirtatious teasing and sincere apologies temporarily forgotten. "Do you mean that?"

Max nodded earnestly. "I do."

For one brief moment, it was as if none of it had ever happened. He wasn't the guy who had called me Hayley and thrown my curry dish at Aguste Bissett, and he wasn't the guy who had taken my anger and turned it into passion in the length of two steps. He was the great Maxwell Cavanagh, whose career I had followed and whose show I had loved—not that I ever intended to confess that to him. He was the youngest chef to ever receive nine Michelin stars. He was a James Beard Award winner. He *was* quite possibly the greatest chef of our time, if not quite of all time—though he wasn't going to get me to admit that to him unless he made me something more substantial than lettuce wraps.

And my dessert was the best he'd ever tasted.

"Thank you, Chef," I whispered.

I'm not entirely sure, but I think all of our history faded for Max too, there in that moment. We were each back to basics, and united in our mutual desire to make an impact on the culinary world we loved so much.

"Thank *you* for creating the dish, Chef."

I smiled at him and savored the moment. I knew it was one that would forever remain in my mental scrapbook of career achievements.

I didn't get to savor very long.

"I think the biggest thing for me—the reason *I* need to practice—is that the way you are on camera, and kind of the way you are in the kitchen in general, really drives me insane."

"Excuse me?"

"I'm not saying that's why I was a jerk to you, but—"

"Wow," I said as I involuntarily took a step back. "You're quite the gentleman, Chef Cavanagh. Maybe you should stick around for dinner and we can talk about how I've gained a little weight, and you can help me decide whether or not the gray hairs I'm starting to get will pass as blonde highlights a little longer."

He lifted his hand to his face and scratched his beard-covered cheek, and then sighed and shook his head. His eyes left mine and traveled down to his feet as his hands formed tightly clenched fists. "I knew it was probably a mistake to bring it up—"

"But you persevered in spite of your doubts, and for that I'm eternally grateful."

His hand lifted before his eyes did, and he held it out in front of him as he said, "Can you just listen to me? Can you maybe just . . . I'm not good at . . ." He exhaled, and finally his eyes lifted. "I'm not always good at *talking,* Hadley.

238

I'm good at talking about food. I'm good at talking about travel and adventure, and what's wrong with everyone else's cooking. But I'm not good at the real stuff. I promise you I'm trying my best here. And I promise I'm not trying to hurt you." His palms reached behind him and grabbed onto the edge of the counter. "Can you just give me the benefit of the doubt for one minute?"

Whatever had happened to lock our eyes in place before happened again, and I couldn't say a word. At least nothing of consequence. I simply nodded—slowly—and said, "I'm going to take the water chestnuts and go sit over here."

A confused laugh bubbled out of him. "Okay . . ."

"I'm going to try really hard to give you the benefit of the doubt and just let you say what you want to say. I just . . . I think a little space will be good." I shakily reached out for the container of water chestnuts and took them with me to the table. "So you just stand there and cook lunch and say what you need to say—"

"Do I have to cook while I say it?"

I nodded. "I'm starving."

A gentle smile spread across his face and I knew he understood, as I did, that cooking would create an environment that made us both more comfortable.

"Okay," he replied. "I'll cook. But I'm going to need the water chestnuts."

"Do you need all of them?"

That smile deepened. "No. Not all of them."

"Let me know when you need them." I took a bite out of one and set the container down on the table as I sat. This really felt like more of a job for popcorn or pork rinds, but Max's ambiguous vegetables would have to do. "Okay. I'm ready."

He chuckled softly, and for a split second there was emotion in his eyes that I didn't recognize. It was gone as quickly as it came.

"So, here's the thing, Hadley. I gave this a lot of thought and—"

"You need to cook."

"Oh. Right. Sorry." He looked around the island and gathered the ingredients he needed right away, and went straight to the pans of mine he intended to use. As he grabbed olive oil from my pantry he said, "Like I said, I just want to be honest. I think you deserve that."

"I deserve to be told everything that you think is wrong with me?"

"What happened to the benefit of the doubt?"

I sighed and gestured that he should continue.

"If I thought any of this was anything that was *wrong* with you, I wouldn't bother. I'm not seeing any of this as flaws. It's not that. It's just . . ." He looked around him and then to me. "Where do you keep your knives?"

"Behind you."

He turned and spotted them. "Ah. Thanks." He

began dicing the raw chicken. "Hadley, the thing is, I think you're remarkable."

I froze. "You think I'm remarkable?" I asked with a mouthful of water chestnut.

His dicing hand hovered a couple inches above the cutting board. His eyes tightened up and his jaw clenched, but then instantly his eyes and his jaw and his dicing all went back to normal.

"To have made it in this business the way you have? Putting up with jerks like me? Yeah. That's pretty remarkable. If anyone knows how difficult it is, and how much it has a tendency to sap the life out of you, it's me. And you deserve more respect than I've given you to this point." He looked at me. "I'm sorry."

I probably would have been moved and honored by his words if the promise of analyzation of my shortcomings wasn't still lingering in the air.

"I appreciate that, Max. Really. But . . ."

His eyebrow rose. "But what?"

"Oh no . . . that wasn't my but. That was your but."

Yeah. That's actually what I said. I kept my head down and held on to hope—for the briefest of silent seconds—that he'd heard what I meant rather than what I said.

His snickering made it very clear he'd heard *exactly* what I said.

"Don't worry. I have no difficulty at all distinguishing between the two."

"I just meant—"

"I know!" He laughed. "But there is no 'but' there."

I shook my head. "That's not true. Apparently, I drive you insane. No matter how remarkable I am."

He began mincing garlic. "It's just that there is a different version of you that makes it to air." He stretched out his hand and calmly said, "I need the water chestnuts. If you didn't eat them all."

"Of course I didn't eat them all." I got up and handed him the container with two or three remaining water chestnuts.

He laughed. "Why are you so upset?"

"I'm not upset," I replied, clearly upset. "As of now, I just don't understand why you find it necessary to come into my house and point out everything you think is—"

"I want to be your friend, Hadley!" he shouted, and then he cursed which, to his credit, I hadn't heard him do very often. Not as often as he always had on *To the Max*. Certainly not as much as he had on the set of *America's Fiercest Chef*. "Though, for the life of me, I can't really remember why right now. You sure don't believe in making it easy, do you?"

I knew those last two sentences would resonate later, but I wasn't there yet. I was still stuck on my observations regarding the foul language he was so well known for.

"Why do you have such a potty mouth?"

Dang it. Why did my *Hee Haw* conversational tactics always rise to the surface when it was most important that I not be viewed as a sheltered fourth grader? Thankfully he didn't acknowledge "potty mouth," apart from the raised corner of his mouth and the amused twinkle in his eye.

"It gets a reaction."

"A good one?" I pushed.

He picked up his knife—*my* knife—and resumed his preparation. "I don't get to just stay home and cook safe dishes that I've been making my entire life, Hadley. My entire career, my entire image, is based on this whole *To the Max* adventurer thing."

I teetered up on my toes. "Oh! So, it's an image? Is that what you're saying? That when the camera is rolling, you flip it on like a switch? How is that any different than what you're accusing me of?"

He kept cutting onions as he looked up at me and shook his head. "It's not." His attention returned to his masterful chopping. "Which is what I was trying to say. Or at least it's what I was *going* to try to say, if you ever let me get there. That's what I thought about last night and this morning. A lot. And so, yeah . . . I meant what I said. I stand by it. But I realized I'm exactly the same. We all are, probably. We probably *have* to be, to an extent. We just handle it differently. I'm a jerk, you're the lost Judd sister."

I had two choices. I could be the girl picking the cut of Wagyu off the floor or I could be the creator of the best dessert the greatest chef of our time had ever tasted.

I cleared my throat and forced myself to sit down calmly. I crossed my legs, composed myself, and said, "Okay, tell me what you mean. I'm Southern, Max. That's always going to be there."

"Yes, you're Southern. And, well . . . at least from this New Yorker's perspective, you have an accent. A *twang,* I guess you would say." He'd said "twang" with as much twang as he could muster, but he'd also smiled a really sweet smile at me. He was forgiven this time. "And it's endearing. Your real accent, Hadley? It's sweet and warm and sexier than I care to admit. It has the power to make me feel like we're living out a Tennessee Williams play. We're Brick and Maggie, sitting out fanning ourselves on Big Daddy's porch, lemonade in hand."

I laughed. "Well, that's about the nicest criticism I've ever received."

Max shook his head. "That's not the criticism. The criticism is that the minute a camera is on you, you become a bad community theatre version of *Cat on a Hot Tin Roof.*"

I settled back into the chair. "Wow."

I wasn't looking at him, but I could feel his eyes on me. "I doubt your viewers see it that way. I think I only notice it—and I think it only bothers me—because I know how nice the real version is."

I took the criticism—which, let's face it, had been pretty nice, all in all—and processed it through my thoughts. The truth is, he was probably on to something, and I knew it was worth considering further.

"Sorry I overreacted."

"I told you I'm not very skilled at this sort of talking." He smiled and then returned his attention to the cutting board. "But, here's the other thing I was thinking about with all of that. With you it's something that happens under the lights, until someone yells, 'Cut.' When it comes to me, I'm not exactly sure when the public persona and I got all jumbled together. I mean, it was always me, just a more exaggerated version, I guess. A more 'out there' version. But at some point I think people began assuming I really lived that wild, reckless, playboy lifestyle all the time. And at some point their assumptions became true." He added under his breath, "I really don't know when that happened."

He was heating olive oil in the pan and grating the ginger, and I finally began to feel calm about the prospect of the lunch. Not the lunch itself, of course. I'd have felt calm about the prospect of a burger. But I watched him and I thought, maybe for the first time, that he and I could actually do this. We could be friends. We could work together. We could be in the same room without jumping down each other's throats or . . . well . . . being all over each other in *any* way we shouldn't be.

"Max?" I began, and he looked up as he added his diced chicken to the pan. "How long has it been since you had a drink?"

He grabbed a wooden spoon from my drawer and tapped it against his knuckles. "Um . . . let's see . . . I guess about four months. Is that right? Whatever day that was that the network shipped me off to Tranquility Peaks. I had some bourbon on the plane. I guess that was the last time." He started moving the chicken around in the oil. "Why?"

"Tranquility Peaks?"

His hand—and, therefore, the chicken—stopped moving briefly, but then he picked right back up. But his voice was different. Like the casual comfort was being choked out of him.

"Um, yeah. You know . . . that's where I . . . well, I thought you knew, actually. During my suspension, I had to—"

"Max, were you in rehab?"

Something resembling amusement skittered across his face. "Not rehab. Anger management."

Oh. Well, that was good. That explained a

lot, actually. The Max I met on the set of *America's Fiercest Chef* desperately needed to learn to manage his anger. Clearly, he'd done it. Tranquility Peaks had done a service for the world, I figured.

"That's great, Max. Really. There should never be any shame in doing work on ourselves and picking up new skills." His stirring had picked up the pace, and amusement on his face had morphed into visible frustration. "Sorry. I didn't mean for that to sound so patronizing."

He shook his head. "It's not you. It's just . . . my manager. I think he kind of forgot there are actual human things at play in all of this. He's always saying, 'Not rehab, Max. Anger management.' " Max's voice had risen about two octaves while quoting his manager. "And sure, maybe that's the better answer for interviews or whatever."

"Your manager has a pretty high voice, does he?"

He looked confused for a moment and then laughed. "Sorry. No. His assistant, Candace, does. She's pretty much the only one I actually get to talk to anymore."

Max Cavanagh had been relegated to his manager's B-list? How was that even possible?

"So . . . you *were* in rehab," I stated rather than asked.

"Yeah. I mean, I definitely dealt with my fair share of anger management while I was there, but it just seems a little misleading, I think, to refer to an inpatient treatment facility in Malibu as somewhere I went to take some classes."

Points for honesty. "That does indeed sound like rehab. How long were you there?"

"Only thirty days inpatient. That was what I had to do for the network to suspend me rather than fire me. And then I stuck around Malibu another sixty days, but that was outpatient."

"Was that your choice, or—"

"Yeah. I had fought it like crazy, of course. In the beginning, I mean. It took me most of those first thirty days to actually start to see some good coming of it. By the time I was able to check out, I could think of a whole lot worse things than sticking around Malibu, spending time at the beach every day, and putting in a little more work at Tranquility Peaks to make sure some of the new habits stuck."

I cleared my throat and thought of my dad. How would he have advised me to proceed? "Good for you. Seriously, I think that was probably a really wise decision. But, um . . . I'm a little surprised, to be honest, that you don't know exactly how long it's been."

My dad had known. My dad had *always* known. Even when the days crossed into the hundreds, and then the thousands, he hadn't stopped counting every single one of them. And never in weeks, months, or years. Each day mattered to him.

"How long what's been?"

"Since you've had a drink."

Max shrugged. "I guess I could look on a calendar and—" His eyes shot up and met mine. "Hadley, I'm not an alcoholic."

"Hey, I'm not judging you. I'm sorry if that was rude. But my dad was an alcoholic, and I know that—"

"I'm not an alcoholic!" he repeated, throwing down his spoon with force. Sauces splattered and the spoon clattered to the floor. He stepped away from the pan—huffed away from it, actually— and took several deep breaths, his back turned to me. But after a few silent seconds, he was putting the spoon in the sink, grabbing a new one from the drawer, and dabbing paper towels on the floor and countertop. He drained his chicken, then added soy sauce, hoisin, rice vinegar, and the things he had minced, grated, and diced. "Sorry," he finally said, quietly, as if that was all there was to say on the matter.

My lower eyelids brimmed with tears, and I turned my head away slightly as one escaped down the side of my nose. I swiped at it as subtly and quickly as I could. I was overwhelmed by the emotion of it all. The familiarity and the newness, all wrapped up in one. I remembered his complete lack of awareness as Stuart and I picked up the Wagyu ribeye he had knocked to the floor, and watched him now, diligently cleaning up every drop he'd splattered. The responsibility had always been his, but now he owned it.

I couldn't help but also think back to what Leo had said to me on the phone the night before.

"Everyone in the business is claiming he has it all together now—has things under control, got help, has dried out, all of that—but you never can tell."

Did any of us really have it all together?

The scent began wafting from the pan, and I was involuntarily drawn to it. I crossed to stand across from him—one of the benefits of having a show kitchen, designed for easy viewing. It was also, as it turned out, designed for easy smelling.

"I'm sorry I upset you, Max. I guess . . . well, with my dad and all we went through there, I guess it's just sort of an involuntary reaction."

"Well, you know what? My dad is an alcoholic too. As far as I know, he still hasn't gotten to the point of counting days. He's still in the passing out and *losing* days phase, to the best of my knowledge. But I assure you, I am not one."

On one hand, he sounded exactly like you would expect an alcoholic in denial to sound. But on the other hand, he hadn't had a drink in months. And on the *other* other hand, which I obviously realize is not a thing, I saw the change in him, and I was looking in his eyes right then. There was no way I could bring myself to *not* believe him.

"I'm sorry, Max. I really am. I just thought that—"

His shoulders relaxed and he began stirring again. "It's okay. I get it." He took a deep breath and kept cooking, but it was as if he was no longer comfortable in his own skin—and I could almost believe he was going to find a way to fidget his way out of it.

I walked around the island, stood beside him, and placed my hand on his arm. The fidgeting stopped immediately. "I mean it. I'm really sorry."

His eyes went first to my hand and then to my face. I smiled at him, apologetically, and fought the temptation to do something zany—cross my eyes, stick out my tongue—to break up the somber feel of the moment. We couldn't keep staring at each other the way we were. I couldn't keep my hand on his arm. And I definitely couldn't pull him close and hold him as long as he'd let me, no matter how much I wanted to.

"So, um . . ." I pulled my eyes away, and then my hand, and returned to my spot on the other side of the island. "I know common ground is usually a good thing, but I'm sorry that our dads' alcoholism is a thing we share."

Way to go, Hadley. That *would break up the somber mood.*

He cut up some green onion and stirred in the remaining water chestnuts. "I haven't seen my dad since I left Ohio, so don't worry about it. It doesn't keep me up at night."

As much as I wanted to say about Max's dysfunctional parental relationships, I chose to react to the more surprising revelation first.

"You're from the Midwest? Seriously?"

"Don't tell. It makes me less intimidating."

I laughed. "Your secret's safe with me."

He pulled out the butter lettuce and began rinsing it. "So what about you? Do you have a good relationship with your parents?"

"I had a great relationship with my dad. He died about ten years ago."

Max glanced at me over his shoulder as the water continued to run. "Oh, I'm sorry."

"No, it's okay." I thought about that for a second and then made the conscious decision to peel away a couple layers of my own. "No. It's not. It sucks."

He gasped and clutched his chest with the hand that wasn't holding the lettuce. "Now who has the potty mouth?"

I rolled my eyes. "Sorry to offend your delicate ears."

He winked and turned back to his lettuce, and not a moment too soon. I can't imagine the expression that must have danced across my face upon realizing that wink had caused my stomach to flutter.

"My dad was the reason I started cooking," I

resumed. "Well, and necessity. He was working all the time—two, three jobs—so I learned to cook. I was nine when I started. Ten, maybe. And even with how busy he always was, even before he got sober, and with whatever drama of the week was going on with my mom, he and I still found time to watch *Renowned* and Julia. Every episode."

As his lettuce dried, he returned to the stovetop to add some salt and pepper and lower the heat on his chicken concoction. He raised his eyes to watch me as he stirred.

"Drama of the week?"

I sighed and quickly reflected on how my very deliberate transparency from just moments earlier had been replaced by natural, involuntary vulnerability.

"She, um . . . she struggles with some mental health issues. Depression chief among them. My dad and grandmother always did all they could for her, but she never really knew how to accept the help, I don't think. That's what I tell myself, anyway. That's a lot easier to deal with than thinking she just didn't want it."

"Hadley," he whispered, and I made the mistake of looking at him. I was the entire focus of those beautiful, stormy eyes, and that realization caused another flutter—this time from head to toe.

"It's okay," I said dismissively with a forced smile.

"No, it's not. It sucks."

"Yeah. It does."

"So where is she now, if you don't mind me asking?"

"Wish I knew. She was in and out when my dad got sick, and then when he died, she took off. We tried to track her down for a long time, but the trail went cold pretty quickly."

"They were still married? When your dad died, I mean."

"Oh yeah. He always told me that before I ever got serious with any guy, I needed to think real hard about the 'in sickness' part of 'in sickness and in health'—he said not to even bother with the 'in health' part. Sickness or health. Richer or poorer. Better or worse." I scrunched up my nose and shook my head, remembering my dad's words. "He used to say, 'Before you get married, you need to make sure you love him enough for a life of sickness, poorer, and worse. 'Cause that's what you're committing to.' " I was once again drawn to the other side of the island, drawn to the irresistible scent of our lunch, and I knew that if it tasted even near as good as it smelled, I was going to be eating crow for a very long time. "That was the legacy my dad left me, I guess. *Renowned*, Julia, an aversion to alcohol, and impossible standards."

"Oh, I don't think they're *impossible*."

"Maybe not. But it kind of takes the fun out of

the thought of just *dating* someone, you know? Just casually getting to know someone, when all you can think is, 'Is this person worth it? The heartbreak? The pain?' "

"So that's the real reason why you don't date?"

I shrugged. "I guess it has played a role. But I meant what I said last night. Who has the time to date when you lead lives like ours?"

His eyebrows rose slowly, and a sheepish grin completely transformed his face.

I shrieked with laughter. "Yet somehow you've always found the time!"

He chuckled. "I used to, that's for sure. You know, at Tranquility Peaks, Buzz would always say—"

"Buzz?"

"My counselor. He would always say that the key to healing is self-realization. And that the key to self-realization is allowing yourself to embrace *nothing*."

I thought over the words as I watched him stir. I didn't want to be disrespectful, but the longer I sat there, trying to figure out a way to respond, the wider his grin spread.

"I'm sorry, but what does that—"

"I have no idea!" He laughed. "I was hoping you could tell me what it's supposed to mean. And then I could stand here and act all deep and philosophical, like I'd understood all along."

"Well, pardon me, but I think it's all a bunch of hooey."

He shrugged and continued to smile. "I do too. And yet, it helped. I mean, I haven't had a drink in however long, I'm not out at clubs, I'm not posing for pictures with different women at different events every night . . . and I don't miss that lifestyle. At all."

"Seriously? Different events every night?"

He nodded. "Pretty much. And do you know what else? I've been sleeping. I mean, not a lot. Still not enough, probably. But I never used to sleep." He shrugged again. "So maybe Buzz's hooey wasn't hooey after all."

I scrunched up my nose. "Well, there's usually some truth to be found in everything, I guess. I mean, Jesus talked about the last being first and the first being last long before Buzz ever said . . . whatever that was. And I think they're basically, in a weird way, maybe saying the same thing."

"You think that's what it means?" he asked.

I buried my face in my hands and giggled again. "I have no idea. But I'll tell you something I do think. I think going away to that place gave you the time you needed—maybe the quiet you needed—to drown out some of that noise. So sure, it helped. Of course it did. Because somewhere in there you were probably able to start hearing yourself again."

He took a deep breath and nodded. "How about you? Are you able to drown it all out and hear yourself?"

"Ah. See . . . my problems are different than yours, Chef Cavanagh. For me, hearing myself is never the problem. The voice in my head is just running nonstop—sometimes telling me the worst things. The challenge for me is shutting myself off for a while and listening for that still small voice that will only tell me the truth."

He stared at me—not unpleasantly, but I couldn't quite make out what he might have been thinking. I wasn't sure if he had any idea what I was talking about or not, but I wasn't out to preach to him. It was such a fine line. I wanted to be unapologetic about my faith, but it was sometimes tricky to keep people listening to you if every time you reached the end of a sentence, you clarified, "I'm talking about Jesus, y'all!"

"Can we eat yet?" I asked instead, dismantling the seriousness with my whimpers.

He held up his finger. "Almost. First, come here."

I was only about four feet away from him, so I wasn't sure what he meant. "Where?"

He gestured in front of him, between him and the stove. "And close your eyes."

My eyes, apparently, didn't like being told what to do, and flew open. "Why?"

He tapped the tip of his nose, as he had the first time we sat down for a meal together. "Every chef's greatest tool."

"Oh. Well, I can already smell it. It does smell really good."

Laughing, he gently pulled me in front of him. He stepped to my side and faced me. "Will you please indulge me for one minute?"

I groaned and said, "Fine," the short little word as long and drawn out as I could make it. "Okay, what am I smelling for?"

"Good grief, Hadley, just your nose."

He was behind me again and his hands were gently covering my eyes. I instinctively raised my hands to his. And the thing is, I meant to brush his hands away. I meant to chew him out for making me feel uncomfortable. But I didn't feel uncomfortable. And I sure didn't brush his hands away. Instead I gripped his wrists and wondered what in the world was happening.

"Now," he said softly beside my ear, "what do you smell?"

I smelled him. All him. Soap and shampoo and fabric softener. Clean. Masculine. But I was pretty sure that wasn't what he meant.

"Umm . . . soy sauce?" I answered nervously, my fingers involuntarily tightening around his wrists.

"What else?"

Okay, get serious, Hadley, I lectured myself. *This is just work. Just a further exploration of the mutual skills we demonstrated at Pancake Pantry.* I took in a few deep breaths and released each of them slowly. Then when I breathed in again, I was able to smell each and every ingredient I had seen him add to the pan. Each of them individually.

"I smell everything."

I felt him shifting from one foot to the other behind me. It seemed there was an excitement bubbling up in him. A giddiness, almost, that seemed to come from the joy of this craft that meant so much to both of us.

"Good! So what's missing?"

I tilted my head and his hands went with me. "What's missing? Nothing, I don't think. It smells amazing—" I stopped abruptly and leaned closer to the pan, with Max accompanying me the entire time. I inhaled as much of the scent as I could, and then I knew. "You cut green onions, but I don't smell green onions."

His hands left my eyes, but my hands weren't as quick to release his wrists. For a moment his fingers rested on my shoulders, but in a flash he was beside me rather than behind me.

"Every chef's greatest tool," he repeated with a smile before tossing the green onions on top, for visual effect more than anything else, and casually adding, "Let's eat."

19. Mix separately.

MAX

After their one day of practice, Max had flown back to New York to get some things squared away before *Renowned* filming officially began. In actuality their one day together had been less practice than therapy, but he still felt pretty confident it had done the trick. He and Hadley were going to face their eight weeks with Marshall Simons as a unified front, he knew. At the very least, he suspected she was going to try not to talk like Blanche Devereaux from *The Golden Girls* every time the camera was on her, and Max was going to do all he could not to lose his temper if she did. The danger now, of course, was that the biggest temptation might be to kiss her just to shut her up. That hadn't ever been a viable option before.

And it still wasn't a viable option, he knew. Hopefully he could remember that.

The day he got back to New York from Nashville, he hadn't had to think very hard about what to write in his Discovery Journal. Oh, there were all sorts of things he could have written, but one stood above them all.

Today, in my ongoing adventure of discovering

who I truly am—the parts I like and should celebrate, as well as the parts I hope to improve—I discovered I hate to fly.

At least he hated flying without having a drink in his hand for the entire flight. Without a drink in his hand there was a feeling that he needed to be on his best behavior. Of course, that feeling may have had something to do with the new way people were looking at him. And the new way people were looking at him may have had a whole lot to do with his first legitimate desire for alcohol in months. He didn't *need* a drink, of course. *Thank you, Buzz. Here . . . please take credit for your accomplishment.*

No, he didn't need a drink. And he didn't need to get angry over his fellow passengers pulling their phones out and snapping photos of him eating pretzels and drinking a ginger ale. That part didn't make him angry, actually. That part was nothing new. What was new was phones being *kept* out, and eyes being fixed on him—not even subtly—as some of his fellow passengers attempted to provoke him.

He felt like Robin Hood. The bounty on his head was increasing the more good he did.

They were just waiting for him to explode. They seemed certain that if they kept talking to him, asking him about Hadley and *Fiercest Chef*, snapping pictures, leaning in for selfies, he would give them what they presumably wanted: at best, bragging rights with their friends; at worst (for him, anyway), an easy payday from some tabloid or other.

He didn't lose his temper once on that plane, but by the time he landed at LaGuardia, it was official. He hated flying and wanted—but didn't need—a drink.

Well, he wasn't going to be put back in that position again if he could avoid it. He would definitely be driving back to Nashville, even though it meant leaving a day earlier.

At least I have enough free time to drive, he thought to himself as he made his way from his apartment to the end of the block, and the private parking garage where his Range Rover lived. What a shock it was to discover he actually meant that. He was grateful for the time. But enough was enough and he knew it was time to get things rolling again. Along those lines, he'd decided he had one stop to make before he got back on the road to Tennessee. He'd been ignored long enough.

"Hey, hey, hey! Good to have you back, Mr. Cavanagh," Bobby, the security guard on duty, greeted him as he entered the code and opened the gate.

"Thanks, Bobby. Good to be back, although now I'm taking off again for a few days. Thanks for taking such good care of the Rover—especially during my long period away."

He laughed. "Oh yes, sir. I talked to her every day and made sure she didn't forget about you, just like you asked."

"Good man."

Minutes later he was zooming through Manhattan traffic—as much as it was possible to zoom through Manhattan traffic, that is—with Ol' Blue Eyes blaring through the speakers. He made his way to the Flatiron District, pulled onto 23rd, turned into the garage near the office building, and after carefully surveying the guy working the valet booth and determining he was trustworthy, handed over the keys.

He whistled "Fly Me to the Moon" as he stepped into the elevator, as content as he could remember being. *In how long?* he wondered. Months? Years? Ever?

Sure, Tranquility Peaks was a hippie haven where dreams and self-assuredness went to die, but there was no way he could deny that his mind was in a better place than it had probably ever been.

He realized he was probably giving Tranquility Peaks just a little more credit than it deserved, but it was easier to acknowledge the role Buzz had played in his contentment than to focus on the role Hadley was playing.

As he rode up to the 42nd floor, he pulled out his phone and reread their most recent text exchange.

I've checked the mail every day for my monogrammed "Greatest Chef Ever" apron, but it hasn't shown up yet. Too bad. I was going to wear it on Renowned.

You know that's not happening, flyboy. I was considering getting you one that says "World's Greatest Preparer of Lettuce Wraps, Not Counting School-Aged Children" but they were going to have to make the font so tiny to fit it all in.

Max wasn't quite sure he'd had any actual hope that the impetuous and extremely uncouth declaration that he wished to be Hadley's friend would even be taken seriously, much less come to fruition. He'd blurted it out in a bit of a panic, after all. It seemed so much safer than "I'm beginning to suspect you may be the most enchanting woman I have ever known, and I'm terrified of the way I feel when I'm around you."

That was really more of a dinnertime declaration.

However, in spite of being increasingly

enchanted by her, and even in spite of the fear—which remained when he was around her, and grew exponentially when he wasn't—they had, in fact, become friends.

"Max?" Candace asked in surprise when he stepped off the elevator and into the office suite. "What in the world are you doing here?"

"Great to see you too, Candace."

She shook her head and laughed as she stood from her desk and walked around to hug him. "Sorry. It *is* great to see you. I just wasn't expecting you, that's all."

And neither is he. That's the point. It's a lot more difficult to avoid someone when you don't know they're coming.

"How've you been?" he asked her, looking around and scoping the place out as he did. There were about a dozen people working in the area, and they all seemed to be taking turns looking at him in a way they no doubt thought was sneaky.

"Good. Good. And you? The beard's new. I like it."

"Thanks. So, is he—"

"Hello, Max."

The voice he'd heard very rarely since being carted off to Tranquility Peaks—though before that it had been the one constant voice throughout his entire career—came from behind him. Max turned to face him.

"Hello, Leo."

"What are you doing here?"

"Well, it's a welfare check, more than anything. Candace has gotten so good at speaking on your behalf that I was beginning to fear she was actually holding you hostage in the break room or something."

Leo sighed. "Come on back."

Max followed him through the peanut gallery back to Leo's office and couldn't help but wonder what he had done to become such a pariah. Obviously, he *knew* what he had done, but why did everyone in Leo's office care so much? As soon as Leo shut the door behind him, he decided to just cut to the chase.

"Thanks so much for all the support you gave me, Leo, while I was in Malibu. And especially since I've been back."

Okay, apparently he was going to passive aggressively cut to the chase.

"Oh, you mean like the support I've shown by keeping your restaurant investors on board when they wanted to drop you? Or do you mean the way I've kept the network from firing you, full stop, after your little stunt? Maybe you're talking about how I got you on *Renowned*, which, just so you know, was the single most difficult thing I've ever managed to pull off."

Max laughed bitterly. "Oh yes, I'm sure that was difficult." He didn't doubt that there was some truth in the first two things—maybe a great deal of it. He wouldn't know. His manager hadn't kept him in the loop on anything. But he was resolute that he understood the situation with *Renowned* better than Leo ever would. There was no way anyone had had to twist Marshall Simons's arm in order to get him to dive headfirst into the season he believed Hadley and Max were going to give him.

Leo stood toe-to-toe with Max and stuck his finger in his face, but Max had a full six inches of height on him, not to mention age and build. Max wasn't any more intimidated by him than he had ever been.

"And don't get me started on all the lawsuits I kept from happening."

"Who? The network?"

"Yes, the network, for one. Your contract has a thing or two to say about you showing up at work drunk and getting drunker throughout a shoot, as you can perhaps imagine."

"They just kept pouring the stuff."

Max caught himself and took a deep breath. Nope. No way. He wasn't going to allow Leo to get the better of him. Not a chance. He took a step back and turned to face the wall. He wasn't handling this at all like he wanted to. He worked to focus his thoughts for a few more seconds and then turned back.

"What?" Leo asked with an irritated shrug.

Max chewed on his lip and knew he was going

to have to pull out all of Buzz's best tricks in order to control his anger this time. He went back to one of the most effective techniques—personalizing the anger, and the results of losing control of that anger. As she had been since the very beginning, Hadley was that personalization. But now, rather than dark circles under bloodshot eyes and shock etched across her face, he saw her in front of him, his hands over her eyes, her small hands wrapped around his wrists—her trust and comfort overwhelming. While she was assigned the task of figuring out what was missing, he had been afforded an unwitnessed moment to take in everything about her.

For the first time, the focus wasn't on what he had lost, or caused others to lose, but on what he stood to lose if he lost control again.

"I'm sorry," he finally said, with surprising calm and true remorse. "That was inappropriate. It's not the network's fault that I drank so much."

Leo did a quick double take, and then just carried on. "That's right it's not. And do you know who *really* almost did you in? Norman Salverno."

Ah, Chef Norman. There was no doubt Hadley had received the brunt of Max's abuse that day, but he probably at least owed Chef Norman a fruit basket or something.

"What do you mean, he almost did me in?"

"He wanted you gone. He threatened to leave

the network unless *To the Max* was yanked from the schedule—"

"Hang on." He wasn't surprised that Norman had pulled something like that. He was a sniveling brownnoser who could burn boiling water—then he'd probably try to serve it on a plate—and he'd perfected his precocious shtick to the point that he'd gotten some equally idiotic food critics to believe he was a genius. What *did* surprise him was that it had worked. "That's why I'm not on the air? They sided with Salverno?"

"Of course they sided with Salverno, Max! You didn't leave them any choice. And then, while you were off at anger camp, who do you think swept in and made a strong case for your time slot? And don't even get me started on Beckett."

The mention of Hadley's name distracted him from all the snide remarks he wanted to make about anger camp, where they would no doubt all sit around a campfire, roasting marshmallows—and their enemies.

"What about her?"

"Well," Leo began, clearing his throat and collapsing into his desk chair. "I'm not sure if you've been paying attention to the world around you, but some of the things you said to Hadley Beckett . . ."

"I know."

"Let's just say you treated her a whole lot differently than you treated the male chefs."

Max stormed toward him. "I said I know!"

"Oh, you know, do you, Max? You're sure singing a different tune now. Do you remember what you said that day?"

"Don't remind me," he said, not as a flippant expression of acknowledgment but as a warning for Leo to stop talking.

"You said being a chef is a tough job and not everyone is cut out for it. You literally said, Max, that if she couldn't stand the heat, she needed to get out of the kitchen. Do you remember that? You also said you didn't remember saying anything to her that you wouldn't have said to the male chefs. But you didn't call Chef Norman 'doll,' Max."

"He was too busy crying . . ."

No. Stop.

Max caught himself again. The heat was rising up to the top of his head, flooding his vision as it went. It was getting more difficult to see what he stood to lose. He had to calm down. He had to put this into reverse.

"I didn't treat Hadley any different because she was a woman," Max insisted as he closed his eyes to block out Leo's face in an attempt to focus on a much prettier one. "I'm just good at knowing which buttons to push, I guess. And that's not justification or an excuse—" He squeezed his eyes tighter. "I'll apologize to Norman. I'll do what I need to do to make it right with the network. And you know I already apologized to Hadley."

Leo sighed. "I must admit, that was good work. I'll give you that."

Max opened his eyes, Hadley finally having solidified in his mind. "I should thank you for that. That was a good idea, me driving to Nashville. Thanks, Leo."

Leo repeated the double take, and then proceeded to stare at Max as if he'd said he was leaving it all behind to travel with the circus. "Okay, what is this?"

"What is what?"

"You! What are you . . ." He looked around the room, maybe hoping the walls could explain it to him. "Are you telling me you've actually changed?"

To hear Leo say the word, Max would have sworn that was a bad thing.

"Wasn't that the point—"

Leo stood up, kicking his office chair behind him. "Who do you think is going to want a nice and friendly Max Cavanagh?" He laughed, and the sound set every nerve in Max's body on edge.

Max flexed his right hand—making a fist, and then releasing; making a fist, and then releasing. "I don't understand what your problem is. You wrote me off because I was out of control, and now you're writing me off because I'm not?"

Leo shook his head, seemingly disappointed

271

in Max because it wasn't all perfectly clear to him. "This isn't about me writing you off. This is about you ruining everything. It doesn't matter what you do now, Max. You've lost credibility, no one wants to work with you—"

He slammed his hand against the desk. "I'm on *Renowned*! Right now. Right now. And it doesn't matter how I got on there. Even if you had to work miracles. I'm on. It's happening. And do you know what else? Maybe I've lost credibility, but everyone loves Hadley Beckett. And maybe no one wants to work with me, but *she is*."

"And she's hating every minute of it!"

Max's breath caught in his throat for a moment, but that cleared quickly. "You don't know anything, Leo. You don't know a single thing."

"Oh, that's adorable, Max. Okay, sure. Yeah . . . you got where you are because I don't know anything." He resumed his earlier posture, finger in Max's face. "Trust me when I tell you she won't hesitate to step on you or whoever else is in her way. She's focused on getting to the top, and I'm the guy who's going to get her there."

Max took a step back. "You're wanting to start representing Hadley?"

"I've been representing her for about a month."

No . . . that didn't make any sense.

"Leo, don't you think that's an enormous conflict of interest?" Max wasn't really sure that it was. Half the top-name chefs in the country were probably represented by Leo. But Hadley? "I mean . . ." He took a deep breath. "How can you possibly do what's right for both of us, when . . ."

When the best thing that ever happened to her career was the worst thing that ever happened to mine . . .

"I got you on *Renowned,* didn't I? I'm doing right by you. At least I'm doing the best I possibly can. But the position you're in? Well, you have no one but yourself to blame for any of it, Max." Leo sighed and placed a hand on Max's shoulder. "Sorry, pal, but you just can't come back from this one."

The words rang in his ears, and they stung anew with each and every ring. *You can't.*

Those were the words that had gotten him to drop from the baseball team so he had time to take home ec. They'd gotten him to turn down an academic scholarship in order to take his chances on culinary school. And they were the words that had helped him decide to sell everything he owned to pay for one month's rent at his first restaurant.

"You can't" was nothing more than a challenge.

Max closed his eyes again, but he didn't see Hadley. Instead, he saw his dad, standing on the street in front of their house, as Max's 1998 Ford Escort drove away. He'd never regretted leaving Cincinnati and heading to New York. Not once. But he'd always regretted leaving on a morning when his dad was actually sober. The odds had been against it, but of course he'd had the bad luck for that to be the day. As much of a lying, manipulative waste of space as he was when he was drunk, at least when he was drinking, he wasn't mean.

It was as if he thought Max's reaction to him telling him how little he believed in him and all the things he wasn't capable of, over and over, would fill the temporary void left by sobriety.

"Why haven't you dropped me, Leo?" Max knew the answer, he just wanted to see if Leo had the decency to confess it.

"Because, in spite of it all, I care about you, Max. You know that. We've been through a lot together, and if I were to drop you right now, well . . ." He offered him a half-smile that Max thought was supposed to pass for compassion. "No one else will represent you. No one else will touch you with a ten-foot pole, truth be told. I want to give you some time to rebuild."

Ah. So it has nothing to do with the massive royalties you get to continue collecting for years of To the Max *syndication? Good to know.*

"That's good of you, Leo. Thanks." He put his hand out and Leo shook it. "Let's talk again sometime soon."

"I'll keep doing my best, pal. If there's any way at all to salvage this, you know I will."

20. Sear evenly and rapidly.

HADLEY

"Thanks again to my very special guests, Nicole and Keith, for spending some time at home with me today. And thanks to *you,* friends. Be sure to check out hadleybeckett.com for bonus recipes, including my sacred family recipe for chicken and dumplings. It's legit. You won't want to miss it."

"And we're out," Stuart called out. Walking over to me, he said, "Well, that's a new one. I didn't know there were any sacred Beckett family recipes. How far back does it go? It's not Twyla's, is it?"

"Of course not!" I laughed at the thought. "I believe my grandmother's chicken and dumplings recipe would just involve some canned chicken and a box of Bisquick." Who was I kidding? "Or, more likely, she'd place an order at Cracker Barrel. This one is just mine that I created."

He gasped in mock horror. "Hadley Beckett! Did you just lie to your audience?"

"I didn't lie! It *is* a sacred family recipe. Just . . . for the future. Trust me, if I ever have kids, my chicken and dumplings recipe is what they're going to be fighting over when I die."

"Well, we'll set up a time to get a crew here to film the heirloom of the future and some other online content, but other than that, we're good to go. That got us up to the hiatus, so you're free to focus on *Renowned* for the rest of the run."

My eyes flew open. "That's it?" I glanced at the clock on the wall and sighed in relief. I was so tired. We had all been up late the night before, prerecording my insufferable special segment with Keith Urban and Nicole Kidman. Keith and Nicole didn't directly cause the suffering. They were lovely. But there wasn't enough coffee in the world to help me enjoy watching Keith Urban butcher my recipe for beef stew until nearly midnight. "Thanks, Stu. You're the best." I took off my apron and threw it on the countertop. "So what are you going to do during the break?"

He laughed. "After you're done cooking—considering all the times you don't know how the appliances work, or when you burn au gratin potatoes—"

"That only happened once!"

"—the shows don't just magically go on the air in a way that makes you look like you actually know how to cook. You do know that, right? It's important to me that you know that."

I smiled. "Yes. I know that. Point taken." I

grabbed my sponge and began cleaning my station.

"How are you feeling about tonight?" he asked as he checked things off his clipboard.

"Good. Nauseous."

"Perfect."

"Just nerves." I smiled. "It's not all that often in your life that you get to achieve one of your lifelong dreams."

"Well, I think it happens to you more than most people, so maybe don't say that on the air. With the hot streak you're on, it could make you look a bit lofty."

I nodded. "Good note."

"But I'm sure you're going to be great. And, I mean, tonight's not such a big deal, right? You already filmed last week."

"Yes. Thank goodness I don't have to meet Marshall Simons for the first time ever again. But tonight's the first *real* filming for an episode. As in, tonight we start filming the episode that will air on Sunday. Sunday! *This* Sunday, Stu. Can you believe it?" I hardly could.

"Of course I believe it. You deserve this, Had! I'm just sorry you have to share—"

I cut him off with a groan. "Oh, let's not do that again."

I hadn't updated him on any of the more friendly developments between Max and me. I knew he wouldn't be pleased, and I just didn't want to mess with it. The friendship, the kissing, the practice . . . Stuart wouldn't like any of it.

Thirty minutes later, the entire crew was gone, my kitchen was ship-shape, and I was exhausted. Miraculously, I had time for a quick power nap. I hadn't taken a nap in years, I was pretty sure. But I decided to afford myself the luxury. I wanted to appear rested and refreshed on *Renowned*. A girl—even this blessed-beyond-belief girl—only gets to tape the first episode of her season of the show she's been watching since childhood every so often. She should look her best when she does.

I jumped off the couch with a start when a bell rang. I looked around in confusion, and I seriously had no idea what was happening or where I was. I certainly had no idea where I was *supposed* to be, and I didn't even understand where the ringing bell was coming from. I looked around for my phone and found it on the floor beside the couch, but that wasn't the annoying sound culprit. I hadn't set an alarm because I was only going to rest for a few minutes, I remembered. I did note the time when I picked it up, though, and that's when the real confusion and panic began. It was 4:45. Wasn't a car supposed to be there about then to pick me up?

The door!

I finally understood where the ringing was coming from, and I ran to the door and threw it open.

"Ms. Beckett?" the man at the door asked as I squinted into the setting sun and tried to make sense of everything. "I'm with the car service and was sent to pick you up. Are you ready?"

Was I? I glanced down at my bare feet. "Give me five minutes!"

I slammed the door shut and realized, as I was walking away, how much nicer it would have been to invite him inside. Let him have a seat, and maybe a glass of lemonade. But I didn't have time to rectify my rudeness just then. We were filming our first episode on location in Nashville, and I had grievously overslept.

I ran to my bedroom and made the mistake of looking in a mirror. I'd gotten a haircut over the weekend, and overall, I was enjoying my shorter hair. But it certainly didn't leave as much room for low maintenance. I ran a brush through it in an attempt to at least tame the flyaways. While I brushed my hair with one hand, I brushed my teeth with the other. My clothes were okay, if slightly wrinkled, but the problem was I knew I shouldn't appear on two television shows in the same outfit.

"Ms. Beckett?" I heard the driver call out. Was I hearing him through the door or out the window? "I'm afraid we really have to be going."

I groaned and began riffling through my closet. I grabbed a red plaid flannel shirt and changed into it, as I took a quick peek down at my jeans.

I was relieved to see they were just plain, boring jeans, and had no distinctive characteristics that would be detected by discerning viewers.

"On my way!" I shouted down as I took one last look in the mirror. Not good. Not good at all.

Two minutes later we were on our way, though I still had no idea exactly where we were heading. But by a couple minutes after 6:00, we had navigated our way through Friday evening Nashville rush hour, and I was being dropped off at the Bluebird Cafe.

When I arrived, Max was standing outside, talking to Chef Simons, who smiled when he saw me and rushed over to greet me.

"Sorry I'm late," I said to Chef Simons.

"No worries, my dear. We're all set up. We're going to film a few minutes inside, to try to really capture a true Nashville vibe, and then we'll move on to dinner elsewhere."

"We're going to dinner?" Max asked. "I thought we'd be cooking dinner ourselves. On a show that is supposed to be centered on our culinary skills—"

"Well, we're probably going to spend some time in the city, enjoying the culture and the traditions. At least, I know that's usually part of the first episode. Right, Chef Simons?" I chose to believe Chef Simons and I had reached a silent understanding the week prior. I would not be calling him Marshall.

"Right you are, my dear," he said as he patted me gently on the back. "This is very much within the scope of all seasons of *Renowned*, and of course we'll be going to New York next week, and experiencing the culture and traditions of *your* home, Chef Max. But for now . . . when in Nashville, do as the Nashvilleians do."

He pronounced it Nashville-ians, but I was still temporarily lost in thought with the fun idea of a group of Southern bad guys called the Nashvillains, who go around wearing fringe and rhinestones, singing country music, and adding sugar to everybody's iced tea.

"Well, aren't you the teacher's pet this evening?" Max muttered to me under his breath. "What happened to not letting them pit us against each other?"

"What are you talking about?"

He adopted a Southern drawl and said, "Yes, Chef Simons. Pick me, Chef Simons. I know the answer, Chef Simons." I laughed as he continued in his normal voice. "Way to show me up, Beckett."

I shrugged. "Well, it wasn't intentional. But all the same . . . sorry. I guess now we're even."

Max crossed his arms, and a smile slowly spread across his lips. "I guess we are."

I nudged him with my elbow. "Hi, by the way."

"Hi, yourself."

"Did you have a good flight?"

He shook his head. "I drove. I'll explain later."

"Excuse me!" Chef Simons called out from just inside the doorway, accompanied by an impatient snap. "Time is of the essence."

"Sorry, Chef Simons," Max and I both called out in unison, in our best teacher's pet voices. We looked at each other and then quickly away, suppressing our laughter. Our newfound secret alliance was potentially going to be more trouble than our rivalry.

"Have you ever been to the Bluebird?" I asked Max as we walked in.

"Pardon me, darling," Chef Simons said, "but we'll be filming soon. Could you please hold off on the conversation, so you and Chef Max have something to talk about? I certainly wouldn't want you to say something interesting to each other without us getting it on camera."

Well, *this* was a strange version of life.

I nodded. "You bet."

Max leaned in and whispered, "What were you thinking? Using all your best material off camera. I mean, asking me if I'd been here before? That was television gold, Hadley."

I giggled. "I know. Silly me," I whispered back. "I almost blew the shoot."

We reached our table, and he pulled out my chair for me.

"Thank you."

He pulled out the other chair at the tiny two-top

and sat next to me, both of us facing the stage. As he scooted his chair in, I got a whiff of him, and I couldn't help myself—I leaned in just a touch to confirm the scent was coming from him.

It most definitely was.

"Golly, you smell good," I said. I instantly regretted it, of course, but unfortunately, I'd still said it.

He smiled. "Thanks."

He was so nonchalant about it. So cool. He was clearly used to people commenting on how good he smelled—and that was understandable. He smelled like wide open spaces mixed with bergamot, a lot of sunshine, and what I imagined Harrison Ford smelled like when he stepped out of the shower after an action-packed day filming *Raiders of the Lost Ark*.

"I don't remember smelling it before. Is it new?"

He shuffled in his seat so he could lean in somewhat and we could hear each other. The crowd was growing, and the noise was increasing proportionately. "Nah. It's what I always wear. I just don't usually wear it in the kitchen."

"Why not?"

He tapped on the tip of his nose.

I cocked my head to the side and laughed. "Okay, so you *really* think your nose is your greatest tool?"

"Not just mine. I think it's every chef's greatest tool. Don't you?"

I considered that for a moment. "You mean beyond your taste buds?"

He chuckled. "No, actually. Including taste buds."

"Well then, no," I said. "I mean, you're right . . . the nose is *so* important. Absolutely. But more important than my sense of taste? Seriously, Max, I can't even wrap my head around that."

I scooted my chair a smidge his way, to get out of the path of a woman who kept walking from the stage to the back of the room, and then back again.

He nodded and smiled. "I get it. And I felt the same way until I went to Morocco for the first time." He closed his eyes and leaned his head back and I could almost see him being transported there. "The spices, Hadley. The spices are everywhere. And they blend together, and yet they're all so distinctive at the same time. I'd walk through the markets and it was just like I didn't have any choice but to close my eyes. The colors, the people, the fabrics . . . they all just stood to distract me from the scent." He opened his eyes and was seemingly back in Nashville. "Have you ever been?"

"To Morocco?"

"Yeah."

I shook my head. "No. I've never really been

anywhere. At least not like that. I went to culinary school in Denver for a while, and I used to film in Brooklyn, of course. And I went to Canada once." I shrugged and he laughed.

"I love Canada. Well, I love *parts* of Canada. I'm not a big fan of the always-cold parts. But there are other places you should go. As a chef, I mean. Morocco is one of them."

"Hey, you two," Lowell interjected himself, crouching down between us. "The singer is going to be out here in just a few minutes, and you can see it's getting pretty crowded. I need each of you to scoot in about half a foot." We did as we were told, and I did all I could to focus on our director's last-minute instructions, rather than "Yummy Indiana Jones" by Dior, which was now just a few inches away and intoxicating enough to make me wonder if I had indeed underestimated the importance of the sense of smell. "We can only have one camera on the back of the stage"—he pointed to it—"and this way we can get you both in the shot."

"Got it," I said, while Max gave a very forced thumbs-up, which made me chuckle. Max Cavanagh was not a thumbs-up kind of guy.

"So, Hadley," he said, taking me off guard. Not the words, just the proximity of them. "Why don't you get out more?"

"My grandmother has been asking me that for years."

He laughed. "No, I mean on your show. Why don't you get out of your kitchen once in a while?"

He suddenly smiled and raised a cool, confident hand in acknowledgment to someone behind me. I turned around to see who was there and caught four college-aged girls giggling and, I think, attempting to flirt with Chef Cavanagh. I turned back toward Max and discovered he had moved on after offering his polite, indulgent greeting.

"Your kitchen is spectacular," he continued, paying no attention to any of it. "But there's so much to taste and see and smell outside of your kitchen. Outside of Nashville. And now's probably the time to get the network to send you wherever you want. For however long you remain the golden child, I'm sure they won't hesitate to add a plane ticket or two onto their mortgage payment."

I was distracted by the college girls doing all they could to get his attention, and I was distracted by Eau de Temple of Doom, but mostly I was distracted by the underlying bitterness breaking through all of the seemingly innocent words he had just said.

"So you said I should go to Monaco," I finally said, attempting to ignore the negativity and pass it off as a result of our chaotic surroundings. "Where else do you think every chef should go?"

A sly grin spread across his face. "I said you

should go to Morocco, actually. But Monaco is nice too. Beyond that, the usual suspects. Vienna, Prague, basically all of Latin America. Basically all of Asia and Europe too, come to that. Madagascar. Paris, obviously. But surely you've at least been to Paris."

I shook my head that I had not.

His jaw dropped. "You're a pastry chef, Hadley."

I scoffed. "No, not really. I just specialize in desserts."

"What do you think a pastry chef *is?*"

"No, I just mean . . . I'm simple."

That sly grin overtook his face again. "I beg to differ."

"I mean my cooking is simple." Out of the corner of my eye I spotted Lowell near the stage, gesturing for me to adjust my position slightly. I did—first my chair and then my body, just a little more in Max's direction. "I'm not like you or Wolfgang Puck or Jacques Pépin. I'm certainly not like Julia." I sighed. "I don't know . . . I just kind of fell into the whole thing. What I do seems to work—"

"But don't you wonder what else is out there? Don't you want to push yourself? Expand your horizons?"

"I *do* that. I'm trying new things all the time."

I resisted the temptation to bring up my Southern/Indian fusion dish from *America's*

Fiercest Chef, and the way it had trounced all over his expanded horizons.

"And that's good," he continued. "I don't doubt that you do. I'm just saying—"

"Hadley!" Lowell called out, and I turned to face him. "We're getting ready to roll, and I had you just where I wanted you, hon. I need you to quit scooting away from Max."

"Sorry," I replied with a wave and a readjustment.

"Look," I said to Max as I shifted back in. "I'm just different than you." I raised my eyes to look at his—I just hadn't really realized they would be so close. But they weren't on me right then. The other table had at least momentarily claimed his attention. I cleared my throat and looked back down at my lap. "You just don't need to talk to me like I'm one of those college girls back there, making googly eyes at you. Okay? I'm doing pretty well. I'm not doing it like you, but I'm doing pretty well."

"I'd say." He shifted in his seat.

"Hey, what's your problem?"

"My problem?"

"Yes, Max. *Your* problem. You're talking to me like I'm your new apprentice, fresh out of culinary school. Believe me, I fully recognize that you're further along and have had more success than I have, but—"

"I'm just making conversation."

"No, you're not. You're talking down to me, just like you always have."

He leaned in closer to me and spoke through his teeth, with great emphasis. "What is happening right now?"

I jumped up from my seat and shouted, "You tell me!"

I saw Chef Simons peek from behind the curtain and then issue a command to Lowell, who promptly ran over to us.

"Everything okay, you two?"

Fillet knife. Grapefruit knife. Herb knife. Ice pick.

"It's fine, Lowell. Sorry. We're just . . ." How could I possibly explain it? "Sorry," I concluded with a resigned sigh. I looked down at Max, who appeared to be extremely focused on taking and releasing deep breaths.

Lowell was as focused on Max as I was. "Are you going to be able to pull it together, Max?" he asked. "Filming will begin the moment Marshall steps out on that stage, which is going to be about thirty seconds after I walk away. So I need you to cool down. Got it?"

My eyes flashed to Max and I saw it. For the first time, I understood, at least somewhat, what his life had become. The stigma and assumptions and rash judgments that had become his constant companions.

I quickly swiped the moisture away from the

corners of my eyes and cleared my throat. "It's fine, Lowell." I sat back down in my seat, hoping to catch Max's attention, but his eyes were still closed, and his shoulders were still rising and falling with regulated breathing. "That . . . I mean . . . Max didn't do anything. That was my fault. We'll be ready. About thirty seconds, you say?"

He looked at Max again, skeptically, and then turned to me. "You're a saint, hon." He smiled and rubbed my upper arm before saying, "Okay, so Marshall is going to get up there, get the crowd involved a bit, explain that they shouldn't ham for the camera. That sort of thing. We'll be filming through all of that, but for all intents and purposes we'll really get going as soon as he steps off. At that point, just dive into some conversation. If you can't come up with anything to say to each other, we'll have someone nearby, prepared to hold up some conversation cues."

"Got it," I said to Lowell with a smile.

"Thirty seconds!" he shouted as he walked away.

I quickly leaned in toward Max and placed my hand on his arm. Under my fingers I could practically feel the frustration and tension coursing through his veins.

"Max, I'm sorry. I shouldn't have—"

His head snapped around toward me and his entire body quickly followed in his chair. "You're so hypocritical. If I call you doll, it's harassment and discrimination. And I'm not saying it was right that I ever did that. It wasn't. But you just *kill* me, because if Marshall Simons calls you darling and kisses you on the cheek, or Lowell calls you hon and rubs your arm, you enjoy every minute of it. You don't even realize that they're being so much more demeaning than I ever was. All you care about is whether or not it's a win in the Hadley column."

"Hadley and Max, please face front. Five seconds!" Lowell called out.

We resumed our choreographed positions as he concluded his attack. "You can be whatever kind of fraud you want to be. I just wish you'd be consistent."

Suddenly Chef Simons was on the stage, thanking the crowd for being there and assuring them they would not be deprived of the up-and-coming country music act they had come to see, despite the chefs and cameras in their midst. He introduced Max and me—Max waved, I smiled, I think—and the crowd cheered. I was doing an okay job—I mean, not really, but sort of—not letting it all break through the surface. I kept it all at arm's length until Max squeezed my hand. His touch surprised me but not nearly as much as the emotion I saw in his eyes once I dared to look.

He mouthed the words, "I'm sorry."

I pulled my hand from his—for too many reasons to count.

All too soon, Chef Simons was off the stage, and it was time for chitchat. It was time for all the brilliant conversation that we'd been urged to save for the cameras.

"So . . ." I began, simultaneously crossing my arms and legs and looking toward the stage. "Have you ever been to the Bluebird?"

21. *Heat to a scald.*

MAX

Well, *that* had been a disaster.

After another thirty minutes at the Bluebird, during which they'd mostly just listened to some awful country music and managed to say approximately nineteen words to each other—none of which were remotely interesting—Hadley and Max had been whisked away for drinks and tapas at some hot spot. The only problem with that was that Hadley never drank alcohol, and Max didn't anymore. And neither of them had much of an appetite after all that had occurred.

Filming was cut mercifully short for the night, since it was easy for everyone to see there was really no point to any of it. They had enough shots of the two of them sitting across from each other in awkward silence to last through multiple seasons of *Renowned*.

It wasn't until the cameras were no longer rolling and everyone was heading home for the night that Hadley and Max once again said real words to each other.

"Sorry again," Max said as Hadley climbed into her car to be taken home.

"Forget about it," she said in response. "See you tomorrow."

That was it, but every word and every tone

was coated in more actual human emotion than anything else that had been said in all of the filmed moments prior.

Max slumped into his hotel room. He was a head-to-toe amalgamation of relief and regret.

He'd left New York in a state of shock that Leo had been managing Hadley's career, and he'd had the entire drive to think through what that meant. By the time he arrived in Nashville, he thought he understood *exactly* what it meant: that Hadley and Leo had been collaborating to, at the very least, use Max's in-motion career disasters to Hadley's advantage; at most, they'd been conspiring to bring Max down, to rocket Hadley to the top. He'd been sure of it, and he'd been ready to confront her, but then he saw her.

She looked so unlike the image she usually put forth. She was always so put together. Simple but meticulous. Not a lot of makeup, but what she wore was always flawless. Flawless hair. Carefully chosen wardrobe. To see her step out of the car with that new hairdo, in that red flannel shirt with the torn hem and the button missing at the bottom . . . he hadn't been prepared for that. It had thrown him completely off his game.

"Stop it," he lectured himself as he collapsed onto his room's king-sized bed and lay back with a sigh. Every guy had a thing for cute girls in flannel.

Except that wasn't true at all, he knew. At least

not for *him*. But now, apparently, he just had a thing for Hadley Beckett. No matter what she wore and no matter what she did. He'd known he had to pull himself together, though. He had to put all that aside and get to the bottom of everything, once and for all.

Unfortunately, he'd realized just a little too late that regardless of what Leo was up to, Hadley wasn't part of it.

With a groan he rolled off the edge of the bed and rubbed his face in his hands. He wasn't sure he'd ever be able to clear away the memory of the suffering in her eyes as he accused her of hypocrisy. As he attacked her with words and emotions she'd done nothing to deserve. It hadn't even taken much effort to get her primed for the onslaught of pain. In his presence, she was no longer the fierce, tenacious competitor she'd been every other time they'd gone to war. And seeing *that* was what made him realize he'd been wrong. So very wrong.

In his presence, she was trusting. Protective—of *him,* not herself. She was sincere, as she had always been. Even the different versions of herself that she presented in different situations, they were all *her*. And not a single one of those versions was out to get him.

Over and over she laid her soul out for him to see—and her soul was the truest, most genuine thing he'd ever known.

"What do I do now?" he asked himself aloud.

He couldn't very well show up at her house again, and he didn't figure there was much chance she'd reply to a text from him. But at least maybe she'd read it. He looked around for a comfortable place to settle in and take a seat. It wasn't that there weren't comfortable chairs in the room. There were. But they all looked so formal. Instead he leaned up against the wall and slid down to the floor and began typing with his thumbs.

And then he stopped. Suddenly. Midword.

What could he say? How could he explain? If he explained to her the assumptions he had made regarding her dealings with Leo, would he give her cause to mistrust *his* dealings with Leo? And why shouldn't she mistrust him? The truth was he and Leo *had* discussed ways to manipulate the situation—no, manipulate *her*—from the very beginning. That's why he'd driven from New York to Nashville the first time. That was Leo's idea, not his. But he'd had no idea Leo was maneuvering the chess pieces on both sides of the board. Did that matter?

Would any of it even matter? How many times would she be willing to overlook his flaws and mistakes before she wrote him off once and for all?

He switched gears, pushed a couple buttons on his phone, and listened in nervous anticipation as it began ringing, and again as Hadley's voice instructed him to leave his number and a brief message.

"Hadley, it's me. Max. Hopefully you'll get this. Look, I said some things . . ." He squeezed the bridge of his nose with his fingers as his eyes clenched as tightly shut as they could. "I've probably said lots of things, but the things I said tonight were just about the worst things I've said. I was . . . well, I was stupid. And wrong. And I feel like half our time together is me apologizing, and the other half is me refusing to apologize, when I really should. And it would be so easy for me to sit here and say we bring out the worst in each other because, let's face it, that seems to be the truth. But the fact is, you bring out the best in me, Chef Beckett. I'm just really sorry that my best isn't . . . better." He leaned his head up against the wall and sighed. "There are some things we need to talk about. Please. Let's talk."

He ended the call and threw his phone onto the bed—but he immediately thought better of it and hurried to pick it up and put it in his pocket. He didn't want to chance not hearing it ring. He grabbed his backpack and pulled out his Discovery Journal. So many options for the day.

Today, in my ongoing adventure of discovering who I truly am—the parts I like and should celebrate, as well as the parts I hope to improve—I discovered:

~~I'm the biggest jerk in the world.~~
~~I'm a pompous, condescending egotist.~~
~~I really hate country music.~~
None of that felt quite right, no matter how true it all was.

He set the journal down in response to the knock at the door and walked across the room with unrealistic hopes and dreams that room service had instinctively known he needed food. He didn't have any more appetite than he'd had at dinner, but his growling stomach had apparently not gotten the memo.

"Hadley," he breathed when he saw her standing there, still in that red flannel.

"Hi, Max."

They stared at each other, and Max felt a combination of joy and misery that he was pretty sure he'd never understand.

"Um, sorry," he finally said as he scooted over and opened the door wider. "Come in."

She shook her head adamantly. "No. Thanks, but I won't take up much of your time. I just . . . well, I got your message, and I was nearby. I was in the lobby, truthfully. I've been debating whether or not to come up, but I just couldn't say what I need to say on the phone. And, well, we need to deal with this now, so that it's not still hanging over our heads in the morning."

"Are you sure you don't want to come in?" he asked nervously.

"I'm sure."

"Look, Hadley, if you're worried we won't be able to keep our hands off of each other—"

"I'm not worried about that." Her gaze was resolute and unmoving. "Not at all."

He opened his mouth to speak, but nothing came out. Well. Okay, then. He scratched the coarse hair on his chin and bit the inside of his cheek as hard as he could without drawing blood.

"I can't do this, Max."

"Can't do what?"

"This. Whatever this thing is that we're doing. This flirtatious, just-friends thing."

He scoffed. "You're the one who wanted to be just friends."

"I know. But I didn't realize just how precarious it would be. Being your friend, I mean." She took a deep breath. "I don't know if I agree with you or not that what you said tonight was the worst stuff you've said, but I know it hurt the most. Not because you said it, but because I was so blindsided by it."

"I really am sorry."

She nodded. "I know. And apology accepted. Truly. But . . . well, it's one thing to have to be on guard against personal attacks from my supposed rival. It's another thing entirely to feel like I can't ever let my guard down because I never know when to expect an attack from my friend."

"Hadley . . ."

She looked down at her feet. "It's just too risky. I, um . . . well, somewhere along the line I started caring too much. I hope you understand."

"Hadley," he repeated. He didn't know anything else to say.

"I'll see you in the morning, Max."

He stood in the doorway—not watching her walk away, not turning away either—until she had almost reached the elevator. Then he found himself in the hallway, yelling after her.

"Your dad really messed you up, didn't he?"

She froze in her tracks and then turned around, her eyes full of fire. "Excuse me?"

He walked toward her in complete dread. He didn't want to fight with her. Not anymore. But she didn't get to have the last word. She didn't get to decide they weren't friends. And it sure wasn't up to her whether or not they cared about each other. It had been decided, and there was nothing either one of them could do about it.

"That whole thing about preparing yourself for a life of sickness, poorer, and worse. I get what he was saying, Hadley, but it totally screwed you up. You're so convinced that a life with someone else has to be awful. That that's the price for caring about somebody."

She shook her head and turned away from him, and continued her walk to the elevator. "That's not true."

He ran to catch up and then stepped in front of her. "It *is* true. I don't know why I didn't see it before, but it's absolutely true."

She stepped around him and urgently pushed the button on the elevator. "How dare you tell me I'm screwed up? You!"

Max laughed bitterly. He just couldn't help it. That one had stung, but he also knew it was fair. "Yep. You bet. You *bet* I'm screwed up. At least I admit it." The elevator doors opened and Max stood in front of the door to block her. Hadley tried to maneuver to get around him, but he wasn't budging. "You can stay here and talk this out with me," he seethed, "or we can talk about it while we film tomorrow. What's it going to be, Beckett?"

She crossed her arms. "Sure. We can talk about it. Here, on *Renowned*, whatever. As long as you talk about what happened on *America's Fiercest Chef.*"

He threw his hands up in the air. "I've talked about it."

"I mean *why* it happened. I've heard more explanation about why you had a breakdown from my *grandmother* than I've heard from you. Why is that?"

"You've never asked."

"I'm asking now!"

"Why does it matter?" he shouted. "It's ancient history—"

"But I deserve to know! Don't you think, Max, that if anyone deserves to know, it's me?"

"How long are you going to use that weapon?" he asked as he clenched his fist and released over and over.

"How long are you going to give me reason to use it!"

He put all the effort he could into breathing deeply. Steadily. But he no longer knew how to personalize the anger. What consequences did he have to worry about? He couldn't imagine that he could possibly do more damage to Hadley than he already had. His career was over, it seemed. Between Hadley and Leo, his already limited friend resources were depleted. Buzz's trick wasn't going to work if there was absolutely nothing to lose.

But then he closed his eyes and felt a familiar rush course through his veins. He saw the dining room of his flagship restaurant in Lenox Hill. He recognized the well-known but never monotonous sensation he always felt when taking one final look around before opening the doors for the dinner crowd. Soon the room would be filled with wealthy diners—the New York City elite—whose names had been on a list for months. Years, in some cases. There would be politicians who came to be seen and celebrities who came simply because they could afford it. Celebrities who would be every bit as impressed by tuna noodle casserole if it cost $200 a plate and had Max's name attached.

But somewhere in the room that night, as he liked to believe there was every night, there would be a twenty-three-year-old kid whose passion was food. That kid had scrimped and saved—maybe even sold their bed—in order to, just once, taste the food of a master. And after that meal, that kid would never be the same. After that meal, that kid's course would be set and their dreams would be solidified. After that meal, that kid would become Max's competition, coming up behind him, ready to change the industry, just as Max had.

In thirteen years he had gone from being that twenty-three-year-old kid to being a written-off man on the verge of losing it all. How had that happened?

In his mind he took one more look around. Each chair, each place setting, each light fixture cost more than that meal had cost him thirteen years prior, but that meal had made every single thing that had come since possible.

He opened his eyes and saw Hadley studying him in what appeared to be complete and utter bafflement.

"Are you okay?" she asked.

Max released a steady breath. "I never meant to hurt you, Hadley. I hope you know that. I'll see you in the morning."

22. *Render and drain.*

HADLEY

From the time I started watching *Renowned*, twenty-five or so years prior, I'm pretty sure I'd never missed a single episode. Not until *my* episode, that is. I was already in Manhattan in preparation of filming, which would kick off there for the week the next day, and during the premiere that Sunday evening, I put the Do Not Disturb sign on my hotel room door, turned off my phone, and took a bubble bath so long I had to refill the tub twice. I knew I wouldn't be able to stand seeing it.

As I thought back over the footage that had been filmed, I couldn't think of a single moment I wanted to relive. Not the annoyance I felt with him as I prepared Bouille Hadley, not our awkward on-camera evening exploring Nashville after our much, *much* worse off-camera squabble at Bluebird Cafe, and definitely not the two days of filming following our hotel confrontation. I knew, more than anything, I wouldn't be able to stand watching Max be . . . fine.

At least he seemed fine. Healthy. Mature, even. And overwhelmingly unaffected by our last off-camera exchange. He walked into my house, greeted the crew, smiled a subdued smile at me, cooked when he was told to, complimented my food on-camera, and willingly took on more of a supporting role when I was the focus of filming.

It was awful.

Early Monday morning, I got a taxi from my Upper East Side hotel to Leo's offices in the Flatiron District. I hadn't seen him in person since I'd thought he was a trained assassin, sent to either kill me or steal my biscuit recipe, and I was pretty nervous walking into the professional high-rise office suite. It definitely gave off a different vibe than meetings with Meemaw in her bedroom while she watched TV.

"Good morning," I was greeted pleasantly by a very attractive woman in her fifties, if I had to guess. "Can I help you?"

I cleared my throat, a bit nervously. "Yes, I'm here to see Leo Landry."

"And you have an appointment?"

"I do."

She regarded me with patience, though I suspected it was waning. "And your name?"

"Oh, sorry. I'm Hadley Beckett."

She nodded and smiled with recognition and pushed a button on the elaborate phone system in front of her. "Leo, Hadley Beckett is here."

"Thanks, Candace. Send her back."

Pointed in the right direction, I walked through the desks back to Leo's office, where he stood waiting at the door, arms outstretched. "How's my favorite client?"

I laughed as he hugged me. "How many times do you greet people that way in a day, Leo?"

"Well, you're the first today! That's what matters." He chuckled and invited me to sit. "Thanks for making time to stop by. I know you have a busy schedule while you're here."

"It's not too bad, actually. We're filming interviews with Chef Simons at the studio on Foodie Row today, and then we're in the kitchen tomor—"

"What's happening with you and Max Cavanagh?"

"Oh, um . . . well, nothing, really. Why?"

Leo leaned back in his chair and laced his fingers behind his head. "The climate. The climate in this industry can change as quickly as . . . well, as quickly as a pie you're making if you accidentally stir in salt instead of sugar."

"Okay . . ."

"Hadley, the network seems to think it's time to boost Max's profile again. They're preparing to revive *To the Max*. They were impressed with him on last night's episode, and based on early viewer reaction, he seemed to rise above a lot of the history and the assumptions people had made. In light of all that, there are probably going to be some tweaks made to the anticipated *Renowned* format for the season."

I hadn't even set my purse down yet.

"But *Renowned* is on a different network. What's that have to do with *To the Max* coming back to the Culinary Channel?"

He stretched his arms over his head and yawned. "Well, it's a small world, this food entertainment world of ours. It's all interconnected. Producers, crews, hosts." He leaned forward over his desk. "Look, I'm just going to give it to you straight. Your biggest asset is how much your viewers love you. You're immensely likable. The problem is that suddenly, as of last night, Max Cavanagh is likable too. No one could have seen that coming. But when he comes across as new and improved, and you suddenly come across as cold and distant for the first time ever . . . well, it's just not giving your viewers what they want."

I was adept enough at holding my own in a roomful of men, but I was really only used to doing it with men who cooked. This was very different. It may have only been one man, but we sure weren't speaking the language of food.

"I was cold and distant?"

"We always knew it was risky, putting the two of you together. Live and learn. But the network loves *At Home with Hadley*. Nothing to worry about there, hon. You're gold. *Renowned* just isn't going the way everyone hoped it would. You haven't really found a rhythm—"

"It's been a week, Leo. Seriously. A week."

And in that week, Max and I had changed our rhythm more often than a jazz trio. "I'm sure it will get better. We're both professionals. We'll do what needs to be done."

"Of course. Of course! I don't want you thinking this is anything to worry about."

"Then what *do* you want me thinking?" I asked.

"I just want you to be prepared that Max may be thrown into a little more of a lead role on *Renowned*. For now. That's all. Really. Nothing to worry about." He picked his cell phone up from his desk and pushed a few buttons. "All right?" he asked, never looking up from his phone.

All right? I had no idea if anything was all right.

"Okay. Sure," I replied. What other options were there?

He set his phone down and stood from his chair. "Seriously, kid, thanks for coming in. I wish you had more time. I'd show you New York."

I followed his cues and stood. "I've seen New York. Um, so we'll talk again, right? Soon?"

He ushered me out the door as he said, "You know, I've got a pretty busy few weeks ahead of me, but I'll definitely have Candace keep you in the loop. Take care."

And then I was standing among a roomful of people at desks, none of whom seemed to know or care in the slightest who I was. I walked back the way I had come in, and waved to Candace as I passed her desk.

"You have a good day, Hadley. Thanks for coming in."

It wasn't until I stepped into the elevator that I remembered.

"Your manager has a pretty high voice, does he?"

"Sorry. No. His assistant, Candace, does. She's pretty much the only one I actually get to talk to anymore."

The doors closed while Candace's high-pitched voice was still echoing in my ears.

23. *While that rests,*
prepare dry ingredients.

MAX

"Max!" Marshall Simons called out from the classy but comfortable *Renowned* living room.

Max rushed over to greet him. "Good morning, Marshall," he said as he shook his hand. In spite of his lifelong daydreams of being best friends with Simons, and going on wild fishing expeditions in Wyoming, Max found himself just happy to be acknowledged. He took it as a good sign that maybe the second week of filming would go better than the first.

"Are you ready for this?" Marshall asked.

"I think so," Max replied with a casual smile. "Just the normal sit-down?"

He nodded. "Assuredly."

"Sounds good. And Hadley? Are we going to film together today?"

"No. Not today. But we'll get you in the kitchen together tomorrow. Which reminds me. Your risotto ingredients list—"

"Already turned in."

Marshall nodded, satisfied, while Max pushed away the disappointment of knowing he wouldn't get to film with Hadley for another day and headed to the couch. He needed to talk to her, but texting wasn't going to cut it.

Since that horrible night in Nashville, a week ago, Max had had time to reflect on all of it. Top to bottom. He now knew the drive from Tennessee to New York like he knew his risotto recipe, so there was plenty of time to process all the stupid things he'd said and done at any given point.

Once he was on the couch, he was instantly surrounded by makeup artists applying powder to his face and hair stylists who always seemed to leave his hair alone but obsessed meticulously over his beard. Within minutes, lighting was set up, Marshall had run through his gargling vocal exercises, and Lowell was calling action.

"Chef Maxwell," Marshall began. "One of the greatest unexpected occurrences ever on *Renowned* has been, in my opinion, the thawing we have all witnessed between Chef Hadley and yourself. Talk about that, if you will."

Talk about that? Talk about the *thawing?* Should he admit that they'd messed up a good thaw by not handling things properly, and what had once been thawed was now spoiled?

"Truthfully, that was pretty unexpected to me too." *You have no idea.* "I'm really grateful that Hadley and I were able to get to know each other and find some common ground."

Wow. That's sexy stuff there, Max.

311

"How would you classify the current relationship between the two of you?"

He shifted uncomfortably in his seat. "She's someone I care about a great deal, and I value her role in my life."

"Chef Hadley having any role at all in your life is quite a feat indeed. Wouldn't you agree? Considering you've put down her food, her cooking style, the way she handles herself in the kitchen . . . You even, as our viewers will see in an upcoming episode, called her a fraud."

Max shot Marshall Simons a look of warning. Yes, the man was his hero, but he was skating very close to the line.

"That was off-camera. That was a private conversation."

"Is there a distinction in your mind, Chef Maxwell, between what is acceptable on-camera versus what is acceptable when the cameras are not rolling?"

Max scoffed and looked toward where he knew Lowell to be standing, near the cameras. He was searching for answers, but he couldn't see anyone in the bright studio lights so he turned back to Marshall.

"What is this? Why am I under attack here?"

Marshall looked briefly down at the index cards in his hands and then carried on. "No one is under attack, and I apologize if you have been made to feel as if you are."

Max was overreacting. He knew he was. There was no doubt Simons had crossed a line by asking about something that had happened off-camera—although they had been miked at the time, Max realized right then, far too late. But Marshall was just asking the questions on his cards. He'd seen chefs take tough questions from him for years. Reputations had been ruined and reputations had been saved on the *Renowned* couch. The last thing Max needed was another breakdown for the highlight reel.

"No, I apologize," he stated, with his best attempt at a humble, contrite smile. "I admit, you did take me off guard, asking me about what I had thought was a private conversation. But, no. There is no difference in what is acceptable when the cameras are rolling. It's just that Hadley and I both said some things we regretted that evening. We have since made amends."

Good save. Even if "amends" stretched the truth a little too far.

"Let's go back a bit further," Marshall continued with a nod, looking up from his cards. "To a conversation that was very public. Take me back to that infamous night on the set of *America's Fiercest Chef.*"

Max should have known, he supposed. He should have known it had to come up sometime. It was relatively miraculous that he hadn't been forced to talk about it until the second week.

But now it was time, and they were no doubt in pursuit of the juicy sound bite that would be used to promo the show throughout the season. *Proceed with caution, Max.*

"I'm pretty sure there isn't much that's left to say on the topic."

"I'd like to know—I think we'd *all* like to know—what was going through your mind?"

Max ran his hand through his hair and shuffled again in his seat. "The truth is, Chef Simons, I don't fully remember. I had admittedly and very clearly had far too much to drink."

"Do you remember interacting with Chef Hadley?"

He'd tried. He really had tried to remember. Oh, he remembered the first day of filming, and part of the second, but he knew Marshall was asking if he remembered the moments when he threw his career into the toilet.

"I don't." He shook his head slowly and deliberately. "To be honest, I do remember cooking. I remember them calling out her name instead of mine as the winner, but my reaction . . ." He shrugged and then instantly regretted it. A shrug probably came across as flippant, so he leaned forward, lowered his head, and rested his elbows on his knees. "Trust me . . . I deeply regret everything that happened."

"I think what everyone really wants to know, Chef Maxwell, is what caused the destructive cycle that finally reached the point of no return on that horrible day?"

Max clenched his hands in front of him and raised his eyes to look at Marshall. "Is that what everyone wants to know, Chef Simons, or is that what you want to know? See, I think that *you* want to know, because you think talking about it will lead to ratings."

"And it wouldn't lead to ratings, Chef, unless people were out there, watching and wondering."

He smiled at his prey in that same iconic way Max had been watching him smile at chefs for years. Funny how, until that moment, he'd never realized what a jerk his hero actually was.

He really should have known. Through the years he'd seen chefs he respected cry to Marshall Simons about the children they'd neglected and the drugs they'd abused; the parents who hadn't loved them. How naïve Max had been to believe they'd all just felt like they could finally be open and honest, because *Renowned* had created a safe environment for them.

Well, it wasn't going to happen this time. If he came across as evasive and withdrawn, that was a million times better than unnecessarily digging up the pain of the past.

"The fact is, Chef Simons, that I've worked very hard to become a better version of myself—"

"Yes, you spent a month in a rehabilitation facility, correct?"

Max sat up straight as heat rushed to his head. "I did go away to work on my anger issues, yes. I know I've done some damage, but I'm really doing all I can to put that all in the past. So, Chef Simons, while completely understanding why there is an interest in all of the drama, I'm afraid that at this time, I'm going to need to respectfully ask you to mind your own business."

"I heard the sit-down was brutal," Leo said to Max as he made his way through the parking lot. He was leaning up against Max's Range Rover, parked in its temporarily designated parking space at the studio.

Max shooed him away as he approached, and Leo snickered as he removed his hands from the sparkling vehicle.

"It got better after I told Marshall Simons to mind his own business."

Leo's jaw dropped. "You didn't."

"I did."

"Max—"

"He went too far, Leo. He was just looking for dirt, and I have far too much respect for this institution—"

"You mean *Renowned*?"

"Yes. I have far too much respect for it to allow it to turn into *Hard Copy*."

Leo laughed as Max reached for the door, and he moved out of the way. *"Hard Copy?*

When was the last time you watched television?"

"You mean television I'm not on? It's been a while. Apart from *Renowned*, of course. And that's the point. I've watched this show my entire life, and I *know* that they air the dirty laundry. But I don't think Simons has ever pushed the way he pushed me today." Leo walked around to the passenger side of the car, and Max stared at him in confusion. "What are you doing?"

"We need to talk, and I didn't think we should necessarily do it standing out in the parking lot."

"Make it quick." Max groaned and they both climbed in.

"So," Leo began, "would you like some good news for a change?" He looked disappointed that Max didn't respond in the manner of a cast member from the musical *Newsies*—"*Would* I? Oh boy, Mister!"—and proceeded on, with just a little less enthusiasm. "The network is ready to bring back *To the Max*."

Max's head snapped up in surprise. "Are you serious?"

"Congratulations, my friend." Leo smiled and slapped him on the shoulder.

"That's . . . I mean, that's great! I didn't expect . . . I hadn't thought . . . I mean, why? Why the sudden change of heart?"

"There was nothing sudden about it, Max. You've been putting in the work I told you to put in, and it worked like I knew it would." He reached behind him for his seat belt and clicked it into place. Max was too lost in thought to comment on the fact that he wasn't planning to go anywhere with Leo as his passenger.

"But seriously, Leo, I didn't even know they were considering it yet."

"Why wouldn't they consider it? The overnights for yesterday's episode of *Renowned* were through the roof, and *you* . . ." He whistled through his teeth. "Max, I tell ya, I wasn't sure you had it in you."

"Had what in me?"

He laughed. "The ability to be likable. But you've somehow managed to completely reinvent yourself. In less than six months! It's remarkable. I really didn't know if you could pull it off."

Nothing he was saying was sitting right with Max, of course. But he couldn't quite force himself to focus enough on what was being said to break it down. In the moment, all he could think about was how grateful he was to finally be walking out of the desert toward water.

But he was also skeptical that his supposed oasis was actually anything more than a mirage.

"As of the last time we talked, you'd completely written me off, Leo. You said I couldn't possibly come back from—"

"Sheesh, Max. Can you please drive while we talk? Or at least turn on the heat? It's freezing."

318

Max started the engine and backed out of the parking space.

"So, you're saying that in the course of a week, everything has changed?"

"Of course not. Nothing happened in the course of a week. It happened over the months of—"

"But you said I was done, Leo." He gripped the steering wheel tightly. "You said—"

"I think the network just needed to see you in action one more time. And with week one of *Renowned*, they were able to see you're still a valuable commodity for them. Simple as that."

Simple as that.

Max scoffed as he aimlessly maneuvered the Range Rover through the Williamsburg neighborhood of the borough. "I thought no one wanted a nice and friendly Max Cavanagh."

Leo laughed. Not ironically, but as if it were all actually funny. "I'll confess . . . I didn't really see it going that way. Of course, I thought you and Hadley would have murdered each other long before we ever got to this point. Way to go, sticking it out. Kudos."

"I think Hadley's the one who deserves the kudos. For sticking with *me* this long."

That statement could not have been more factual in his mind. He thought back over it all in a way he never really had before—through the lens of "What in the world was she thinking?" What was she thinking, replying to his text that night? What was she thinking, agreeing to share an opportunity with him that deservedly could have been hers alone? What was she thinking, forgiving him, time after time? The way he had come to care for her, he knew that he would strongly advise her against ever coming into contact with anyone who had treated her the way he had to that point, and yet she'd given him the benefit of the doubt. And then she'd given him chances piled upon chances.

"Yes. Absolutely. Hadley's a good kid. She's going to be fine," Leo stated flippantly. "Which reminds me, since we are apparently going with nice and friendly, you could warm up on her a little more still."

Max turned his head long enough to observe Leo's expression. His tone wasn't telling him if he was serious or not.

"What do you mean? Warm up? Warm up how?"

He couldn't imagine being much warmer on Hadley Beckett than he already was.

"Marshall told me you didn't really speak to each other the last couple days. You may need to carry her for a while. Silence doesn't exactly make for compelling television, Max."

"Well, there are sometimes more important things in life than making compelling television," he replied scornfully.

Leo laughed. "Since when?"

They came to a stop at a red light, and Max turned to face him. "What did you mean when you said Hadley's going to be fine?"

"That she'll be fine. She's got a bright future ahead of her."

Max felt his pulse quicken, simultaneously with all of the blood draining from his face. "Tell me Hadley didn't lose her time slot so I could get mine back . . ."

Leo replied, "Wow. Ego's still in check, I see. No. *At Home with Hadley* is safe. It's got good numbers and a loyal following. Admittedly, I'm very interested to see what happens once the network's true number-one show is back on the air. We all are. But no, all I meant is that it seems Marshall Simons has cooled on her—"

"What are you saying?" Max jolted at a car honk behind him and faced the now-green light.

"Isn't it obvious? *Renowned* is yours, Max! I mean, she'll still be there, of course, but they're definitely adjusting the focus for the rest of the season."

No. No, no, no.

After a quick examination of his rearview mirror, Max screeched his way onto the side of the road and slammed the brakes.

"What are you doing here, Leo? This doesn't make any sense! Hadley's your client too. How can you be happy about any of this? How can you just cast aside whoever isn't flavor of the month?" That was being generous and giving Leo points for loyalty that he did not deserve. "Or flavor of the *day!*"

Leo turned in his seat and faced him. "How dare you! I'm not casting Hadley aside, and you know full well I have never cast you aside."

"You told me I was done. You had completely written me off. You told me no one else would work with me—"

"Because I know you, Max! You're the most self-sabotaging person I've ever met. With every new thing you accomplish and each higher level of stardom you reach, you get more and more complacent. And the more complacent you get, the harder I have to work to keep you from losing it all."

"That's not true."

"Oh no?" Leo laughed bitterly. "Then you tell me how you think it would have played out if you had come back from rehab knowing that the network was actually desperate to get you back on the air. Tell me how long you think the new and improved Max Cavanagh would have lasted if you'd discovered that, as it turned out, there was nothing you could do to make the network turn its back on this multimillion-dollar empire we've built. I was just giving you something to fight for. It was the only way to keep you from self-destructing. Again." He shrugged. "*Renowned* was the only tricky part. Simons wanted you, but he was nervous. We all were. We just couldn't be sure at first how audiences were going to react to you. But you *and* Hadley? Well, that was too good to resist. Mario Borjomi got the boot—"

"Not tuberculosis?"

Leo smiled, and for a brief moment Max wondered if his agent had resorted to biological warfare to get him on *Renowned*. "No. Not tuberculosis. I just thought Hadley might be too nice to go along with it if she knew she was taking someone else's spot."

Max felt more anger stirring inside of him than he'd ever known in his entire life. "So you used Hadley . . ." His voice trailed off.

"Look, you getting *Renowned* without her was iffy. Her getting it without you? Not a chance. Not yet. So you used each other, really. It's the nature of the business, and you know it."

"She didn't deserve to be dragged into any of this." Max's knuckles had turned white, but he still wasn't able to grip the steering wheel tightly enough to dispense with the building rage.

Leo laughed again. "Your concern is touching. Surprising, but touching. But, hey, she got the house, I'm finalizing a much better contract for her, she'll have *Renowned* on her résumé . . . and what's more, she'll finally be taken seriously. Did you know she didn't have a manager before me? It was just her grandmother, taking meetings on her behalf." As he talked he appeared to send a text. "Would I have loved it if she had it in her to become more of an entertainment mogul like you? Sure. But it turns out she's really just a chef. And she isn't very interesting outside of the kitchen." He looked up from his phone. "Did you notice she seemed *less* Southern on *Renowned* than she ever has? What's that about?" Shaking his head, he gave his attention back to the phone in his hands. "Poor girl. I don't think she's figured out *who* she wants to be."

This guy, this creep he'd trusted with his career for more than ten years, who had been, at alternating times, father and friend and confidante and mentor, was now a stranger to him. But all the anger Max was striving to control came from the realization that Leo hadn't changed. Not one bit. Who he was in that moment—tap, tap, tapping on his phone, playing with people's lives as if they were nothing more than pawns in his game—was who he had always been. And Max had accepted him. Revered him. Paid him and paid him well to dash dreams, if necessary, on his behalf—all in the name of the genius of Chef Maxwell Cavanagh. The one-of-a-kind talent. The once-in-a-generation superstar.

"Get out," Max told him through clenched teeth.

Leo looked at him in bewilderment. "What?"

"You heard me. Get out."

He looked around. "You've lost your mind. You can't just drop me off in the middle of Brooklyn, like I'm some—"

"It's Bedford Avenue and you're about three blocks from the subway. I daresay you'll live." He fiddled around with the controls on the vehicle's console until he found the one he wanted. At the touch of a button, the passenger side door opened. "Now get out."

Leo sneered at him as he removed his seat belt and stepped out. "You're making a big mistake, Cavanagh. If you think you can treat me this way, after all I've done—"

"I *would* like to thank you for getting me this Range Rover though," he interrupted with words and another push of the button. As the door latched shut, he smiled and added, "I like it very much."

24. *Sweat until translucent.*

HADLEY

"Hello?" I answered my cell phone.

"Ms. Beckett? This is Graham from Legacy Car Service. I'm downstairs."

"Thanks. I'll be right down."

I took a deep breath as I looked in the mirror one last time before leaving my hotel room. *Not good, but it will have to do.* I'd wrestled all night with the choices I had to make, and by the time I rolled out of bed at sunrise, I hadn't made a single decision.

I'd almost texted Max at least a dozen different times, but I figured I'd lost the right. Besides, I don't know what I thought that could possibly accomplish. Did we need to talk? Probably. Did we need to confuse matters further by hiding behind our indestructible force field of friendship and flirtation that seemed to be activated by text messages? Probably not.

My phone buzzed and I pulled it out of my pocket as I grabbed my bag and threw my jacket over my arm. *Hmm. That's a surprise.*

"Hello?" I held the phone between my ear and my shoulder and shut the door behind me, verifying it was locked before I began walking toward the elevator.

"Hey, kiddo. You're not to the studio yet, are you?"

Sure enough, it was Leo. I'd half-expected it to be Candace, using his phone.

"No. I'm just getting ready to leave the hotel."

I smiled at a gentleman who was holding the elevator for me and held up my index finger and mouthed "First floor. Thank you" as he pushed the button for me.

I heard Leo let out a big gust of air. "Okay, good. Glad I caught you."

Why? Should I not even bother going in? Had they just decided to bring in the cardboard cutout of me that's standing next to the Hadley Home bakeware sets at Target for the rest of the *Renowned* shoot?

"What's going on, Leo?"

"I just . . . well, I just wanted to connect with you. I'm worried about Max."

The gentleman was holding the elevator door for me again, this time so I could step into the lobby, but there were too many people and too much noise out there. And I needed to focus.

"I'm going back up," I mouthed and waved, and then pushed "32."

My stomach began to feel queasy. "Why? Why are you worried about Max?"

"I think he's drinking again. Or, I don't know . . . something's going on, that's for sure. He was saying all sorts of crazy things last night."

"Like what?"

He sighed. "I really shouldn't get into it. I wouldn't want to betray his trust that way. But I just wanted to warn you. I know you'll be in the kitchen with him today, and there's just no telling—"

"Hey, Leo . . ."

"Yes?"

"I didn't realize you and Max were that close." I bit my lip and measured my words very carefully. "I didn't realize you knew him at all, actually."

I used the moment afforded by his silence on the other end of the line to try and figure out if that had been a lie. I *hadn't* known until I put it together about Candace the day before. And, even then, I didn't *officially* know that it was the same Candace with a high-pitched voice who got assigned the task of dealing with the clients her boss no longer cared enough about to deal with personally. That could have been anyone.

Yep. I was pretty sure I was still on the moral high ground.

"The truth is, we have worked together. Mostly with his restaurant interests. He's been coming to me for advice lately, looking for ways to get his career back on track."

I suddenly felt pain in the palm of my hand, caused by my fingernails clawing away inside my tightly clenched fist.

"Well," I began with an exaggerated kind and Southern tone. "You really are the best then, aren't you?"

"Now, Hadley." He chortled. "I hope you're not insinuating that anything you and I discussed yesterday has anything to do with my dealings with Max." He had begun the sentence with laughter, but by the end, his voice had morphed into a tone of insulted consternation—as seamlessly and fascinatingly as one of those time capture nature videos of a caterpillar becoming a butterfly.

The door opened in front of me, onto the 32nd floor, and I waved an apology to the people waiting there before closing the doors and once again beginning my descent to the first floor.

"I'm not insinuating anything, Leo. I'm just wondering what you think Max is going to tell me today, and why it's so important that I believe he's lying or that he's been drinking." A realization suddenly flooded my thoughts, and I gasped in response. "Did he know you were my manager?" I shook my head. "Never mind. Don't answer that." I knew I couldn't believe anything he told me anyway. "Did he think that you and I were . . . ? That I was . . . ?" My voice trailed away and my eyes clouded. "He didn't think that I would ever . . ."

My head was so cluttered and my heart was so heavy at the idea that Max had ever thought, for even a moment, that what he and I shared wasn't real. He *couldn't* have thought I had used him to get ahead. Could he?

"Leo, you're fired."

"I'm *what?*"

"It doesn't matter what you say. I trust Max. Believe me, no one's more surprised by that than I am, but facts are facts."

Come on . . . come on . . . come on. I pushed the button for the 1st floor over and over, as if that would make my descent back down go faster.

"But Leo?"

"What?" he asked shortly.

"Thank you for getting me the house. I like it very much."

25. *Blend until smooth.*

MAX

"Where is Chef Hadley?" Marshall roared for the fourth time in as many minutes.

"I'm here! I'm here!" she called out as she ran into the studio, threw her purse and jacket onto the floor, and skittered across the set to the kitchen.

Max took a deep breath and braced himself for whatever the day held. He'd hoped they would have some time to talk before the cameras started rolling, but apparently that was not to be. And, as everyone knew, they were just *the best* at having honest, rational, nonconfrontational conversations on-camera.

"I'm sorry I'm late," Hadley said to the room in general. "Some things came up, and then there was construction on the bridge. I tell y'all, I'm just not used to all this big city traffic. I don't how you do it."

It was undeniable. The stressed-out, running-late, impatient vibe in the room completely dissipated as everyone smiled at Hadley and told her it was no big deal.

Max looked down at his countertop and smiled. She was good. He directed his eyes upward to discreetly glance at her as she took her place at the separate kitchen island beside his and caught a sheepish grin on her face. She was good and she knew it.

Hair and makeup surrounded her and prepared her for the harsh studio lights while Marshall crossed to them and laid out instructions for the day.

"As you're aware, chefs, yesterday we discussed which dish should be prepared today, and you both agreed on risotto. And then you were each asked to provide the recipe for a risotto you wished to make, so we could acquire the necessary ingredients. Are we all on the same page thus far?"

Out of patience with Chef Simons after the events of the day before, Max replied, "It's tough, but we're trying to keep up." Once again, he saw a subtle smile dance across Hadley's lips.

Ignoring him, Marshall continued. "We decided, however, to try something new and have a little fun with the two of you. As a tribute to your competitive cooking history, you might say." He turned to Max, eyebrow raised, and said, "Not as simple as you thought, perhaps. But don't worry about a thing. Just make the best risotto you can. If yours is better than your opponent's, you win. Simple as that. There will be a few little twists thrown in there, but since we're running behind schedule, I'll just explain them to you as I explain them to our audience."

Hadley and Max shot quick glances at each other, and then back to Chef Simons. It was a trap. Max knew it *had* to be a trap of some sort. From the expression on her face, it seemed Hadley realized it too. At the very least, he assumed Marshall Simons was bound and determined to get *some* traction from their *America's Fiercest Chef* history.

"Are we ready?" Lowell called out from his chair as Marshall took his mark in front of the camera.

Nope. They weren't anywhere close to ready. But Max just wanted to get it over with. The past week and a half had felt like the longest year of his life.

"Today, in the *Renowned* kitchen," Marshall said as soon as the cameras were rolling, "Chefs Hadley Beckett and Maxwell Cavanagh are going head-to-head, each of them putting their own unique spin on the same dish: risotto."

They each stood behind their individual islands, aprons on, knives at the ready. She was facing Marshall and smiling, while Max was doing the best he could to remember the cameras were rolling and that he couldn't just stare at her the entire time.

Marshall approached her and asked, "Chef Hadley, why did you and Chef Max choose risotto as your competition dish? It seems a bit simple, does it not? For two of the greatest living chefs?"

"In fairness, we didn't know it was a competition dish," she began, accompanied by a rather nervous-sounding laugh. "But risotto's simplicity is actually why we chose to make it, Chef Simons. Chef Max is still learning, so . . ."

She flashed her eyes toward Max, and he was taken off guard by the twinkle in them. She was *teasing* him? He'd thought those days were over.

Max cleared his throat. "All joking aside, we chose risotto because it's one of the most deceptive staple dishes out there. It's tricky to make a truly great risotto, but it seems so simple that everyone tries. As a result, there are a lot of horrible risottos being served in restaurants around the globe. I suppose we wanted to prove that none of those horrible risottos will be found in *our* restaurants."

"And hopefully our risottos won't be as dry as our reason for wanting to *make* risotto," Hadley added, apparently feeling the need to turn *Renowned* into an open mic comedy night.

"Chefs, you were asked for your ingredient lists yesterday, and the ingredients from those lists are in the baskets in front of you. If, by chance, you forgot any of your ingredients or wish to make any changes, you may choose from anything available to you in the *Renowned* kitchen—but only twice. Additionally, one of your requested ingredients has intentionally been left out of your basket—it may or may not be an ingredient that can be found in this kitchen. You may be forced to improvise and make a substitution. Regardless, that is a total of three ingredients you may pull from the *Renowned* kitchen, but no more." He turned to face them. "Are you ready?"

"Ready, Chef," Hadley answered enthusiastically, doing everything but saluting and clicking her heels.

"And Chef Maxwell?" he asked.

"Sure, why not." He stifled the miserable groan that wanted to break free.

Hadley's head snapped in his direction, and he looked at her and shrugged in response to her wide-eyed—but seemingly amused—dismay.

Marshall stepped to the side of Hadley's island. "Tell us about the risotto you will be preparing, Chef Hadley."

"I'll be preparing my attempt at Chef Max's signature wild mushroom risotto."

Marshall laughed while Max did a double take.

"I admire your pluck!" Marshall exclaimed through his laughter. "What, may I ask, compelled you to attempt Chef Max's signature dish, in competition *against* Chef Max?"

"Again . . . didn't know it was a competition. But it's a tribute, actually. He and I do not always agree on food—in fact, we rarely do. But the first risotto I ever attempted was this one, from Chef Max's very first cookbook."

"Tell us your thoughts, Chef Maxwell."

Marshall crossed to the side of Max's island. "Chef Hadley is preparing her dish in tribute to you. I can't imagine you expected that."

"No," he replied softly. "I didn't."

What in the world is she up to?

Max weighed his options. If *he* had been the one with the plan to prepare *Hadley's* signature dish, everyone would have thought he was being manipulative—and let's face it, not all that long ago he probably would have been. And not all that long ago, he probably would have assumed that was what Hadley was attempting as well. She wouldn't have been, but he would have taken it as an attack and responded in kind. The problem was how well he knew her now. There wasn't an ounce of manipulation in it, and *that* made it difficult to know how to respond.

"I'm genuinely moved by this." He hated that he had to reveal his true feelings about it all to Marshall and everyone else, but he needed Hadley to know. "I had no idea that Chef Hadley ever used any of my recipes." He turned to face her and smiled. "I am a little depressed, however, at the thought of how old I must be now. Either that or you were shockingly late to the risotto party."

"A little bit of both," she countered with a smirk.

"And as for you, Chef Maxwell? What will you be preparing in competition against your own recipe?"

Well, he'd planned on preparing his signature wild mushroom risotto, of course. It was a lose-lose. Hadley was a brilliant, remarkable chef. He had come to know and truly believe that. But she wasn't going to beat Max at that dish. He didn't doubt her abilities for a moment, but he'd had ten years of perfecting that recipe before it ever appeared in the cookbook where Hadley found it. And he was shocked by just how much he didn't want to upstage her that way.

At the same time, the thought occurred, she had to have known she couldn't win. Was it some sort of olive branch? Did she want him to win so they'd be one-and-one in head-to-head competition? Was it all about balancing the playing field between them?

Except we didn't know it was a competition! he had to remind himself. It was more than a little bit worrisome to him how quickly and easily he fell into the competition mind-set. Especially when Hadley was his competition, it seemed.

But as he prepared to say *something* that would hopefully be ambiguous enough but also somewhat realistic, one final thought popped into his mind. What if she hadn't submitted ingredients for wild mushroom risotto, but had decided at the last minute to make use of her three allowed wild card ingredients from the *Renowned* kitchen? And she was banking on being able to find some wild mushrooms?

No, Hadley wasn't manipulative, but she was driven and unexpectedly fearless in certain circumstances. Was it possible that she actually believed she could out-Max-Cavanagh *Max Cavanagh?* He didn't have a difficult time believing that she could have rolled out of bed, ready to take him down—even if she hadn't known they'd be competing.

"I'll be preparing a Southern, down-home, comfort food risotto, Chef Simons."

It was Hadley's turn to whip her head around in surprise, and Max had to admit to himself that he was very gratified by her reaction. Whatever she'd expected him to do, that wasn't it.

"Well, well, well," Marshall reveled. "This is a fine turn of events!"

Max glanced over at Hadley, who was attempting to neutralize her expression, but it was plain as day. He'd taken her element of surprise and upped the ante.

"Chefs, you have one hour until your risotto dishes will be judged by a panel of experts. You may now begin."

Max opened up his basket and quickly surveyed the ingredients. He was desperately hoping that the mushrooms were what was missing, so he could pick out all three of his wild card ingredients for his new dish, but alas, no.

"Which ingredient are you missing, Chef Maxwell?" Marshall asked.

He sighed and squeezed the bridge of his nose. "That would be rice, Chef Simons."

"Ah. That will most assuredly be needed." He nodded and flashed a smarmy smile. "And you, Chef Hadley?"

She was already digging through the kitchen, on the hunt, while Max was still standing over his basket, attempting to figure out what two ingredients he needed to get—along with *rice,* of course—in order to have any hope of turning his gourmet plan into comfort food.

"Well," she drawled with a bit of a frustrated tone. "I'm missing wild mushrooms, Chef Simons."

"I believe I spotted canned mushrooms in the pantry," he contributed, most unhelpfully.

"Yes, Chef. I saw those too. But I would sooner turn this into a dessert risotto than ruin Chef Max's legendary recipe that way."

A smile spread across Max's lips and he turned to look at her. She was on her knees in front of the open refrigerator, digging through the crisper. He glanced down at his own basket and the bowl of beautiful, fresh wild mushrooms he wasn't going to use.

"Here, Had," he called out as he set the bowl on her island. "Take mine."

He'd shown her his hand and made it very clear that he'd had every intention of making wild mushroom risotto, but that didn't matter.

Nothing mattered apart from the expression of pure, unadulterated gratitude on her face as she climbed out of the fridge.

She ran over and quickly kissed him on the cheek. "Thanks, Max."

Okay. That mattered too.

Of course, Marshall didn't want to let it all be that easy. "That's very generous of you, Chef Maxwell, but I'm afraid the rules state—"

"These rules, which supposedly exist for this impromptu competition, state she can take three separate ingredients found in the *Renowned* kitchen, I believe. My basket is sitting here in the *Renowned* kitchen, so . . ."

Marshall nodded, not looking at all pleased. "Of course."

"But you'd better believe that counts as one of her three," Max added, resulting in another beautiful grin from Hadley.

Max pulled out a Dutch oven as his comfort food plan began to come together in his mind and placed it on one of the burners. He hurried over and grabbed rice from the pantry, and then gathered chicken breasts from the refrigerator. His basket already had vegetables he could use and plenty of Parmesan cheese, and of course some white wine, so he decided to err on the side of caution and save his third ingredient for any potential inspiration that might come along. Bacon, perhaps.

But his mind was quickly changed when Hadley appeared in the open refrigerator door beside him. "You need butter," she whispered.

"I've got olive oil."

She nodded. "I know. But no brilliant comfort food has ever been created by a chef who said, 'I don't need butter. I've got olive oil.' " She shrugged. "That's all I'm saying."

And just when he'd *almost* stopped thinking about trying to kiss her every moment of the day. But he didn't want to give Chef Simons the satisfaction of letting him air it on *Renowned.*

"Do you have any idea how much I adore you?" Max asked her, staring straight into her eyes, grabbing her hand with his free hand, and raising her knuckles to his lips. "Thank you."

Hadley responded with flushed cheeks, and then Max released her hand, grabbed the butter, winked, and returned to his station. Her own return to her station was slightly delayed, but since the refrigerator was behind him, Max could only hope that had a little something to do with him. He made a mental note to pay special attention to that moment when the episode aired on Sunday evening.

For a few minutes they each paid silent, diligent attention to their dish preparation. Max couldn't remember the last time he had cooked in silence. On his show he was talking to the viewers the entire time, and on *Renowned* he and Hadley had spoken to each other—of course the *way* they spoke to each other had varied greatly—or Marshall had blabbered on about something to try and fill the awkward pauses. Even in his kitchen at home, he rarely cooked without music blaring in the background. The silence felt unnatural.

"How's it going, Chef Beckett?" he asked her. "Are you putting me out of a job?"

She chuckled. "Not likely. My food is probably a little too flavorful to ever make it onto your menu." He grinned and stirred in his shallots. "And you, Chef Cavanagh? Have you found a way to ruin your risotto by adding tofu yet?"

"Well, it's deep-fried tofu covered in gravy, so I think it will work perfectly."

Now *that* was natural. *They* were natural. Who would have ever imagined?

He glanced up at her—she was adding her rice, right on schedule—and looked at the way she connected with the cameras. Even when she wasn't looking at them or speaking toward them, or even acknowledging them in any way, she seemed to be instinctively aware of them. And of course, they also seemed to be instinctively aware of her. You talk about natural. Hadley Beckett in front of a camera was perhaps the most natural thing Max had ever witnessed. It was her tool, and she used it masterfully, and Max felt like an imbecile for ever having questioned her.

He didn't labor under the misapprehension that

he and the camera shared any such magnetism, but he began to wonder if he could make it work for him this time.

"Chef Simons, I fear I've been a bit obstructive when it comes to talking about some of my past struggles."

"I'd say obstructive is an understatement, Chef," he replied as he approached and stood behind Max's island. "But it's certainly understandable that you wouldn't want to dwell on mistakes of the past."

It's understandable, is it? You didn't seem quite as understanding yesterday.

"Thank you for understanding that," he muttered, as kindly as he could. "But I think I'm now ready to discuss what caused my . . . what did you call it? 'Destructive cycle,' I believe? You know, that finally reached a boiling point that day on *America's Fiercest Chef*." Hadley was trying to act uninterested, it seemed, but her head kept tilting in his direction as she tended to her mushrooms. "I'm not sure if this is the time—"

"Au contraire," Marshall said, most pretentiously—undoubtedly desperate to keep his big scoop from slipping away. "You know as well as anyone, Chef Max, that *Renowned* is about capturing the chef as an artist *and* as a person."

Max shrugged with nonchalance as he finally added his rice—running a little behind, unlike Hadley. He took a deep breath. He was willing to do what needed to be done, and the fact that he was even considering talking about any of it cemented in his mind, once and for all, that he was not the same person he once was. But actually *saying* it . . . actually allowing Hadley and Marshall Simons and the entire world to see inside the most damaged, sheltered parts of him. Not even Buzz or his Discovery Journal had been told this story yet . . .

Don't think about that, he lectured himself. *You're only letting Hadley in. Everything else is just the means of allowing that to happen.*

"Well, it was a couple things, actually." He attended to his sautéing chicken breasts. "I had just proposed to my girlfriend at the time, and she turned me down because I was going to insist she sign a prenuptial agreement." Hadley's subtle tilts had been replaced by her full attention. The emotion in her eyes was almost more than Max could endure so he turned his focus back to the risotto. "It was all for the best that she said no, of course. We'd only been dating a few weeks, and I was drunk when I met her, truthfully. *And* when I asked her to marry me, come to that. But when she said no, for the reason she said no—straight out saying the entire relationship had been a colossal waste of time, once she figured out I wasn't going to make her rich—I guess I took it kind of hard."

"Max . . ." Hadley breathed his name.

Max cleared his throat. "That was two days before *Fiercest Chef*. And then one day before filming started, my dad called me for the first time in . . . oh, about eight years, I guess. His wife—not my mother, but the one he 'actually loves,' he says—needed surgery. He wanted money, of course. The timing wasn't great, I guess you could say. I wasn't feeling very charitable." He chuckled bitterly as he removed his chicken from the heat so it could rest. "So, when I refused to pay for my stepmother's nose job—a stepmother I've never met in my life, mind you, and who is nearly a decade younger than I am—he disowned me for probably the fifth time in my life."

He looked up at Marshall, who looked positively giddy with only just-contained excitement, and then he looked over at Hadley, whose eyes—focused entirely on him—were brimming with tears that seemed like they were barely managing to hang on.

"I think your wine has reduced, Had," he told her, his heart threatening to burst with the affection he felt for her. But no amount of affection, in his opinion or hers, he knew, justified a destroyed risotto on *Renowned*.

Her eyes flew open wide and she turned to her pan, which was beginning to smoke a bit more than it should. She quickly took care of that, and Max faced Marshall again.

"There is no justification," he resumed. "None

345

whatsoever. But you wanted to know what the final straws were that led to the crash and burn, and I suppose that's the answer to that."

He took a deep breath. He knew Marshall was going to step in and ask for more details, and he knew he could probably anticipate exactly what those requested details would be.

Deciding a preemptive strike was in order, he said, "I don't have a drinking problem. At least not in the traditional sense. Alcohol isn't my problem. My temper isn't even really the problem. According to my counselor, at *rehab,*" he added freely and emphatically, looking straight into the camera, "I'm attempting to mask the pain . . . *that's* the problem." He poured more chicken stock into his rice, kept his head down, and stirred. "Last night I almost went for a drink, without even thinking. And it's not that that was bad, necessarily. It's just that without even realizing it, I almost took the easy way out. It would have been so much easier to not have to feel everything I was feeling. But then I thought of all the pain I'd caused by being a drunk idiot, and of course all the pain my dad had caused by being a drunk idiot. And in that moment, the thing that stopped me from potentially allowing myself to turn into that idiot again was asking myself, 'What would Hadley do?' "

He had to clear his throat again. The power of the memory was enough to overwhelm him. He tilted his head to wipe his eyes with the back of his hand, and as he did, he looked up at her. He just couldn't help himself.

He kept staring at her and her beautiful, tear-stained face as he said, "So I went home and got online and printed out some of your dessert recipes. And I don't know if that's really what you would have done. I mean, I know you wouldn't have gone to your website and printed out your own recipes. You know what I mean. But it felt good. It felt good to go back to my first love. To cook because I wanted to cook."

"Which of Chef Hadley's recipes did you attempt to conquer, Chef Max?" Marshall asked, his tone and volume having completely transformed into something much kinder and more compassionate.

Max laughed and swiped at his eyes again. "Well, actually, I didn't have the right ingredients for any of them."

"Such as," Marshall prodded.

Max turned back to face him. "Sugar. Butter. Enough cream to take a bath in." Hadley began laughing and Max added, "That's actually how she has it written in one of the recipes. 'Enough cream to take a bath in.' I don't know the last time I came up with something truly new, before last night. It was . . . well . . ." He looked at Hadley and matched her smile with his own, and whatever words he'd been preparing to say faded away.

The two of them stared at each other in silence—and somehow the crew's silence was even quieter than theirs—until Marshall asked Hadley, "Chef Hadley, do you have anything you wish to say in response?"

She smiled and sniffed, and then half-heartedly stirred her dish as she said, "I'm pretty sure these risottos are going to be as unimpressive as all get-out."

26. *Reduce and set aside.*

HADLEY

"Not bad," Max said as he tasted my risotto, after filming had wrapped.

I laughed. "You're being generous. I hate that the first time I cook one of your dishes for you, *this* is what we get."

"Hey, don't worry. You haven't tasted mine yet. Actually, I haven't tasted mine yet either."

"You didn't taste it?"

He shook his head. "I was so behind, and I had to get it plated. The whole thing was just a disaster."

I leaned down and put my elbows on the island. "Yeah. But we should be really proud of ourselves. I doubt any other chefs have ever had a judge say things to them like, 'This dish is clearly not up to the caliber we traditionally find on *Renowned*.' We broke new ground, my friend."

A laugh burst out of him. "Was that for yours or mine? I can't remember."

"Oh, who knows! Now we have only to hope that we will be remembered for our contributions prior to today."

"Here, here! A lofty goal indeed!" He took my fork and got a scoop of his risotto on it, and then repeated the action for himself. "Together? On three?"

On the count of three we both tried a Max Cavanagh attempt at comfort food, and it took everything in me not to spit it out.

"Oh Max, that's awful!"

He laughed as I attempted to rub the horrible aftertaste off of my tongue. "That's right. *That's* what they said about mine. Yours was the 'not up to the normal caliber' thing."

We stared at each other for a moment, the smiles remaining on our faces, until I sighed and set down my fork. "Well."

"Well," he echoed.

We both removed our aprons in silence and handed them off to a production assistant passing by. And then my desire to alleviate any perceived awkwardness grew too strong to ignore.

"I wonder which moments from today are going to make it into the promos for Sunday?"

He laughed, but there was an unmistakable edge to it. "Yeah, I don't know. Do you think we gave them anything to work with?"

I put my hand on top of his and hoped my touch would somehow relay the comfort I didn't quite know how to give him with my words. But in an instant his fingers had spread and mine willingly eased into the gaps he had created for me, and they all curled and interlocked in a way that made it difficult to tell whose were whose.

He was looking down at our hands as he said, "I can just picture it now." His voice took on the timbre of a voice-over announcer. "Hadley Beckett and Maxwell Cavanagh, as you've never seen them before. Finally, it's all out in the open."

"You didn't have to say all of that, Max," I breathed. "I can't imagine how difficult that was. And I know you didn't want everyone to know—"

"No, but I wanted you to know."

"You could have just told me."

He smirked as his thumb began gently tracing meaningless patterns on my skin. "We weren't really talking . . . except when the cameras were rolling."

I suddenly felt exhausted at the thought of all that had happened between the two of us in such a short period of time. "About that. I'm really sorry I—"

"No." He shook his head. "I was way out of line." He took a deep breath and then his eyes, which had still been cast downward, began lifting to look at me. "I have to tell you something."

I chuckled nervously in response to the foreboding expression on his face. "Should I sit down for this?"

"Maybe."

He didn't seem inclined to let go of my hand, but he also made no move to accompany me to a seat, so I just steeled myself and asked, "What is it?"

He took another deep breath and then let it out

so slowly. "I'm not quite sure how to say this, so I'm just going to say it." With his free hand he rubbed his knuckles against his beard. "See, the thing is, Leo Landry . . . well, he started representing me when I was twenty-five years old. He's pretty much the reason anything *ever* happened for me in my career, and I guess at some point—well, I'd say he changed, but I don't think he did. Anyway, the point is—"

"Max." I released the breath I'd been holding and smiled. There was a little part of me that wanted to watch him keep digging out and sorting through everything that had to be going through his brain, but there was a bigger part of me that wanted to put him out of his misery. And the biggest part of all knew that Max's misery and concern would have just taken away any lingering doubts or questions I had—if there had been any. "I know that Leo is your manager. I figured it out yesterday."

He finally released my hand and began pacing slowly in front of the island. "I didn't know he was your manager until a little over a week ago. I swear I didn't. By the time we were at the Bluebird, I had myself convinced that you'd known all along, and that you and Leo had actually been conspiring against me."

I closed my eyes and bit my lip as that thought registered, and then I began nodding as it all started making sense. "That explains a lot."

That fear had flooded my mind, of course. On the phone with Leo, my heart had broken at the thought of Max thinking he couldn't trust me. Knowing that was *exactly* what he'd thought didn't make me feel all that great, but at least I understood why he was so critical of me that night at the Bluebird.

What I didn't understand was what had made him back down and apologize.

"So, what changed?"

He stopped pacing and faced me. "You were so hurt. It was . . ." He shook his head and looked down at his feet. "I said those awful things I said, and you looked . . ." His voice trailed off again and his shoulders drooped. "When I looked at you, I had that feeling you get when you write a text bad-mouthing someone, and then realize you accidentally sent it to that person. You know?"

I didn't bother telling him that I didn't know. I understood what he meant, and I understood how he felt, and right then that was all that was needed.

"What?" he asked.

"What *what?*"

He smiled. "I don't know. You're looking at me kind of funny."

Was I? Hmm. My thoughts certainly hadn't been humorous.

I took a step toward him. "Max, I think I'm gonna kiss you now, if that's okay."

His eyes widened, and it was very clear he suddenly didn't know what to do with his arms. He crossed and uncrossed them, put them behind his back and then in front. It was pretty fun to see him flustered. Maybe I needed to tell him I was going to kiss him more often.

He cleared his throat. "Yeah. That's fine with me." The way his lips curled and his jaw clenched gave me the impression it may have even been slightly better than fine.

It only took one more step to get close enough to touch him, and then I felt all of my boldness begin to slip away. I wanted to kiss him, and the way he was eyeing my lips made it plain as day he wanted to kiss me. But there I was, close enough to notice he was holding his breath, and my brain started to get in the way.

I don't know how much time passed with us awkwardly standing there, inches apart.

"Um, Hadley?" I was so close that I couldn't see his entire face, but his eyes were smiling at me.

"Yeah?"

"When you said you were going to kiss me, did you mean you wanted me to kiss you?"

"No."

He nodded. "Okay. Because I'd be happy to—"

"I'm getting there," I whispered.

The smile in his eyes grew. "Okay. Take your time."

"It's just . . . I don't know . . . I'm having a difficult time shutting my brain off."

"I think I could maybe help with—"

"I said I'd do it. I'll do it."

He began chewing on his lip, probably to keep from laughing at me, I figured. "I have complete faith in you. But I have an idea. No big deal. You're definitely going to be the one to do it. But maybe I can just . . ." He placed his hands just above my hips and slowly pulled me closer to him. "How's that?"

I instinctively rested my hands on his chest. "That's good."

"Good," he whispered, nearly brushing my lips with his. "If I can offer any further assistance . . ." One of his hands stayed on my waist while the fingers of the other began tracing the line of my jaw.

"Max?"

"Hmm?"

"I need you to know something."

He traced the outline of my lips. "Okay."

"When I found out Leo was your manager, I trusted you. I didn't wonder. I didn't doubt. I just . . . trusted you." My hands eased their way up and briefly combed through his hair before looping around his neck. "And I have to tell you, even *as* I was trusting you, I realized how weird it was that I was trusting you."

He laughed a little too loudly, considering how

quiet our whispers had been. When I saw the redness of his eyes I understood. Emotion was threatening to break free in all sorts of ways he couldn't control.

"Hadley Beckett, I'll give you about three more seconds and then I'm taking over here."

Just then the studio lights shut off with a whoosh that, in the context of how intimate our thoughts and conversation had become, sounded like I imagined New York City would at the moment of total blackout.

The darkness gave me the confidence boost I needed, I suppose, and I closed the minimal gap between us. And I quickly discovered that it didn't matter who initiated. When Max and I kissed, his lips were in control.

"Is someone here?" Lowell's voice called out.

"Don't answer and maybe he'll go away," Max somehow muttered, though he never really stopped kissing me.

"And we'll be stuck here all night," I replied, pulling away slightly.

He attempted to pull me back. "We have a fully stocked professional kitchen. We'll be fine."

I planted one quick peck on his lips and laughed. "We're here, Lowell! Heading out now!"

A light flipped on in the kitchen set and Lowell appeared just after Max and I fully separated. "Hadley, I'm so sorry. I didn't realize anyone was still here." It seemed to dawn on him that I wasn't alone, and he looked from me to Max and back again. "Everything okay?"

"Yep. We were just . . ." I glanced at Max, who crossed his arms, quirked his eyebrow, and was generally no help whatsoever. "We were just working through some things before tomorrow's shoot."

Not a lie. Moral high ground maintained yet again!

"Okay, well, do you want to share a cab?" Lowell asked. "I'm heading to Midtown so—"

"Thanks, Lowell," Max responded. "But I live in SoHo, so . . ." He lifted his hands and became the perfect personification of the shrugging emoji.

"Oh, well, um, I meant Hadley, since she's staying on the Upper East Side, but if you need a ride—"

"Nah. I'm good, but thanks. Actually . . ." He turned to face me, and even though I knew he was looking at me, I couldn't wipe the stupid grin off of my face. "I can drive you to your hotel."

I just nodded. So many thoughts were intersecting in my mind that it seemed my brain had turned into a bumper car track. On the one hand, I definitely had feelings for Max. I was well past the point of being able to deny that. But on the other hand, absolutely none of the reasons I knew I couldn't date him had gone away.

Nothing had changed except now I apparently had taken to kissing him whenever I felt like it. Because *that* was going to make it easier to not date him.

We got out to the parking lot and said good night to Lowell, and by then some time and distance, not to mention the cool Brooklyn evening air, was allowing me to think a little more clearly.

"You know, I have a guy."

"You have a guy?"

"I mean, I have a driver guy. A driver. *Renowned* gave me a driver while I'm here. You don't need to go out of your way just to take me home."

His key fob caused his vehicle to beep, and he stepped in front of me to open my door. "I was actually hoping we could grab some dinner. I'm starving, and all I've had is some really bad risotto."

I smiled as I climbed in. "Okay, but it's pretty late. Are places still open?" I closed my eyes and shook my head, instantly realizing how silly my comment had been. "Don't mind me. Remember, I have the nightlife of a sunflower. I suppose there are probably a few places that stay open past 10:00 in Manhattan, right?"

He winked at me and, just before closing my door, said, "I know a place."

27. Season to taste.

MAX

"Are you trying to impress me?" Hadley asked as Max pulled her chair out for her and then scooted her in like a pro once she sat. "Because if so, it's working."

His flagship restaurant in Lenox Hill was indeed impressive. Occupying the 44th floor of the Talbot, one of the most luxurious hotels in the world, Cavanagh's was a sight to behold. The hotel itself was an art deco masterpiece, but Cavanagh's—with its opulent gold-on-white at every turn and breathtaking views of Central Park—took it to another level. Max knew there was probably no better restaurant anywhere for a man to take a woman on a first date, if impressing her was the goal. Although, considering the menu prices, most men would be wise to consider what they thought the odds were of getting the woman to agree to a second date. Cavanagh's was too pricey to be considered a good idea for *every* first date.

Of course, Max didn't know if he was actually on a date at all. Good thing he didn't have to worry about the bill.

"I am, as a matter of fact," he acknowledged. "I hope this is okay. If you were just wanting to run by Shake Shack or something . . ."

Hadley laughed. "I enjoy Shake Shack, thank you very much. But, no. This is great. I've actually never been here before. I've been to a couple of your restaurants that run more on the 'mere mortal' side of the price scale, but Cavanagh's . . . wow." She looked around the room and then back at him. "Is it any good?"

He smiled with all the humility he could muster, but when it came to the crown jewel of his career, there really wasn't much point or hope of modesty. His first three Michelin stars were obtained by Cavanagh's, and they'd been maintained for the seven years since. It had also been at Cavanagh's that Max had earned his first James Beard Award, as well as his most recent. Hadley, no doubt, knew all of that. And yes, of course he was trying to impress her. But he also could think of no better way to let her see the most genuine parts of him than by sharing with her the thing he was most proud of in the world.

"Good evening," their waiter greeted them. "Welcome to Cavanagh's, madam." He bowed slightly toward Hadley, and she smiled and put her hand out to shake his. Such an unusual move. Such a heartfelt attempt at connection beyond what normally existed between diner and waitstaff. So unmistakably Hadley. In kind, the waiter, Vikram Kaur, kissed her knuckles in genteel fashion. "Chef Beckett. An honor."

Max watched her and beamed as she chatted

with Vikram. How could it still be a complete shock to her to be recognized and respected?

"And, sir," Vikram said, turning his attention to Max. "Is this your first time dining with us?"

Max scrunched up his nose. "I hear it's overrated."

"I must respectfully disagree, sir. Cavanagh's is not overrated. Now, our founder, on the other hand . . ."

Max laughed and shook hands with Vikram. "How are you, Vik?"

"I'm doing very well, Chef. Thank you. And you?"

"I'm great. Sorry you drew the short straw tonight."

Vikram smiled and turned to Hadley. "He's very demanding and he doesn't tip very well."

"That is not true!" Max exclaimed as Hadley laughed. "Demanding, okay. But I do tip well. I mean, not *here*. Here I tip with Christmas bonuses and a very competitive insurance package. But other places . . ."

Vikram ignored him with a roguish smile and asked Hadley, "What can I bring you to drink, Chef Beckett? Would you care to see the wine list?"

She shook her head. "Thank you, but I'll just have iced tea."

"Same for me, please," Max said.

"He's great," Hadley began as she looked over

her menu, as soon as Vikram had gone. "He's worked here awhile, I assume?"

"Since the beginning. I've tried to promote him about ten different times through the years—to maître d', house manager, you name it. I'd let him be the sous-chef if he wanted, at this point. But he loves being on the floor, and there's a part of me that's glad he's turned down all of the offers. He's as much a factor in this place's reputation as the food."

"Well, I don't know about that," she countered. "This menu is amazing. What do you recommend?"

"It's all pretty decent, if I do say so myself."

Hadley laughed. "I have no doubt." She set her menu down and looked around the dining room. She seemed to be taking in the details of the high, ornate ceilings and the chandeliers that hung majestically from the center of the room, but then her gaze lowered to the tables around them. "So, um, Max?" She faced him and leaned in slightly. "You do realize that every eye in this place is on you, right?"

"Probably on *us*."

"Well, maybe that would be the case a lot of places. At Cavanagh's, I think all eyes are on Max Cavanagh. Should we maybe sit somewhere less out in the open? Like the kitchen?"

He chuckled. "This from the girl who sat front and center at Pancake Pantry without a care in the world."

"And I don't have a care in the world now. I'm just thinking of the guy who wore his sunglasses and kept his head down the whole time at Pancake Pantry."

He felt his throat tighten and he swallowed a few times to try to loosen it up. He didn't have much luck.

"Chef Beckett." He cleared his throat. "What did I do to deserve your friendship?"

She lowered her head briefly, but then she met his eyes and smiled. "I'm torn between saying something very heartfelt and taking the easy way out and saying something smart-alecky instead."

Max leaned back in his chair and crossed his arms. "Well, I'd hate to miss out on either."

Hadley's eyes twinkled as she said, "I haven't fully worked it out, but it would be something about how you've done nothing to deserve my friendship, and how I'm a saint for putting up with you."

He nodded. "And the smart-alecky comment would be . . . ?" Max savored the gratification he felt as she laughed, and then prodded, "But seriously . . ."

She stopped laughing at once, but the smile remained on her face as she said, "I'm proud of you, Max. Getting to see you become this guy has been one of the greatest pleasures of my life. And I'm not quite sure what either one of us has done to deserve the other's friendship, but I know I wouldn't trade it for anything."

There was no one in the entire world who meant more to him than she did. There was no one else in the entire world who made him feel the things she made him feel. And the only thing stopping him from telling her that was the fear that if he made a move for more and she wasn't ready, he would lose everything they had between them, right then.

Vikram appeared with their iced tea, while Max noticed Hadley was right. Every single table was watching them. But it was definitely *them,* not just him. How strange it had to be for all those people to see the two of them sitting together, laughing together, enjoying each other's company.

"Are you ready to order, Chefs?" Vikram asked. "May I provide any recommendations, Chef Beckett?"

"Actually," Max interjected, looking at Hadley. "If you think you can trust me, I'd love to have the honor."

Her eyes flew open and color rose to her cheeks. The lighting at Cavanagh's was all about ambience, not clear viewing of your tablemate's face when it flushed, so he couldn't quite decipher her reaction.

"You mean . . . you want to order for me?"

Uh-oh. He shuffled in his chair and leaned in.

"I'm sorry. I didn't . . . I mean, it's not that I don't think you're capable of deciding for yourself—"

"No." She shook her head gently. "I didn't take it that way. I was just . . . surprised. Yes. Please. By all means."

Max took a deep breath and began, without ever looking at a menu.

"To begin for Chef Beckett, Vikram, let's have the confit bouchée à la reine. For main course, the chateaubriand with béarnaise, but instead of the salade périgourdine, which I would usually recommend, of course, let's pair that with the cauliflower au gratin. Finally, she and I will each have poire belle Hélène for dessert."

"Very good. And for your other selections, Chef?"

"Foie gras torchon for starters and, let's see . . . let's go with the roasted guinea fowl, accompanied by the wild mushroom risotto."

"All excellent choices, Chef," Vikram said as he gathered the menus. "As you are fully aware."

As Vikram walked away, Max silently pleaded with the kitchen for everything to be perfect—this night of all nights. Then he faced Hadley and was surprised to see her leaning in, resting her chin on her folded hands, staring at him with warmth in her eyes.

"What?" he asked, smiling.

"Nothing. That was just, um . . ." She cleared

her throat. "Well, frankly, that was the sexiest thing I've ever seen in my life."

Max felt his shoulders relax. "Oh, good. I was worried."

"Worried? Why were you worried?"

"Oh, you know."

She shook her head. "I don't."

"I just didn't want you to think I thought I should order because I'm the man or anything like that." He looked around the room and saw the darting eyes surrounding them, so he leaned in a bit closer and spoke quietly. "I'm going to be very honest with you, even if it gets me into trouble. The fact is, I really wish there were some pamphlets or something we could use to help us, as men, to know what's considered chivalrous and what's demeaning."

Hadley bit her lip and smiled. "I'll just tell you right now, anytime you want to order for me, you go right ahead. I haven't even tasted anything you ordered yet, but I'm a believer. But I get it. It's a tough distinction sometimes." She sighed and sat up straight. "It's kind of like what you said at the Bluebird. About how hypocritical it is that I—"

"No. I didn't mean that. I was just in a bad place because of all the Leo stuff."

She shrugged. "Whether you meant it or not— which I think you did—it's true, Max. Or at least I'm sure it seems true. That I pick and choose what I'm insulted by. You weren't right, however, when you said that when Simons or whoever calls me 'darling' or 'hon' I love every minute of it. I don't.'"

"Then why do you put up with it?"

"Same reason you put up with all those parties you don't want to go to, I guess. And honestly, more often than not, it doesn't really matter to me too much. I mean, I don't like it. I see it happening and I wish it wasn't. But, Max, I'm still in that kitchen. I'm on *Renowned*. I won *America's Fiercest Chef*." She tilted her head and smirked. "Sorry."

"I've come to terms," he said with a laugh.

She took a sip of her tea and brushed her bangs out of her eyes before continuing, a little more somberly. "I just want to keep getting into the room. Getting into the kitchen. And I don't want to be invited in because I threw such a fit that it was all men in there that they *had* to invite me. I want to be invited because I deserve to be there. And I want all the other women who deserve to be there to be invited in. And people like Marshall Simons? Well, he could use a gender etiquette brush-up, for sure, but he's giving me a fair shake. And that's all I'm asking for."

"But is he giving you a fair shake, Hadley? Leo said Simons had cooled on you—" He froze in panic as he realized he'd just said something he'd never intended to say. He didn't know if she'd been given the information that Marshall's focus had shifted from Hadley to Max, and he definitely didn't want her thinking he and Leo had spent a lot of time sitting around, discussing her career trajectory.

She flapped her hand in front of her face and scoffed. "That doesn't have anything to do with me being a woman though. It just has to do with me making you look so good that they've all momentarily forgotten what a pain in the neck you are to work with." An enchanting smile spread across her face. "Besides, like I said earlier, I trust you. I do *not* trust Leo." She emitted a noise that sounded something like a growl, and her face took on the countenance of a six-year-old unwrapping socks for Christmas. "You know, I generally like most people. At least I don't *dislike* them. But I don't mind telling you I do *not* like Leo Landry."

"Good call."

"I fired him this morning, by the way."

"Took you long enough," Max teased. "I fired him yesterday."

"For goodness' sake. Is everything a competition with you?"

Hadley reached across the table and placed her hand on his, as she had several times before. Each touch of her hand had brought comfort and excitement, simultaneously. But this time, they were the centerpiece of a crowded and interested dining room, and that carried with it a new sensation he couldn't quite put his finger on. All he knew was that he was a fan of the sensation.

With only a quick consideration of the potential public reaction, during which he promptly determined he didn't care what the reaction was, he scooted his chair around so he sat beside her at the two-top rather than across from her.

Her eyebrows perked up and she whispered, "Well, if they weren't looking at us before . . ."

"Let them look. I'm not going to kiss you or anything." He leaned his shoulder in and nudged her playfully. "Unless you want me to."

She laughed gently and nudged him back. "Whether I want you to or not is not the point."

"Oh, I beg to differ."

"Seriously, Max. There were guys I dated for months in college—including Stuart—who I never kissed as much as I've kissed you."

"And that's a problem?"

Again, she laughed. A little more nervously, he thought, which made Max nervous as well. Maybe he needed to take his foot off the gas. He felt so thrown off his game when it came to romancing Hadley. Probably because, for the first time in his life, there were no games involved. He sat up straight at the thought, and then he took a deep breath in, held it, and released it slowly.

No games.

"Look, Hadley, I'm crazy about you."

His eyes were closed at first. He thought that would make it easier. But then he realized that part of the whole "no games" thing should be knowing and understanding how she felt. He couldn't do that without looking at her. He opened his eyes and immediately returned his chair to its original position across from her and took in everything about her reaction, which so far was nothing more than wide eyes and a bottom lip captured by her teeth.

Max inhaled and continued. "And I know we talked about all the reasons now isn't the time to try being anything more than friends, but—"

"Those reasons are still there, Max."

"I know. I know. But so much has happened since then—"

"Yeah . . . like neither of us have a manager anymore!" She laughed and swiped at her eyes. "I don't know what's going to happen with *At Home with Hadley*. I mean, Leo had already arranged a few things, like the house and the crew, but we were still in the middle of contract negotiations. And you—they're bringing back *To the Max*, right? What do you think that would look like, with you traveling all over the world, and us trying to carry on any sort of relationship?" She sighed. "I'm crazy about you too. I am. But I can't date. Not right now. Remember how I talked about being confused before? What do you think today has done for my confusion level?" With a sad but determined smile, she continued. "And the fact is, even just a couple weeks ago I was being handed everything I had ever worked toward, but now I may have to get a little scrappy."

He was more impetuous than she was. He knew that. But even he had to admit she brought up some very valid concerns. Concerns that he knew he could dismantle one by one, if given the chance, but they were valid nonetheless. And at the core of it all was that unrelenting fear that he could lose her from his life altogether. He just couldn't let that happen.

He noticed Vikram exiting the kitchen with their starters so he sat up straight and prepared the table for the food's landing.

"Okay," Max said as he smoothed out the tablecloth and raised his eyes to meet hers. "For now. We'll take some time. Sort some things out." Regardless of anything else either one of them had going on in their careers, he had six more weeks with her. Six weeks in which he got to spend at least three days a week with her. That would have to be good enough for now.

He'd even try to refrain from kissing her, but he made no guarantees.

28. Let rest. Serve warm.

HADLEY

> Where are you? You Know
> Who is about to blow a gasket
> because we're already ten
> minutes behind and WE
> HAVE SO MUCH TO DO! (His
> shouting. Not mine.)

It was time to begin our last night of filming for *Renowned*, and Max was not yet at my house.

> Why do you always call him
> You Know Who? Are you afraid
> Marshall Simons is intercepting
> our texts?

> > Would you put it past him?
> > Now, Maxwell Cavanagh,
> > WHERE IN TARNATION ARE
> > YOU? (My shouting.)

> I'm just crossing over the
> bridge into Brooklyn. Be there
> in ten minutes.

I grinned. Sometimes he had the sense of humor of a dad from an eighties sitcom. I walked out of my bedroom, where I had been hiding from the panic of You Know Who, and headed downstairs to the front door. I ignored the shouts as I passed and opened the door with a grin.

"You're so predictable," I greeted him.

He smiled as he stepped inside. "How are you?"

"Nervous. You?"

He took off his leather racer jacket and hung it up as I closed the door. "Why are you nervous?"

"You know how these last interviews go," I replied through clenched teeth. "Do you remember Wolfgang Puck's season?"

"You mean when Simons had him so flustered, Wolfgang kept mispronouncing Spago?" He threw his arm over my shoulders and we walked toward the kitchen together. "Nothing to worry about. There's nothing left for him to throw at us."

"At you, anyway. You've talked about everything—anger, your dad, rehab . . ." My voice trailed off, though I silently added, "Miss Fancy Pants Kitty Cat." "But he hasn't asked me to dig very deep yet."

"That's just because you're boring and the world's interest in you is only skin deep."

"Oh! Is that what it is? Well, that makes me feel much better. Thanks for that."

He planted a quick kiss on my temple and said, "Anytime."

When the news broke to the world, about five weeks earlier, that *To the Max* was returning to the Culinary Channel, it hadn't taken much time at all for Max Cavanagh to become *Max Cavanagh* again. At least in the world's eyes. He was once again in demand for social events and interviews and various television appearances. And, as Leo had forewarned me would be the case, Max definitely became the star of *Renowned*. But I don't think anyone knew quite what to do with a Max Cavanagh who didn't shout or throw things, and who turned down almost all of those events and interviews and TV appearances.

We had meteoric ratings success with episode one, and climbed even higher with episode two, of course. And then most of those viewers stuck around for episode three. But since then, we'd fallen sharply. Ratings were still very solid by *Renowned* standards, but Chef Simons had abandoned *Renowned* standards. I'm pretty sure he'd been hoping for some amalgamation of *Survivor* and *The Bachelor*, in which Max either gave me a rose each week or I extinguished his tiki torch. The *Renowned* Max and I loved so much—in which food was the focus, as well as the catalyst to discovering the heart and soul of the chef—had seemingly disappeared before our eyes under the pressure to produce ratings and viral clickbait.

"Chef Max!" Chef Simons exclaimed as soon as we walked in. "Where have you been? We have so much to do!"

"Yes, so I heard. Apologies, Chef. I got tied up on a business call."

"All right, let's get you both in the living room," Lowell commanded.

I had very mixed emotions about the season wrapping. It would be nice to have my house back—or at least have it down to sharing it with only one film crew. And I wouldn't be sad to see Chef Simons go. I'd reached the conclusion he was sort of like the Wizard of Oz—seeing the man behind the curtain had been extremely disenchanting. And it would be nice to have more time available again to focus on restaurants and the magazine.

Beyond that, I wasn't allowing myself to think about what life would look like once filming wrapped.

"This is either going to be fun or a train wreck," Max said to me as we sat on the loveseat together.

With all that we'd had thrust upon us over the course of eight weeks, we hadn't had a single joint interview, outside of the kitchen. Apart from that, though, we'd been run through the entire *Renowned* gamut. From increasingly absurd cooking competitions to visits with chefs we'd competed against on *America's Fiercest Chef*; hidden cameras that never caught anything of consequence to on-location filming scenarios that reinforced the feeling that we were on the first-ever season of *The Bachelor: In the Kitchen.* Max and I had joked that they'd probably have us cooking in a hot tub before all was said and done.

"I'm leaning toward train wreck," I whispered. "Don't you think it's weird that we're just now sitting down with Chef Simons together? Doesn't it feel like we're about to have the rug pulled out from under us?"

"When did you turn into such a negative Nelly?"

"When did you start saying things like negative Nelly?"

Max laughed as his nose was powdered and his already perfect beard was fussed with ad nauseum. "I guess you're rubbing off on me."

"I don't say negative Nelly."

"Maybe not, but you most definitely say things *like* negative Nelly."

Chef Simons sat in the chair strategically placed across from us and said, "Okay, Chefs. This is it." He reached out and grabbed my hand and Max's and squeezed them both. "I simply don't want to believe that our time together is over."

Max could only move so much, due to the fuss that was being made over his face, but he managed to shoot me a look that I had no difficulty at all interpreting. The new and improved Max Cavanagh—whose potty mouth had very nearly disappeared—would never actually say it, thank goodness.

"We just can't thank you enough for the opportunity," I said, and I meant it. Even if I also would have meant a cleaner version of what I was pretty sure Max was thinking.

"Ah well. There is no time for sentiment," Chef Simons said, yanking his hands away. "If I'd known Chef Maxwell was going to treat the call sheet as only a loose guideline, I would have had Lowell pad the schedule. Lowell!" he shouted, and Lowell came running.

As they whispered intensely—probably about how western civilization was on the brink of collapse because we were behind schedule—Max and I leaned closer together and did some whispering of our own.

"At least he hates us both now," I said.

"That is nice," he agreed.

"I just never understand the need for the whiplash. Either we're his teenagers going off to college for the first time or we're the bedbug-infested hotel he's checking out of. We can't possibly be both."

More than anything, over the course of the eight weeks prior, Chef Simons had seemed annoyed by us. I think he thought we were always on the precipice of doing something he thought was really interesting, but we never quite took the leap. At least not since the risotto episode. Since then, there had been no major revelations, and Max and I had mostly managed not to fight in the kitchen. In the kitchen and everywhere else, he was respectful and considerate, and when he did make fun of my cooking, it had nothing to do with the fact that I was a woman, or that I was the less-experienced, not-yet-as-successful chef.

It was usually just related to the amount of butter I used.

Who could have imagined, all those months ago, that the drunk, obnoxious, sexist chef who threw food and couldn't remember my name would actually be a joy to cook and create alongside? Or that he would become one of my favorite people in the world?

"All right, let's go, people. Hadley? Max? You ready?" Lowell asked.

The hair and makeup artists scurried away, and Max and I nodded. Max leaned back slightly into his corner of the loveseat and crossed his ankle onto his knee. He looked so relaxed and casual, while I was pretty sure I gave off the vibe of a sixteen-year-old boy in an uncomfortable suit, meeting his date's parents on prom night.

"You okay?" Max asked me in response to my slight fidgeting.

"Sure. I'm fine."

"Quiet everyone!" Lowell bellowed. "Counting down . . . Chef Simons, we're on you in five . .

. four . . ." His fingers took over the count at the same time an expression of serenity overtook the one of vexation on our host's face.

"And here we are. The final episode of this season of *Renowned*. A season which I dare say none of us will ever forget." He spoke to the camera and came across just like the Marshall Simons I had watched and respected for years. "Chefs Hadley Beckett and Maxwell Cavanagh walked onto the *Renowned* set two months ago as bitter rivals. And today they sit here as . . . well, let's allow them to tell us. Shall we? Chef Hadley, how would you categorize your relationship with Chef Max?"

Oh boy. "Wow. Not even a warm-up question, Chef Simons?" I chuckled and began fiddling with the hem of my blouse as the thought occurred that maybe that *was* the warm-up question. "Well, the truth is we've become very good friends."

"And that's been truly beautiful to watch," Chef Simons said. "And, frankly, surprising."

"I'm pretty sure no one's as surprised as we are," I added with a smile.

"So how did it happen?" he asked.

I shrugged. "I think everyone *saw* it happen, actually—"

"No." He shook his head. "I believe our viewers had the privilege, as I did, of witnessing milestone moments, but what was happening behind the scenes?"

I glanced over at Max, who, as was usually the case in these sorts of moments, provided no help whatsoever. He just raised his eyebrow, tilted his head, and smiled.

"Well," I croaked, and then cleared my throat. "We were getting to know each other—"

I think Chef Simons was already bored with my answer. "But to move past your public shared history could not have been an easy thing."

"No. It wasn't. But—"

"And then to be forced into a situation in which you had to share the *Renowned* stage—"

"We weren't *forced* into—"

"Still, to know that your nemesis—"

"Max was *never* my—"

"To know that he was also reaping the benefits of—"

I let out a frustrated growl and jumped up from the loveseat. "For cryin' out loud, Marshall! Are you going to let me finish one single thought?"

Mandoline. Nutmeg grater. Oven mitt. I performed a quick inventory. Maybe . . . maybe . . . nope. Not enough. *Poultry shears . . .*

Max's hand enveloped mine as he said, "Will you excuse us for a moment?" And then he pulled me into the kitchen. He looked around the room which, with my dazzling open floor plan, didn't do much to keep a cameraman and his equipment from rolling on in there. "Get out," Max ordered.

"We have every right to film right now, Max,"

Lowell said. Then he added, more quietly, "I'm sorry, but this is the show."

I turned my back to the camera and leaned forward against the sink, but I wasn't there long. Max pulled me away again, and I did all I could to keep up with him as he hurried up the stairs, down the hall, and into my bedroom. As soon as we got inside, he closed the door and locked it. He dropped my hand, but then he looked at the door, back to me, and then to the door again. Then I was once again being pulled, into my bathroom. He shut and locked that door, and then he looked instantly calm.

I separated from him and buried my face. "I can't believe I lost it like that."

"I'm glad you did."

I shook my head inside my cupped hands and groaned. "No, that was bad. That was so unlike me."

"Not really."

I lowered my hands and placed frustrated fists on my hips. "Yes, it was. I've never lost my temper like that. Not on television anyway. Not with Marshall Simons! Oh my gosh, Max. What did I just do?"

He sat down on the edge of my bathtub and smiled at me. "You stood up for yourself."

"And *you!*" I walked toward him, my pointer finger flailing wildly. "You didn't say anything! You just sat there and let him push and push."

His smile grew wider. "You didn't need me to say anything. You handled it just fine on your own."

I laughed bitterly. "Clearly not."

He stood from the bathtub ledge and crossed the room. When he reached me, he opened his arms and pulled me against him. "Can you still pronounce Spago?" he asked against my hair, and my laughter grew less bitter.

I sniffed and rested my head against his shoulder. "I just didn't want to give him what he wanted. You know?"

"I know."

"And, let's face it . . . if anyone was going to lose their temper, best odds were on you."

I felt his chest and throat rumble with laughter against me. "You know what my favorite part was?"

"That I called him Marshall?"

He threw his head back as the laughter exploded out of him. "Yes! It was such a perfect Hadley Beckett insult. The worst name you could possibly call him was the name he'd been telling you to call him since day one. It was so polite, but still scathing!"

And then I lost it. We both did. I buried my face in his chest and we laughed until we couldn't breathe. Finally, our breath began to regulate, and he gently rubbed my back as he softly said, "We should probably get back down there."

I let out another groan and pulled away from him. "This is so embarrassing."

"Don't be embarrassed. Seriously, Hadley. You said you didn't want to give him what he wanted. Well, I don't think you did. Do you think for one minute that's the reaction he thought he was going to get out of you?"

It was hard to imagine he'd seen that coming. I sure hadn't.

"Probably not."

"You know what I think?" I shook my head and he continued. "I think he was hoping to make you cry. But you didn't cry. You didn't back down when Marshall Simons underestimated you any more than you did when *I* underestimated you. That's nothing to be embarrassed about." He shoved his hands in his pockets and I sighed— the combination of all the sweet words and my favorite Maxwell Cavanagh posture almost more than I could handle. "In fact, I think you should be proud of yourself. I know I am."

I looked down at my feet and noticed they were close enough to kick his, so I did. "Thanks." There was no way I was going to ruin that moment with some emotion-deflecting attempt at humor.

"Welcome," he said, kicking me back.

I took a deep breath. "Shall we?"

"Ready when you are."

I looked up and smiled at him, and then

unlocked the door and made my way out. But he stopped me just before I got to the second door standing between us and the cameras.

"Hey, Hadley?"

"Yeah?"

"Do you remember when I ordered for you at Cavanagh's and you said it was the sexiest thing you'd ever seen in your life?"

I felt my cheeks flush—for many, *many* reasons. "I do."

"Well, you standing up to Simons like that?" He stepped in front of me, unlocked the door, and opened it. Sure enough, there was a camera waiting for us just on the other side. But that didn't stop Max from saying, "Ditto."

After my makeup was retouched and lint rollers and other magic tools were used to remove my powder from Max's shirt, we were ready to roll again. And neither Max, Chef Simons, nor I said a word until the cameras were rolling.

"Chef Hadley," Simons began as soon as Lowell had counted us down. "Your friendship with Chef Max seems to matter to you a great deal."

I nodded. "Of course it does."

"And Chef Max." He slightly adjusted his angle in the chair to have a better view of Max and, more importantly, the camera over Max's shoulder. "After your nervous breakdown on

America's Fiercest Chef, resulting in one of the most spectacular falls from grace I've witnessed, very few in the industry believed you would ever again be considered reputable. Respected."

"Is there a question in there, Chef Simons?" Max asked calmly.

"Well, my question would be how did you ever convince Chef Hadley to trust you? To let you in. To, somehow, become a friend?"

Max leaned forward—calm, cool, collected—and rested his elbows on his knees. I found myself repositioning my body so I could see him better. My trust in his transformation was absolute, but I was endlessly fascinated by it, nonetheless.

"That's a great question, Chef. One I've asked myself many times. And the truth is—"

"Because you have to admit, Chef Max—"

Max held up his hand and Simons stopped speaking at once. I couldn't quite see Max's eyes, but there must have been something in them that our host took seriously.

"Let's not do that. What do you say? Maybe you can ask questions, we'll answer them, and *then* we can move on to the next? I'd say that sounds like a good plan."

Well, doesn't that just beat all? I chewed on my lip to keep from laughing as Chef Simons sat back in his chair and plastered on a fake smile.

"Indeed. Please proceed, Chef."

Max nodded. "The truth is, Hadley and I were

able to become friends because of Hadley. It had very little to do with me. I mean, forgiveness. I don't know if I'd ever really seen it in action before. But she didn't hold a grudge, she didn't punish me for what I'd done in the past—"

"Oh, I think I did," I said quietly.

"I don't think so, Hadley." He turned to face me, and for a moment it felt like it was just the two of us in the room. "You didn't act like it never happened, nor should you have. But you gave me a chance." He turned back to Chef Simons. "At rehab I had this counselor who said that the key to healing is self-realization, and that the key to self-realization is allowing yourself to embrace nothing. Hadley and I joked about how we didn't really have any idea what that meant, but I think I've figured out that it's completely backward."

"What do you mean?" Chef Simons asked.

"I don't think the key to healing is self-realization at all. I think you've got to realize that there are other people out there, and they matter more. And I think you realize that not by embracing *nothing,* but by embracing *something.*"

I caught a single tear with the back of my hand before it rolled off the tip of my nose. Without thinking, I stretched my other arm out and almost placed my hand on Max's arm. It had become instinctive. Second nature. But just in time I caught sight of Chef Simons's gaze following my hand. No. I wouldn't give him the satisfaction of digging up any more of my very private emotions.

But Max would, apparently. Before I could pull it away, he had clutched my hand in his.

Looking like a kid in a candy shop, Chef Simons asked, "Chef Max, have you found religion?"

He shook his head. "I don't know. I don't even know what that means. I'm not going to act like I have things all figured out, or that I even understand what all there is *to* figure out. I just know that Hadley has something that not everybody has. And whatever it is, I think it's at the core of why we were able to become friends. So, I'm grateful to whatever or whoever made that possible."

I squeezed his hand and I didn't care who saw. I also blinked my eyes furiously to try to keep more tears from falling, but it had the exact opposite result. I couldn't bring myself to care too much about that either.

Nearly thirty minutes later we were nearing the end, and it was taking everything Max and I had in us to keep it together.

"We have one final Tweeter message for our chefs," Simons was saying, as he read from the cards in his hands.

He'd called it Tweeter four times already, and not a single person on his crew had spoken up to correct him. At first, I thought maybe they didn't know either, or that they were too scared to speak up, but the smirk on his face made it clear that at least one cameraman was fully aware, and perfectly willing to let Marshall Simons embarrass himself.

"This message is from 'At Symbol Foodie-Shipper'—ah! A member of the food industry, perhaps?" he asked Max and me.

It was all just too good. I wished I was still holding Max's hand so I would have something to squeeze. As it was, the inside of my cheek was probably going to be bruised in the morning.

"Actually, Chef," I replied, turning away from Max so I couldn't see his only moderately successful attempts to contain the laughter—currently consisting of a vicious rubbing of his face with both hands. "I think 'shipper' is a slang term for someone who wishes two people or characters would get together. As in, 'relationshipper.' "

And it's Twitter. And you can just say "At" rather than "At Symbol." "Hashtag"—not "Pound Sign."

"Is that so? Interesting," he said, clearly not interested. "Well then, 'At Symbol FoodieRela-tionshipper' says, 'At Symbol TVRenowned, Pound Sign HadBeck has rewritten the recipe of At Symbol ChefMaxCav's life. Pound Sign MaxandHadley. Pound Sign FoodieLove." He stared at his card, and then his lips began moving in silence. Finally, he looked at Max and me with a smile. "Indeed. Thoughts?"

Too much! I crossed my legs and shifted around uncomfortably. My stomach was beginning to cramp from maintaining my decorum.

"Thank you for that, FoodieShipper," Max said into the camera, the hilarity etched all over his face. We were gone. One hundred percent. "You're right. HadBeck"—he turned quickly to me—"Although, shouldn't you be 'At Symbol HadBeck' rather than 'Pound Sign Hadbeck'?"

I squeezed my fingernails into my knee as his twinkling eyes and mischievous grin pulled me into the conversation. "I'm not on Tweeter, actually."

He shrugged. "I'm still going to start calling you HadBeck." Then back to the camera. "HadBeck *has* completely rewritten the recipe of my life. She took her sloppy, delicious, maddening technique and got flour all over everything. And now I can't even imagine a version that doesn't have as much butter."

I don't know how he managed to keep such an earnest expression on his face, but I was completely done for. I grabbed a pillow and put it in front of my face, but there was no way to hide my bouncing shoulders.

Why, oh why, did Max and I have to be the subjects of *Renowned*'s first horrible attempt at being hip and modern?

Chef Simons carried on, oblivious. "And with that, it is now time to say goodbye. And not just until next season. *Renowned* has been a staple of culinary entertainment for nearly forty years, and I've savored every moment."

I grabbed Max's arm and dug my nails in. All the humor had vanished for both of us.

"Being invited into your homes, year after year, was an honor I will carry with me always. But all good things must come to an end. As for this season's featured chefs, you know where to find them, of course. Continue to follow Chef Hadley Beckett on her hit Culinary Channel series, *At Home with Hadley*, and we're just a matter of weeks away from the hotly anticipated return of Chef Maxwell Cavanagh on the highest-rated cooking program of all time, *To the Max*."

Max cleared his throat. "Actually, Chef Simons, *To the Max* will not be returning."

My head jerked around to face him. He looked at me and smiled nonchalantly, and then turned his attention back to Chef Simons.

Chef Simons, meanwhile, had just given up. He stood from his chair, muttered, "I'll record a sign-off in postproduction," and walked out the door without another word.

"Well, how do you like that?" Max mused as

the crew began feverishly breaking down the set. "We killed *Renowned*."

"Did we also kill *To the Max*?" I asked, pulling him aside. "I'm so sorry. What happened?"

He opened his mouth to speak, but instantly shut it again. We simultaneously offered sideways glances at the camera about three feet away from us.

"What are you doing?" Max asked.

The operator shrugged. "Lowell said to keep rolling."

Max and I both groaned and, without a word, took off together toward my bathroom. Once we were locked behind two doors I repeated, "So what happened? Did I make you too boring when I rewrote the recipe of your life?"

He grinned. "Something like that."

I hopped up on my vanity and continued to prod. "But seriously. What in the world happened? I thought you were heading off to the Great Barrier Reef next week."

He returned to his position on the edge of my bathtub. "I was. Now I'm not."

For the first time in probably twenty years, my stomach experienced the precise messed-up gravity sensation that used to occur when we'd hit the top of the Dulcimer Splash log-flume ride at the Opryland USA amusement park. He wasn't going away. And the way those blue eyes were staring intensely at me, dancing with humor and challenge under cocked eyebrows, made me think maybe it had a little something to do with me.

"Why not?"

"I don't want to. Not right now." He took a deep breath. "Things are settling down. You have a new manager; I have a new manager. Not the *same* manager, thankfully. Your *At Home with Hadley* contracts are settled, you're keeping the house, things are good with all the restaurants—yours and mine. Let's see . . . did I forget anything? Oh yeah. *Renowned* is over. For good, apparently."

He stared at me and I just stared right back. I had thought that when *Renowned* wrapped, life would go back to normal. But for the life of me, I couldn't remember what normal looked like. Normal had been replaced by Max, and when I looked at him, looking at me, it seemed like he mattered more than anything else that I'd considered normal before.

"Okay, Max . . . say for just a second that you and I gave this a shot. Say we figured out how to keep from fighting—"

"We don't fight much anymore," he protested, rising from the tub.

I laughed. "We fought *yesterday!*"

"You overcooked the polenta!"

"Say we didn't have to be rivals and we didn't have to compete for the best time slots. Don't you think, even if all of that was out of the way, you and I both carry around too much baggage to try and store all in one closet?"

"No. I don't. I think we would just need to build a bigger closet. Or sort through all that baggage and see what we can get rid of. We could just store it all in your shower." He looked behind him. "That thing is enormous."

"I know. It's like a whole room. But it would always be difficult for us. You know that as well as I do."

"I don't."

"You *do!*" I laughed again and jumped down from the vanity. "We both have trust issues, we don't agree on much, we live two very different lifestyles in very different places—"

"I like Nashville." He shrugged. "It's not that hard."

I scoffed at his attempt to make it easy. It could never be easy. "It *is* hard. And even if we sorted that out, we will both always want to win—especially against each other, I think."

"Nothing wrong with a little friendly competition."

"But can you really see yourself dating someone who is as busy as you are? Maybe even as successful as you are, eventually?" I sighed. "I've tried to make it work in my head, Max. I have."

He crossed his arms and shook his head. "No, you haven't. It sounds to me like you've just worked out a lot of excuses. You've even worked quite a few out for me, and while I appreciate you trying to save me the trouble of thinking it through myself, I really think you should stop now."

I swallowed hard and darted my eyes away from his. "I don't want to lose you. As a friend, I mean."

"Why would you?" he asked, taking a step toward me. I told my feet to step back in response, but I think they must have been too busy admiring Max's folded arms—as I was trying not to—because they ignored the snot out of me.

"What happens when we date for a little while and then it all goes horribly wrong—as, let's face it, it probably will? We had to get past a whole lot to become friends. Do we really want to add a breakup to that?"

"See, that's the problem. Right there! You've already played it out in your mind. You're so convinced there can't be a happy ending that you don't even want to keep reading to find out. But it hasn't even occurred to you that we get to write this story, Hadley."

"No, I do understand that. It's just that—"

"Oh, good grief, woman," he muttered as he looped one arm around my waist and pulled me against him before hooking his other arm around my neck. Then he bent me back and kissed me in a manner worthy of Rhett Butler. His lips were unrelenting until I finally threw my arms around him and started giving as good as I took. It was then that he brought me back to a self-supporting posture (though my knees took a little longer to catch up) and kissed me one more time, briefly and gently, before taking a couple steps back, leaving my lips numb and my arms missing him.

Well, fiddle-dee-dee.

"Would you please just listen? Just for a minute?" he asked, and since my brain was incapable of forming words anyway, I just nodded silently. "Okay. Thank you." He took a deep breath and another small step back from me. "You think you don't want any of this."

"Any of what?" I asked quickly, before he could stop me.

His hands gestured back and forth wildly between the two of us. "*This,* Hadley. The pain and struggle and heartbreak that goes along with loving somebody. And I get that. All you've ever seen is the pain and struggle and the heartbreak, so of course you're scared." He ran his fingers across his chin and scratched his cheek. "And me? Well, I've never even seen the love. I've never even seen anything to make me believe that it can ever work. To make me think it's ever worthwhile. That there's any point to any of it." He took a deep breath and his eyes locked with mine. "But in spite of that, in spite of having no idea what's happening or what to do about it, I know you and I've got a pretty good shot at making this work. Because I get it now."

"What?" I whispered. "What do you get?"

He smiled and took a step toward me. "I get that it's not about having it all figured out. It's just about knowing there isn't anyone else on earth I want to be standing beside while we figure it out together. It's about believing in something that . . . Hadley . . ." He bit his lip. "I believe you and I can be something so good. And I know that maybe I'm supposed to make all these promises to you. Promises to never let you down, and to be the man you need me to be. All of that. But the thing is, I don't feel like I have any chance at all of not disappointing you if I make those promises. Because I'm going to let you down. And, sure, I'll *try* to be the man you need me to be. Always. But I don't think life together really works that way. I'm not even sure it's supposed to. So, I can't make those promises. But I can promise I'll do all I can to protect you. And that I'll always respect you. And I can promise I don't want anyone but you. I can promise to be honest with you—whether that's admitting when I make a mistake or saving your poor patrons from coronaries by making sure you know when you've used too much salt."

I laughed with him and, as much as I didn't want to stop looking at him as he said the most beautiful words I'd ever heard, I couldn't resist the offer of his open arms. He pulled me against him—I never would have imagined we would fit together so well—and I rested against his chest. He kissed the top of my head and leaned his cheek against my hair.

"In sickness, poorer, and worse, right?" he said softly. Gently. "Just give me the chance to love you through all the *worse* that life can throw at us, Hadley. I can promise I'm not going to get scared off by any of that. Because I'm not willing to miss the *better* that I know is going to be there."

I lifted my head from his chest and reached up to run my fingers through his hair, then I wrapped my arms around his neck and tilted my chin toward him.

His finger slowly traced the outline of my mouth. "So what do you say?"

I sighed as nonchalantly as I could as my hands made their way to the back of his head and began to pull his lips toward mine. "I guess we can give it a try."

Max's eyes sparkled as he seemed to take in everything about the moment—everything about *me*—and he was finally close enough for his lips to brush against mine. Briefly. Perfectly. Frustratingly.

"I love you, Chef Beckett," he whispered.

I pulled out my tried and true method of listing

things found in the kitchen to help me remain calm and focused—*Max. Max. Max.*—but it just wasn't getting me very far.

"I love you too, Chef Cavanagh."

I expected a smile, but the emotion that danced across his face wasn't playful in the least. It was raw and intense, and carried with it the promise of a love I never thought I wanted.

"Well . . ." he said, and then the smile appeared—and it was *everything*. "Just remember who said it first."

He pulled me to him, in a style that was perfectly all his own, and I realized that if this was what losing to Max Cavanagh looked like, I had no desire to ever win again.

Epilogue

HADLEY

Six Years Later

"I don't *at all* understand the concept of this show," Stuart said as he looked around the new house.

I took his jacket from him and hung it on the coatrack by the door. "It's not that hard, Stu! It's just *life,* you know?"

"See, that's a reality show. Not a cooking show."

We walked into the bustling kitchen, and I gestured with my arms like Vanna White. "And that's where you're wrong. It is a cooking show. And maybe also a reality show—but only in regard to food. Cooking, meals, travel, adventure—"

"Ah." He nodded. "Okay. I get it now. It's *At Home with Hadley . . . To the Max!*" He laughed. "Why didn't you just say so?"

I shook my finger in his face. "Nope. That's not it. Not at all—though, believe you me, the network executives would have peed themselves if we'd gone with that as the name. But it's really not that. It's so different. It's more about the role that food plays in people's lives." We walked further into the kitchen, and Stuart shook hands with various members of the crew—most of whom we'd both worked with repeatedly through the years. "Sometimes it might be like something you would have seen on *To the Max*, back in the day—"

"Like figuring out ways to use every part of the goat for a celebratory dinner with Bedouin nomads in the Negev?"

I laughed. "Exactly. But then we also got the opportunity to spend the day cooking with a Make-a-Wish child and her family. Because that was her wish, Stu! To learn to prepare Thanksgiving dinner for the less fortunate people in her community. I mean, can you believe that? And it's because food matters. Food brings people together." I shook my finger at him again. "There is power in food, my friend." We stepped behind the island and I pulled my apron out from a drawer. "And how about you? How's LA?"

He nodded. "Good, actually. Just before I flew out here, I got a pretty exciting call. Steven Spielberg hired me as second AD for his next film."

I squealed as I jumped into his arms—which he'd instinctively known to throw open for me. "Stu! That's amazing! I'm so proud of you!"

"What's going on here?" Max asked as he stepped into the kitchen and caught sight of Stuart twirling me around. "Should I be concerned?"

"I'm stealing your wife," Stuart replied with a smile as he set me down.

Max shrugged. "I knew it would come to this eventually." He put his hand out, and Stuart shook it. "It's good to see you."

"You too, man."

"Stuart's directing a Spielberg movie!" I exclaimed proudly.

Stuart laughed. "Well, not exactly. *Spielberg* actually tends to direct Spielberg movies." He turned to Max and humbly clarified. "Second assistant director."

"Wow!" Max replied, genuinely impressed. "Okay, then I take it back." He wrapped his arms around me from behind and quickly kissed me on the neck. "You can't have *everything*." He released me and playfully whacked me on the bottom with one hand and grabbed an apple from a bowl with the other. I faced him with mock horror just in time to catch him waggling his eyebrows at me mischievously as he took a bite out of the apple.

Stuart grinned at me and I chuckled as I repositioned the remaining fruit in the bowl. "Seems like you guys are pretty happy."

"We are."

He leaned in to speak discreetly. "And Max is doing okay with this life?"

I sighed dramatically. "Well, times are tough, but somehow he gets by . . ."

He chuckled. "You know what I mean. You traveled so much for the first couple years . . . I just know you were kind of worried about how he'd be with settling down. The great adventurer Maxwell Cavanagh—ensconced in the suburbs of Nashville, Tennessee, of all places. I mean, let's face it. He's a great guy, but you don't exactly look at him and think, 'Now *there's* a guy who loves to spend his Saturdays tailgating and playing cornhole.' "

I guffawed at the thought. "No, I suppose you don't."

A soft, disgruntled cry began to emanate from the baby monitor on the counter but quickly grew in volume and intensity.

"On it," Max called out as he reappeared in the kitchen, to cross through to the stairs.

"Hey!" I grabbed him from behind, by the waist of his jeans, as he passed, and he walked in place for a moment—as if he wasn't strong enough to escape me. Then he grabbed my chin and planted a kiss on my lips as the doorbell rang. "Actually," I muttered against him, "I'll take care of Jules." He shook his head and laughed as he began pulling away. "I'll even make sure Harper and Elijah are dressed!"

"Already done, baby." Max continued to laugh as he unlatched the baby gate and began up the stairs. "Dad of the year!"

I ran over to the stairs and looked up at him.

"For a month! I'll take care of getting the twins dressed for a full month!"

"You lose, Hadley!" his distant voice rang out. "Go answer the door!"

The doorbell chimed again, and I looked back over to Stuart, who was leaning against the counter, a bemused and knowing expression on his face. "You ready for this, people?" I called out to the crew, who all laughed in response. I took a deep breath and walked to the door. And then one more deep breath before I opened it.

"Hi, Meemaw. Come on in."

It wasn't that I didn't love seeing her. I did. It was just that, well . . . we saw her *a lot.* And the older she got, the more comfortable in her own skin she got. And that was great. But, well . . . who knew she could get even more comfortable than she had already been?

"I don't know how you live in this neighborhood," she began as soon as she walked in.

"What's wrong with Forest Hills?"

"No, not Forest Hills. Forest Hills is fine. I just mean *this* part of Forest Hills. There are kids everywhere. On bikes, in yards . . . do you ever get any peace and quiet?"

No. No, I did not. But that was just *inside* the house.

"Hey, look who's here, Meemaw!" I directed her toward the kitchen and held in my laughter as Stuart shot me an expression of betrayal. "You remember my old friend Stuart, don't you?"

She offered him a wave and sat down at the dining room table with the magazine she apparently had stashed in her handbag.

"Good to see you too, Twyla!" he called out, causing me to giggle and resulting in no reaction whatsoever from my grandmother. Then he looked around the place and threw his arms up in the air. "Had, how in the world are you possibly going to be able to film a show with all of this chaos?"

I grabbed his face in my hands and said, "The chaos *is* the show, Stu." Then I patted him on the cheek and added, "Now you'd better get off my set unless you want to make an appearance." Never having had any desire to be in front of the camera, he was standing with the crew within seconds.

"You ready, Hadley?" Jerry, who was now my director, asked.

I offered one emphatic nod and straightened out my shirt. "Ready."

"Okay, everyone," Jerry bellowed. "We're rolling. And we're on Hadley in five, four . . ." His fingers took over for the words and I smiled at the camera.

"Hi, y'all. I appreciate you making a little time in your busy lives to spend some time with us and be a part of *our* lives." Just then, three-year-old Elijah came up to me, and I hoisted him up onto the counter so he could sit beside where I stood. "As you can see, we're just hanging out at Casa de Cavanagh today, and I thought we might make . . . well, what do you think we should make today, Eli?"

Max walked into the kitchen, Eli's twin sister, Harper, in one arm, ten-month-old Julia in the other. "How about some superhealthy smoothies, Mommy?" Max said in a high-pitched voice meant to imitate our toddler son. "With lots of antioxidants. And kale!"

Eli and Harper giggled, and I scrunched up my face at them. "Daddy's silly, isn't he? You know what *I* think we should make?" I slowly pulled the container out from the cabinet, to build suspense until they could see the cookie cutters.

"Cookies!" they both shouted excitedly.

Max set Harper down and I helped Eli off the counter, and they went running toward the dining room.

"You know," Max said, wrapping his arm around my shoulder but talking to the camera. "I think it would be a great day to teach the kids how to make macarons. I mean, we can't let them start preschool without knowing how to properly *macaronage*, as it were. And we'll even start simply. We'll work on perfecting their French buttercream filling later. For today, we'll just pull together a basic ganache and—"

"The boy one is standing on the table!"

Meemaw shouted loudly, but pretty nonchalantly, from the dining room.

Max and I looked at each other and then back at the camera. "Oh. And my grandmother is here," I explained to our audience. I put my hands out, and Julia dove from Max's arms to mine.

"You know what sounds good?" Max mused as he backed away to go see what the boy one and the girl one were up to.

"Chocolate chip cookies?" I asked.

"Chocolate chip cookies," he agreed, before running into the dining room, roaring like a dinosaur preparing to attack—resulting in giggles and screams that filled the house with beautiful chaos.

Out of the corner of my eye, I spotted Max lying on the floor, the twins climbing all over him. Clearly the great dinosaur hunters had captured their prize.

I understood the feeling perfectly.

"So, business as usual for the Cavanagh clan today." I hoisted Julia higher up from where she had slipped down on my hip and turned to the camera once again. "Thanks for spending some time at home with us."

Acknowledgments

With each book, I tell myself that next time I'm going to do something really creative for the Acknowledgments. Maybe I'll write them all in haiku, or to the tune of the theme song from *The Golden Girls*. But then each time, I find myself short on time and overflowing with appreciation for all the people who have contributed not only to the writing of the book but also to my life in general. That list just keeps getting longer and longer, and the gratitude gets more and more profound. But there are quite a few people who played a role in the writing/publishing of this book specifically. Everyone in my life who isn't listed . . . I owe you my eternal love and appreciation. (And a haiku.)

For this book, we have to kick it off with my editor, Kelsey Bowen. I handed her a first draft that I knew wasn't good. But I believed in the potential and had complete trust that she would know just what was needed. And, of course, she did. She talked me through it, gave me two-and-a-half weeks to get her a completely different book, and, more than anything, believed I was capable of getting it done. I'm so proud of what we've been able to create together and so grateful that she continues to believe I can get it done.

That crazy trust that we had in 2016 as practical strangers sharing an Airbnb has only grown, and I consider that trust and friendship among the greatest gifts of this writing and publishing journey.

Another of the greatest gifts is my agent, Jessica Kirkland, who is an amazing sounding board, a fierce advocate, and a treasured friend. (Also, sometimes I wonder . . . are we *supposed* to laugh as much as we do when we're "working"?)

I love (love, love, love) the brilliant team of people I get to work with at Revell. Brianne, Karen, Kristin, Michele, and Gayle . . . you do amazing work, and I'm continually amazed by the heart and kindness with which you do it.

David Ramsey—your influence on this book is bigger than I'll probably ever confess to you in person. We both know I'd just cry the whole time, so let's agree to never speak of it. But every single time I sat down to write, I listened to country music artists I'd never heard of before you took the time to help me shape Hadley's personality through the music she would listen to. I didn't really know who she was until I listened to her favorite songs. Thanks for helping us get acquainted.

Jenny Todacheeny—Max was born over breakfast at Beny's. This story simply wouldn't exist without you. And I think I could honestly say that about every book I've written.

Secily Toles and Jacob Plemons—I can't. I can't even. I don't even know where to start with the two of you. I'll just say that I look at that picture of our shoes—each one distinct but also sort of seamless in how they overlap and intersect—and I think, "That's us."

LeeAnn Ramsey—so much of my affection and inspiration for Hadley's Nashville sprung from our trip. It was so fun to think back to that treasured time as I wrote!

Susan May Warren and Rachel Hauck—the two of you have mentored and inspired so many that you probably don't even know when you're doing it! But that day at Cafe du Monde, you unleashed a new fire in me. I'll never forget it.

There are so many other people to thank, and I'm (always) so afraid of missing someone, but without the following friends who brainstormed with me, allowed me to vent, read, critiqued, or just made me laugh when I needed it most, I'm just not sure I would have survived the writing of this book (or at least Hadley and Max may not have survived!): Sarah Monzon, Nicole Deese, Carol Moncado, Anne Jessup, Mikal Hermanns, Melissa Ferguson, Tracy Steel, Janine Rosche, and all of my Monday Night Book Club peeps!

As someone who has been heavily influenced by pop culture, I would be greatly amiss if I didn't thank a few people who provided inspiration for this story, even if I've never met them personally. Yet. (That's right, #12. It's going to happen.)

- Gordon Ramsay, whose recipes gave me clues to Max's brilliance, whose potty mouth gave me insight into Max's public persona, and whose demeanor with kids clarified for me that Max wasn't just who the world had decided he was.
- Julia Child, who, by being Hadley's inspiration, became my inspiration as well.
- Michael Martin Murphey, whose recording of "What's Forever For" made me feel all the things I needed to feel, on demand.
- Aaron Rodgers. Just because.
- Nora Ephron, who is *always* my inspiration for all things romcom.
- Colin Firth. Also just because.
- The Beast from *Beauty and the Beast*. Forever and always.
- John Stamos, who started it all.
- Chris Pratt, John Krasinski, and Dan Stevens, who have taken turns being pinned to my corkboard as character inspiration.
- Gillian Jacobs, Claire Foy, and Jessica Capshaw, who also provided character inspiration, but for some reason didn't stay pinned to my board for nearly as long.

Don and Bev Whitis—thanks for life. Thanks for bringing me up to love movies and TV and story, and even more importantly, Jesus. Thanks for telling everyone you know that they need to buy my books. Thanks for asking every library and store if they carry my books (and if not, *why* not?). And thanks for always demonstrating what "for better or worse" is all about.

Missy Whitis—you will never read my books. But I love you still. For you I wrote a haiku.

Ethan Turner and Noah Turner—you both support and encourage me in so many ways, and you probably never realize it. Even just your chants of "Book! Book! Book!" mean more to me than you know.

Kelly Turner—every book begins and ends with you believing in me, and every day begins and ends with me loving you.

Throughout the process of writing this book, God and I wrestled. Every single time I thought I had things figured out, he said, "See! I am doing a new thing!" And the new things scared the living daylights out of me. But day by day, I fell even more in love with him and his new things. Thank you, Jesus, for scaring the living daylights out of me with your boldness and truth. Please never stop.

Bethany Turner is the award-winning author of *The Secret Life of Sarah Hollenbeck*, a finalist for the Christy Award, and *Wooing Cadie McCaffrey*. When she's not writing (and even when she is), she serves as the director of administration for Rock Springs Church in Southwest Colorado. She lives with her husband and their two sons in Colorado, where she writes for a new generation of readers who crave fiction that tackles the thorny issues of life with humor and insight. For more, visit www.seebethanywrite.com.

Books are produced in the United States using U.S.-based materials

Books are printed using a revolutionary new process called THINKtech™ that lowers energy usage by 70% and increases overall quality

Books are durable and flexible because of Smyth-sewing

Paper is sourced using environmentally responsible foresting methods and the paper is acid-free

Center Point Large Print
600 Brooks Road / PO Box 1
Thorndike, ME 04986-0001 USA

(207) 568-3717

US & Canada:
1 800 929-9108
www.centerpointlargeprint.com